Please return/renew this item by the last date shown.
Items may also be renewed by the internet*

https://library.eastriding.gov.uk

* Please note a PIN will be required to access this service
- this can be obtained from your library

BOOKS BY CLARE CHASE

Death Comes to Call

CLARE CHASE

Bookouture

Published by Bookouture in 2019

An imprint of StoryFire Ltd.

Carmelite House
50 Victoria Embankment
London EC4Y 0DZ

www.bookouture.com

ISBN: 978-1-78681-812-6
eBook ISBN: 978-1-78681-811-9

To the wonderful Westfield gang

CHAPTER ONE

Detective Constable Tara Thorpe's eyes ran over the abandoned room. The light levels outside were already low, and a tall Anglepoise lamp shone out from one corner. The shadows it cast, thrown by a pair of easels and some high stools, ran like outstretched fingers across the room. The space was gloomy, and filled with canvases, rags and half-used bottles of turpentine. The smell of the solvent mingled with that of oil paint and dust. On a scuffed wooden table next to her sat a coffee-stained sea-green mug. There was a dead spider next to it, so insubstantial it looked as though the slightest breeze would turn it to dust. It wasn't often that she got such an instant feeling of unease about a place.

The paintings she could see, stacked up against one wall, looked just as threatening as the weather outside. There had been a bitter cold snap over the last week and a half. It felt nothing like March and dusk was already taking hold though it was still afternoon.

The canvases were thick with paint in dark colours – indigos, greys, black and midnight blue. A lot of the images were of stormy fenland skies, reeds and waterways. She could see one of St John's College Chapel, shown in near darkness, rain reflecting off its roof. Luke Cope – an artist and the missing occupant of the house she was standing in – had made it look like a place of evil. What kind of a person imbued everything they depicted with such an ominous atmosphere?

'For God's sake, I just need you to *do* something.'

Very understandable, of course, but the flak was undeserved. She evened out her expression and turned to face the man who'd spoken. Matthew Cope was tall, with deep brown eyes. His lips were white, his jaw set, cheeks tinged red. The rest of his face was pale. He was agitated all right. Agitated and angry.

'I reported my brother missing over a week ago, and they send me you!'

The words came out in a rush, his pitch rising and uncontrolled as he finished his sentence. He took a deep breath – to steady himself, Tara assumed. She hoped it did the trick. She could understand he was concerned, and she could rise above the way he was treating her, but she'd rather not have to.

'Have people told you Luke's unreliable? Is that the problem?' Cope didn't pause long enough for her to answer. 'Take it from me, this is completely out of character.'

Tara had read the case notes when she'd been sent to talk to Matthew Cope after the latest approach he'd made to the police. He'd been forced to admit that his brother had gone missing of his own accord before – but never for more than a night or two.

Cope paced up and down next to the table, which Tara now saw was makeshift – the planks of wood were balanced on piles of bricks. After a moment, he stopped and closed his eyes. 'I want him found. I've got the worst possible feeling about his disappearance. Why the hell doesn't anyone understand?' He went on to bad-mouth the first officer who'd been to see him and 'clearly done nothing'.

Tara decided to let him vent for a bit. She could appreciate his anxiety, but his lack of control over his temper was annoying. It was pointless to address his criticism of the police until he'd calmed down. Wade in now and she'd just be stoking an argument. She made use of her time by continuing to size up the room they were standing in.

The contents of the studio were incongruous with Luke Cope's stately Cambridge villa. The other rooms she'd walked through were grand and elegant, but this large space at the back of the house was spattered with paint and full of clutter. That was fair enough; everyone had the right to do what they damn well liked in their own home. But there was something about this area that felt out of control; as though the occupier had been living on the brink. The carpet had been taken up to reveal bare, unvarnished boards. It was still rolled up at one end of the room, with paint spatters on its woven reverse side. The studio was just off the kitchen and Tara guessed it might once have been a very large utility room. *Who could possibly need that much space to do their chores?* There were cupboards on the walls – their paintwork chipped as though they'd been there for some years – and a lopsided wooden laundry pulley dangled from the high ceiling. All around there were bits of paper that had been torn or crumpled up tight and tossed here and there. Something about the way they'd landed spoke of a man with a short temper. Perhaps the brothers had that in common. She could see plates of half-eaten food dotted around: toast with a single bite out of it; an apple, nibbled on one side, then left to go brown. It must only be the cold that prevented the room from smelling of decay as well as the artist's materials. A Stanley knife stood at a forty-five-degree angle to a work bench – its blade had been jammed into the wooden surface. She could imagine someone ramming it in like that in a moment of frustration.

Matthew Cope had stopped pacing. She met his look, keeping her eyes sympathetic, whatever she felt inside. Her journalist's instinct, ingrained and automatic, served her well now she'd retrained as a police officer. She wanted him to open up, because this place gave her the creeps like nobody's business. Luke Cope's case wasn't an official priority, but her antenna told her something was off.

At last her patience had the desired effect. He pushed his fingers through his thick hair. 'I'm sorry. Sorry. It's just – well.' He stopped for a moment. 'Truth to tell, my brother's caused me a lot of grief over the years. I'm anxious, but I suppose at least part of me is angry at him for causing me so much worry.' Tara reckoned the anger was winning. 'If I could just be sure people are actively looking for him… It feels as though everything's gone quiet.'

'It can seem like that when everything's happening at arm's length,' Tara said. 'I'm here to make sure we've covered all possible angles of enquiry.' But Luke was an adult and not considered vulnerable. She knew her colleagues had already followed the standard procedures. It was chilling that someone could just walk out of their life like that and – unless they were seen as at risk – there wasn't much you could do about it. For a second she imagined it being someone she loved – Bea, for instance – the woman who'd brought her up whilst her mother had been busy with her acting career. It didn't bear thinking about: the not knowing.

The man was shifting his weight uneasily from foot to foot now. 'I thought maybe they'd send someone more senior at this stage. I wanted to…'

She longed to tell him he was lucky to have her. She wouldn't stop digging if she thought something was off, even if it meant working in her own time.

Tara waited for him to continue but it was clear he'd changed his mind about confiding. She could see he was chewing the inside of his cheek. What had he been going to say? Something he felt he could only raise with a higher-ranking detective?

'Please, tell me what's on your mind, Mr Cope. I can either handle it or pass it on. If you've got extra information, it can only help your brother.'

The man shook his head sharply. 'I'm not sure that's the case.'

Interesting… She waited. He was close to coming across with extra information, she could tell. Pausing for long enough usually did the trick. Most people were amazingly uncomfortable with silence.

'I was worried about Luke before he disappeared,' he said at last. 'About the way his mind was working.'

'Why was that?'

He frowned, opened his mouth to speak and then closed it again before taking a deep breath and starting afresh. 'I hadn't really intended…' He broke off and pursed his lips, shaking his head. 'Dear God, this is no good. It might be best if I show you. It's not something I wanted to share, but if it'll make you take this seriously…' He turned his back on her and strode to the opposite side of the space, where he began to rummage through a series of paintings. The pictures were facing away, towards the wall that they leant against, so that she could only see the frames and the backs of the canvases. Matthew Cope had crouched down and was pulling them back one by one, resting them against his knees as he scanned the compositions.

At last he selected one from the pile, lifted it free of the others and let the rest fall back again.

He stood up. 'Possibly I should have mentioned this when I first called. I'm quite sure it's not directly relevant to Luke's disappearance. But, if I share it with you in confidence…'

Before she had time to warn him it might have to go further, Matthew Cope had turned the canvas so Tara could see the picture. For a second, before she looked down, her eyes were still on his. He averted his gaze.

The painting was of a woman with shoulder-length blonde hair, her head resting on a scarlet cushion. The picture only showed her head and shoulders, but she looked as though she was naked.

And around her neck was a pair of hands, tightening over her windpipe…

CHAPTER TWO

It wasn't just the subject matter of Luke Cope's painting that was shocking; it was the feeling he'd managed to put into the image – the raw violence. 'Who is she?' Tara said, slowly. 'And how is she connected with your brother?'

'Her name's Freya Cross. She works at a gallery called Trent's just outside Cambridge, where Luke shows his paintings.' He hesitated. 'They're friends, too.'

There was nothing friendly about the scene in the painting, but the nudity made Tara wonder. 'She and Luke are in a relationship?'

Matthew Cope looked uncomfortable. 'Freya's married. But – well – I'd suspected there might be something going on before I saw this.' He indicated the painting. 'Of course, I knew Luke couldn't have acted on what he must have been imagining when he painted her. It would have been reported if anything had happened to Freya. But the idea that he'd been having that sort of thought just before he disappeared makes me think he was close to the edge.'

No kidding…

'How did you come to see the painting?' She couldn't imagine Luke Cope showing it off.

'I was round here one night. He'd been ranting on about Freya all evening. They'd clearly quarrelled about something. Luke had drunk a lot and after a while he fell asleep on the couch there.' He pointed to a sort of day bed at one side of the large room, covered in a tattered throw. 'It was only then that I spotted it. The paint was still wet.'

'He didn't give any hint about why they'd fallen out?' Tara's stomach was tense.

Matthew Cope shook his head.

'Have you ever known him to be violent… apart from in his imagination?'

'No.'

Tara looked at him sharply. Had he answered too quickly? 'All right,' she said at last. 'Could you take me back to the beginning please?' Having read the case notes was all very well, but hearing Cope's account face to face would be much better. She wanted to see the subconscious signs he gave off as he talked. What did he really think of his brother? 'You realised something was up around ten days ago?'

She walked up and down the room to try to keep warm. She was only one step away from shivering. She was wearing a hazelnut-brown tweed trouser suit – a present from her mother which she secretly rather liked. It was more flattering than she'd expected, and warm too, but still no match for the current temperatures.

Matthew Cope nodded. 'That's right. We were meant to be meeting up for a drink at the Snug, a week ago Saturday.' Tara knew the place. A trendy little bar that described itself as bohemian, and a home for intellectuals… *Enough said.* 'When he didn't show up I called his mobile first, but there was no reply. After that, I came round here and knocked. When I got no answer I wrote him a note – asking him to call me – and pushed it through the letter box.' Cope paused to drag in a deep breath. 'The following day I called him again, four times. It was then that I started to feel really uneasy. No replies to any of my attempts to reach him and my head was still full of that damned painting. What is it that they say about the balance of someone's mind?' He put his hands up to his face for a moment. 'By the Sunday evening I'd decided to let myself in, using his spare key. It felt like an intrusion, but I didn't know what to think. Even when I managed to ignore the most dramatic thoughts I was having, the more mundane ones still worried me. My father died falling down the stairs.' He paused. 'Given Luke likes the odd drink, I wondered if he could have missed his footing and shared the same fate. But once I got inside there were no signs that anything was wrong. He'd just disappeared and my note was still sitting on the doormat.' His eyes met Tara's. 'You can see there's good reason to make a concerted effort to find him.' His strident tone was making a comeback.

In fact, it was the woman, Freya Cross, who was the vulnerable one as far as Tara was concerned. But Matthew Cope was right: she was sure they'd have heard if something *had* happened to her. After all, she was local and had someone at home to raise the alarm if she went missing.

'Okay. We need to take this step by step and look at all the options.' She'd already read his answers to the standard questions, from whether he'd checked the local hospitals, to if there were any signs Luke had intended to stay away overnight. And when he'd first made the report he'd confirmed that he'd spoken to Luke's friends too, but time had passed between now and then.

'Have you called his contacts again, to see if they've heard anything from him?' She glanced around at the evidence of Luke Cope's career. 'I presume he's freelance, so there's no place of work to check?'

Matthew nodded. 'He sells his artwork for a living – or tries to – he doesn't make much. His work's first class, but he's no salesman. You have to be hard-nosed – or team up with someone who is.'

Again, she could hear Cope's frustration. But his brother must be doing all right, to be living in a place like this. Tara ran her eyes over the expansive room.

'The house was handed down by my parents.' Matthew must have read her thoughts. 'It was here that my father fell down the stairs. It's not officially Luke's yet – we each had property left to us in trust until we're forty.' He raised an eyebrow and gave her a look that challenged her to make a comment. 'Some people feel that's rather Victorian, but my parents didn't want us to have too much too soon.'

She looked at the room again. For a moment she wondered what the Copes senior would have thought – having part of what had been their smart Cambridge home turned upside down like this. Tara's own mother was always incredulous about the way Tara chose to live – though she fondly imagined she managed to hide the fact. Tara's house wasn't chaotic though – just lonely and in a poor state of repair.

Matthew Cope's sigh – short and sharp – brought her focus back to him. 'But to answer your question, I've called round the friends I know about, and they haven't heard anything from him. This is going over old ground. I assumed when I showed you the painting things would move up a gear.'

'So, you've contacted Freya Cross, I presume, to see if she knows where your brother is?' Tara kept her tone calm, despite the rising annoyance in his voice.

She'd wrong-footed him by the look of it. His haughty, irritable expression morphed into one of uncertainty. In spite of the situation, Tara found it hard not to feel pleased.

'I didn't like to. It might have sparked gossip if I called her at work, and I don't have any other number for her.'

The missing man probably had a lover – a lover who he'd quarrelled with – and Matthew Cope hadn't approached her…

'But her name was on the list I gave to your colleagues,' he added quickly.

Tara nodded. 'That's good, but if you told them you'd already had a ring round they wouldn't have immediately followed up on those names.' *How much spare time do you imagine we have?* 'But it's useful to know,' she added, burying her irritation deep. 'It's a fresh line of enquiry. I'll see if I can reach her at Trent's.' She met his eye. 'You needn't worry – I'll be subtle about it. And I'll keep you up to date.'

Inside her car, Tara reached for her coat, which she'd left on the back seat, and wriggled her way into it, tying the belt round her waist.

Five twenty. A quick google on her phone told her Trent's – owned by one Jonny Trent – would be closing in ten minutes. She'd call them now, before she returned to the station to report back and then swap her work car for her bike to cycle home.

The phone rang for a minute before a man's voice answered, rich and plummy.

'Trent's.'

'Please could I speak to Freya Cross?'

There was a pause. *'Who's that calling?'*

The voice was cagey now. Tara frowned. She'd love to be economical with the truth, but saying she was a friend would look suspicious. Any mate of Freya's would call her on her mobile. Her DI, Garstin Blake, would no doubt point out it was against protocol to lie, too.

'My name's DC Tara Thorpe. Is she around please?'

'Police? Is something wrong?'

'Not at all. My call doesn't directly relate to her. I'm just hoping she might have some useful background information that would help with a case I'm working on. Is that Mr Trent?'

'Yes, yes, Jonny Trent speaking.' He sounded a little less bristly now. *'I'm afraid Freya's away from work at the moment.'*

Tara felt the hairs on the back of her neck rise. 'On leave, you mean?'

'That's correct,' Trent answered after a second.

'Could you tell me when she'll be back?'

'*It's uncertain.*' There was a momentary pause. '*She's been feeling the strain – pressure of work – the usual story. I understand from her husband that she's gone to stay with a friend. She knows she's welcome to take as long as she needs. I've got plenty of cover. I'll ask her to call you when she returns, shall I?*'

He was all bonhomie now, but Tara's adrenaline was ramping up further. An open-ended time away from work, under the circumstances, made her want to speak to the woman immediately. She presumed the story of her absence due to stress was true, given that the information had come from her husband, and her boss didn't sound surprised. But what had caused her emotional upset? Had it been related to Luke Cope? The timing was suspicious.

'I'd be grateful if you'd text her to ask her to give me a call.' She reeled off her mobile number. 'Even though my enquiry doesn't relate directly to her, it's urgent.'

Jonny Trent heaved a heavy sigh. '*I don't like to bother a member of staff when they're on leave, but I'll try for you. I can't guarantee that she'll reply.*'

She thanked him and hung up. His responses made her frown. Someone calls to speak to an employee, but they're away on leave. Wouldn't you normally say as much first off, without any fuss? *I'm afraid she's away at the moment. Who's calling? Can I take a message?* That's how Tara would have dealt with it.

She wondered what Blake would think, back at the station. She was sure he'd be interested. As she turned her key in the ignition and began her journey, her mind was on sharing the information she'd gathered. Thank God it was her DI that she was reporting to at the moment, and not her immediate – and currently suspended – boss, DS Wilkins. Hunches based on people's behaviour weren't something Wilkins took seriously. A momentary shudder went through her as she thought of the day when he might be back in his post. But it would be a while yet, by the sound of things. Despite her worries over Freya, she found herself smiling fleetingly as she turned right at the roundabout, back towards the centre of town.

The room where Blake's team worked was oddly quiet that evening – so much so that when Tara walked past the DI's office door she could hear immediately that he had someone with him. It was often the case, of course, but she still felt thwarted. She'd have to wait to fill him in on the afternoon's events – or else email him, but that wasn't the same as discussing something in person.

She wondered who was inside. The soundproofing for his office was good enough to keep what was being said private. All she could hear were murmurs, and they didn't give much away. She hung her coat on the stand in the corner, dropped into her chair and logged back into her computer.

She was part way through writing up her report when Blake's door opened. She glanced up quickly, but in a second her eyes were down on her screen again. It wasn't Blake who'd appeared, but a woman she recognised as his wife, Babette. 'Babette the babe', Wilkins used to call her – secretly, with a low laugh – before he'd been put on the disciplinary for unrelated misconduct. Tara had an alliterative pet name for Wilkins too, but it was too obscene to utter out loud.

It was amazing how much you could observe in a split second. Tara only recognised Babette at all because she'd accidentally caught sight of her, Blake and their daughter Kitty outside what was clearly their family home in Fen Ditton. She'd never seen her at the station before. And she'd got the impression – for many different reasons, from Wilkins' gossip to the way Blake sidestepped conversation about her – that their marriage wasn't strong.

But now, here was Babette, looking what Tara's mother would call 'ravishing', all of a glow, and clearly… very much pregnant. How quickly did you get that big? Tara was no expert but she guessed the woman had to be six months along at least.

Which meant Babette and Blake must have already been expecting when she'd glimpsed them outside their house at the start of December. And certainly just before Christmas, when Blake had held Tara tightly in his arms, just after she'd escaped from a burning building…

Shaky marriage, huh? Catching that one glimpse of Babette, smiling, putting a protective hand on her bump – glowing – made things look rather different. If your relationship was washed up, you didn't try for another baby.

She was conscious that Blake was standing outside his office now too. She could see his legs out of the corner of her eye; he must be facing in her direction. She kept her head down and carried on typing. Hopefully he'd assume she was too absorbed to have noticed him.

After a moment, she heard Babette speak.

'Come along, darling! You said you were ready to leave. We're due to pick Kitty up from Esme's in ten minutes. Don't you want to see your daughter?' She laughed.

At last, Tara raised her eyes slightly, to see if the coast was clear. The pair of them had already turned towards the exit, but, just before they left, Blake glanced over his shoulder.

'Good night, Tara.' He sounded uncomfortable.

Tara sat there for a full five minutes, digesting what that meant.

That night, as she lay awake in her cottage with its draughty sash windows, her mind was on Blake rather than Luke Cope and Freya Cross. She thought back to that last look he'd given her as he'd left the station that evening. If he felt awkward about her seeing Babette then maybe she hadn't misread his actions before Christmas.

She tried to put a stopper on the thoughts that were invading her headspace; what he'd done back then had simply been an impulsive response in the heat of the moment. Except it hadn't just been relief she'd seen in his eyes as he'd held her… why had he radiated such intense emotion when he'd *known* Babette was pregnant?

You ought to have behaved better, Blake. You were in shock, but I was the one who almost died.

At last she must have slept. It was still – ridiculously – the first thing in her head when she woke again. Talk about a waste of time. No amount of dwelling on the situation would alter the facts.

But the focus of the day changed very quickly.

The call from her colleague DC Max Dimity came in at seven thirty. Blake wanted them both over at the Paradise Nature Reserve.

A dog walker had discovered a body.

CHAPTER THREE

Paradise Nature Reserve lived up to its name in spring and summer – a secluded overgrown haven with boardwalks skirting round its dense interior. It was just across a branch of the River Cam from Sheep's Green, but DI Garstin Blake couldn't see any animals grazing there today. The was no grass to be had – it was still buried under the compacted snow.

Sue and Barry – the uniformed cops who'd been dispatched when the call came in – had done a good job in securing the scene so quickly. The entrances to the reserve were taped off – both at the end nearest Lammas Land, with its ancient willows and playground (thankfully deserted, due to the weather), and where the area met Owlstone Road in the well-to-do district of Newnham. They'd put tape along the river's edge too, using the ivy-covered tree trunks as posts to which to tie the plastic. Anyone could reach the nature reserve by boat – or punt, it being Cambridge – but Blake wasn't expecting many curious river-goers on a day like today.

He'd already pulled on the requisite white overalls – handed to him by one of the CSIs, who'd filled him in briefly – when he caught sight of Agneta Larsson, the pathologist. She was dashing towards the police barrier from the direction of the Lammas Land car park, her blonde fringe flying in the strong breeze.

It was the first time they'd seen each other since he'd confided to her over the phone that his wife, Babette, was pregnant again. Hell, it wasn't his fault, but he was still embarrassed – ashamed even – about the state of affairs. When he'd been to dinner with

Agneta and her husband Frans just before Christmas, Babette had already been three months gone, but he'd had no idea. That evening, he'd confessed to Agneta that he didn't want another child. Or at least – not with Babette. And when he'd explained – for the first time ever – just why there was such a rift between him and his wife, Agneta's white-hot anger – felt on his behalf – had shocked him. But it had also reflected his feelings of four and a half years earlier, when he'd found out how Babette had planned to betray him. Agneta was the only person he'd fully confided in.

She was pulling on her overalls now, whilst nodding at him. 'Blake. Where do we go?' They'd first met through work, and she still called him by his surname, just like most of his friends. The only people who habitually called him Garstin were his mother and Babette, which was ironic. He had complex relationships with them both. His sister used the pet name Gar, which he could just about cope with – because it was her.

Once Agneta was ready he led her along the route the CSI had described, following the icy raised path away from the river, then stepping off it and into the snow-covered undergrowth. A very slow thaw was taking place. The compacted flakes on the upper side of the tree branches glistened with a covering of meltwater, but the wind still made it bitterly cold – intense enough to have numbed his feet already, and to have worked its way through his clothes.

On the other side of a tree that had one long, low branch sticking out at right angles to its trunk, lay the body of the woman identified as Freya Cross. Sue had found her handbag nearby, containing all the usual ID. There was nothing obviously missing from it: her phone, purse, cards and keys were all there. Her driving licence showed she'd lived in Newnham and Blake already had reports coming in on everything from her line of work to her next of kin. She'd been very close to home when she'd been attacked. She was fully clothed in a high-quality grey woollen coat. The skin that was visible was blue-white, and snow had built up around the outline of her body. He shivered. When they moved her she would leave behind her imprint.

Freya Cross had worn a scarf, too, which was now loose around her neck. But Blake could see without Agneta's help that it had been tight at one point. Too tight. There were abrasions round her throat, and her open eyes were glassy and bloodshot. Her tongue protruded a little. Some bastard must have taken her by surprise. Someone she'd agreed to meet? Or someone – a friend or a stranger – that she'd been unlucky enough to run into by chance?

'The CSIs told me it's Freya Cross. I see it's not manual strangulation, then.'

He'd been so deep in thought he hadn't heard footsteps behind them. The snow had likely deadened them anyway. He didn't have to turn to know it was Tara. Her voice was shaky and when he spun round her green eyes were on the dead woman.

'What did you say?'

Tara recounted the interviews she'd conducted the previous day. As she described Luke Cope's painting of Freya Cross, Agneta put a gloved hand to the area of her mask that covered her mouth. 'My God.'

Tara was white-faced. 'If I'd pushed harder yesterday – called her home, gone to look for her in person – she might not be dead. I just went back to my cottage. I poured myself a glass of wine, for God's sake.'

Blake cursed inwardly. Tara's revelation had caught him off balance too. Normally, he'd have read her report the previous evening, but he and Babette had got into one of their 'discussions'. It had gone on into the night.

'Remind me again when Luke Cope went missing?' he asked.

'A week ago last Saturday.'

Blake looked at Agneta. She was already crouched over the dead woman's body, examining her, gingerly touching her unyielding arm.

Now the pathologist turned to meet his gaze. 'Well,' she began, 'she's rigid. In temperatures as cold as this rigor mortis can last way longer than usual – up to three days or so potentially. But in this case, she is simply frozen stiff. There's nothing to say she hasn't been here since the same Saturday the artist went missing.' She glanced up at Tara. 'You can set your mind at rest. Searching for her yesterday evening would already have been too late, though I may never be one hundred per cent certain on the timing. This weather is no help. We can at least say she died after the first snowfall. Her body was warm enough to melt the flakes beneath her torso when she fell, but there's thick snow under her hands and boots that stayed frozen.'

'What about the method, using the scarf rather than bare hands? Would that make Luke Cope less likely to be the perpetrator?'

Agneta shrugged. 'I wouldn't say so. What seemed appealing in his sick dreams might not have been practical in reality. Manual strangulation takes a lot of strength, and it's harder to control someone if they're standing, and on a slippery surface as well. Whoever your killer is, they probably realised the scarf was a surer option and went for that.'

Blake nodded. 'The bastard who did this got lucky. If the weather had improved she'd probably have been discovered the day after she was strangled – possibly by some cheery family with kids scrambling over the tree trunks, looking for beetles.' He closed his eyes for a second, imagining six-year-old Kitty faced with such a horrific sight. 'As it is, the trail's likely to be as cold as the weather – and if Luke Cope is the guilty party, who knows where he might have got to by now?'

'You're not certain it's him.' Tara's eyes were on Blake.

He shook his head. 'And you're not either.' He could see it in her expression.

She raised an eyebrow. 'Her husband told her boss she was staying with a friend for an indefinite period. If his wife's been here all this time he can't have spoken to her to check how she was doing. That seems odd for a start.'

Blake agreed. 'And you said her employer was cagey when you called?'

'Yes. He didn't respond in the way I'd have expected.'

Blake looked down again at the body. He thought of the stilled blood in her veins, the life that had been cut off so violently.

'Her other half is one Professor Zach Cross, apparently. I'll be watching him very closely when we go to break the news,' he said, turning to Tara. 'The family home is just round the corner, so we haven't got far to go. And then we'll want to talk to Matthew Cope again too, to find out more about his brother.'

Tara nodded, but already she'd turned away from him. The action seemed pointed to Blake.

Agneta looked up. 'I should have more for you by late afternoon. I'll call you when I have a firm time for the post-mortem.'

'Thanks, Agneta.'

She nodded.

'Tara, will you join Sue and talk to the woman who found the body?' He nodded over to where a grey-haired lady in a Barbour jacket, brown skirt and wellington boots was speaking to one of the PCs. 'I'm going to explore this place – get my bearings – and then we can get going.'

She'd turned to face him again. 'Sir.' Just that one word of acknowledgement… but then she smiled. It wasn't a genuine one though; she was being professional.

He watched her duck under the police tape before removing her mask and pulling down her hood. Her movements were controlled, even in overalls. He wondered if it was down to the honed spatial awareness that had come from the self-defence training she'd done.

She'd been stalked as a teenager and taken steps to protect herself. The offender had never been identified, and he suspected she'd been on her guard ever since.

He wished he'd known Babette was going to drop into the station the evening before. *If I had I would have—* But he cut off the thought. Focusing on anything but finding Freya Cross's killer was a betrayal of the dead woman.

Blake took the circular path that ran round the outer perimeter of the nature reserve. When he reached the exit that led towards Newnham he realised that the walk to Freya Cross's home was even shorter than he'd thought. And the house where the missing man, Luke Cope, lived wasn't far off either – though in the opposite direction. His brother Matthew had clearly thought they'd been having an affair and although it didn't sound as though there was proof, a painting of the woman naked in his house was pretty suggestive. And they'd fought, if Matthew Cope's report was accurate… Maybe he'd asked to meet her there, out in the wilderness, to sort out their differences. Perhaps, given the location, it was a favourite rendezvous point of theirs – part way between their two homes. Luke Cope could have reached it quickly on foot from Trumpington Road, cutting along Vicar's Brook through the meadows of Coe Fen, and then over the two footbridges, with their steel frameworks and timber decking, to reach the nature reserve. Maybe Freya Cross had arrived from her quiet, respectable street, all ready for a reconciliation. Only Luke hadn't come in peace after all…

What could have made him angry enough to paint that picture? And then –

perhaps – to have made the imagined scene a reality?

But he agreed with Tara – Zach Cross was of interest too. Could the man be responsible for a double murder? The circumstances would fit with a crime of passion, and it would explain Luke Cope's disappearance just as neatly.

He walked back towards the spot where Freya Cross lay, via the path next to the river.

'How's Babette?' Agneta asked, glancing up at him as he approached. She was still crouched down by Freya Cross's body.

'She's well.' The adrenaline started up the moment Agneta mentioned her name. There was a long pause. 'Nearly six months along now.' The pregnancy had gone fast – mainly thanks to him not knowing about it to start with. He sighed. 'I'd made up my mind to leave,' he said at last. 'On my way home, just before she told me she was pregnant, I realised that was the only way forward. But as soon as I heard the news everything changed.' He met her eye. 'It had to. Kitty's really happy. You can imagine how delighted a six-year-old is at the thought of a baby in the house.'

Kitty was his and Babette's first. Only it turned out she wasn't his at all, but some other bloke's – he still didn't know whose. He adored her just the same. Babette hadn't told him the truth about her parentage until she was eighteen months old. At which point his wife had secretly planned to take her abroad to be with her natural father. She'd gone, in fact – made the flight to Australia, leaving him alone in their cottage in Fen Ditton, the last memory of Kitty's face imprinted on his brain. But for whatever reason, Babette had decided within a fortnight that she'd made a mistake. Blake had wondered more and more over the intervening years why that had been. Whatever the truth, Kitty was the main reason he'd agreed to give their marriage another go. That and the sight of Babette in their sitting room, sobbing and clearly in such anguish. Or so it had seemed at the time.

'Blake.' Agneta stood for a moment and her blue eyes met his. 'We're old friends. You don't have to explain anything to me. I'm glad Kitty's pleased.' But her expression was serious. 'I just hope you're okay too, you know?'

He nodded. 'Thanks, Agneta.'

Her eyes were still on his. He could tell there was another question coming.

'You really think it was an accident, her forgetting to take her pill?'

Blake remembered Babette's sheepish look as she'd trotted out that excuse. He'd immediately felt that she'd done it on purpose – to try to cement their relationship maybe? The thought made him feel desperate. But he'd been primed to blame her by that point – furious because of her dishonesty and her unwelcome news, tying him to a marriage that was no longer working. The thought that the new baby might not be his lingered too – though if she'd been having an affair, he imagined she'd have been more careful about contraception, given what happened last time. A DNA test was still an option, once Babette had given birth, but what would he do, if the answer proved he'd been betrayed again? Walk out, leaving Kitty? And a new baby too? 'I'm honestly not sure. In a way it doesn't matter. The result's the same.'

But of course it did matter really. His suspicion and anger weren't healthy for him, her, the baby or Kitty. And his attitude was the reason he hadn't told his colleagues at work that he and Babette were expecting another child. He'd somehow hoped to find a way out of the situation – except there wasn't one.

Agneta patted his white-suited arm. 'Come round again soon for fish and chips. Frans and I need adult company and he liked that you were so appreciative of his cooking.'

They had a small baby, Elise. Agneta claimed her conversation was becoming limited to 'Look, Elise, there's a duck. Ducks go quack.' She didn't get to chat much at work, given her main contact was with corpses.

'I will. Thank you.'

At that moment he looked up and saw his DC, Max Dimity, had turned up. He was approaching Tara, who'd finished talking to the dog walker. Max looked calm, as usual, but there was something in his eye that caught Blake's attention. Tara glanced up at Max, and, as he spoke, her expression changed. It was like watching storm clouds scud across a clear sky. He strode over to them – avoiding the tangled slippery roots at his feet.

'What's up?'

Max frowned. 'Sorry, boss – no idea how, but the press have got hold of this. Shona Kennedy from *Not Now* magazine is at the barrier towards Lammas Land, asking if someone will give her a comment.' His look matched Blake's feelings.

'I'll talk to her,' Tara said. But her expression spoke of what she'd like to do to the woman, rather than say to her.

Not Now had once employed Tara. She and the magazine's editor, Giles Troy, hadn't parted friends. And then Shona Kennedy – one of his staff reporters – had written a poisonous article about Tara's handling of the last murder case she'd worked on. Shona had been eagerly helped by Blake's now suspended DS, Tara's boss, Patrick Wilkins. Wilkins' leaks had been hugely damaging to the case and a massive abuse of his position. Blake had always disliked the smug idiot anyway. He'd never trust anyone who paid that much attention to their appearance. How could you be serious about your work if you whipped out a comb every time you passed a mirror?

Blake mostly tried to ignore the fact that Tara had already made a few enemies. He admired her for the reasons behind it, even if it was disruptive. She was clever, uncompromising and although she was smooth as hell when she wanted to get information out of a suspect, she could tell it very straight when she saw no need for tact.

Having her talk to Shona about the current case seemed like a bad idea.

'I'll deal with her.' He gave Tara a look.

'You can trust me, you know.' Her voice was tight.

Tara had once got into a fight with a fellow journalist, resulting in a broken finger and a black eye for him. But she'd only lashed out because the man had been following her. She'd thought he was the stalker who'd plagued her during her teenage years. Extenuating circumstances.

Blake sighed. 'It's not you I'm worried about. Whatever you say to her she'll twist it. She's on a mission and she's guided by Giles Troy. Max – would you come and listen in? You can witness what I say, in case she takes the same tack with me.'

Max nodded. 'I'd be glad to.'

Blake turned to Tara again. 'I want to starve the flames she's fanning of oxygen, that's all.'

He'd managed to keep his tone calm, but Shona Kennedy was a serious threat. Not only had she rubbished Tara's professionalism in her article back in December, she'd also hinted at some kind of improper relationship between him and his DC. In the event, Tara's theories about that case, which they'd derided at the time, had proved to be entirely correct. He smiled for a fraction of a second. *Not Now* had been made to look like a pack of fools. It had been satisfying, but it would have left Giles Troy with a new score to settle. Blake suspected he'd already been prepared to stop at nothing to bring his former employee down, and he certainly wouldn't worry about the fallout.

CHAPTER FOUR

Tara wanted to explore the murder site like Blake had, but she'd only got halfway round when she saw that he had returned. The 'chat' with Shona Kennedy had taken all of two minutes. Max was no longer with him.

It was Blake's turn to avoid her eyes as he strode past her. 'We're going out the rear way,' he said, nodding towards the Owlstone Road end of the nature reserve. 'I've sent Max back to the station to talk to Fleming and prepare the incident room.'

Karen Fleming was the detective chief inspector. She attacked each new case with ruthless efficiency, driven by personal ambition and the welfare of the victim in fairly equal measure.

'Hopefully the very unlovely Shona Kennedy will follow Max,' Blake went on. 'If not, Sue and Barry will keep her at bay. There are plenty of our people out front. I want to make damn sure we get to Professor Cross before he gets wind of his wife's death on the local grapevine. It won't take long for the rumours to start circulating. Sue looked him up. He's based at the faculty of History, but the administrator there told her he's working at home this morning.'

Tara kept pace with him, watching his expression. 'You managed to deal with Shona pretty quickly.'

'Said she'd have to wait for the press conference like everyone else.'

His jaw was tight, and wondering what Shona's response had been set Tara's pulse racing. Maybe she could persuade Max to fill her in later. There was no way Blake would tell her, even if she asked – he'd see it as 'fanning the flames'. And she wasn't in the mood to coax the information out of him, anyway.

'Congratulations on your news, by the way.' The words came out quickly but she reckoned she'd managed to keep her tone nonchalant. 'I caught a glimpse of your wife as you were about to the leave the building last night.'

Blake's brown eyes met hers for a long moment, but he didn't speak.

'When's she due?'

'The end of May.'

They were on the path that led round the nature reserve's interior, away from the river. The raised boardwalk wove its way through the tangle of ice-covered fallen leaves from the previous autumn – a decayed bed under the trees. Here and there a snowdrop showed there was new life to come. The white petals made Tara think of Freya Cross. They were the same colour as her skin. The fact that someone had cut her time on earth short, whilst everything else was rejuvenating, gave Tara a heavy feeling inside her chest. She blinked away the emotion that threatened to break cover – sorrow overlaid with a thick dose of fury, partly at herself. However long Freya had been dead, it didn't change the guilt she felt. She should have looked for her the evening before.

After a moment she and Blake ducked under the police cordon at the nature reserve's exit, nodding to the uniformed officers stationed on Owlstone Road. Then they stood there in the street, peeling off their masks and overalls, ready to hand them back to the CSI team. Having Blake there in front of her, suddenly revealed in all his scruffy glory, was unhelpful. Tara had a strong desire to share and offload after what they'd just seen, but her automatic reaction to him ensured she held back.

As she finally stepped out of her protective suit, she caught a glimpse of a man with a tote bag over one arm, glancing back at the spectacle from the corner of the road. When he caught her eye he turned away hastily and carried on walking. *Believe me, you don't want to know...*

The narrow lane was lined with evergreen hedges and trees, still coated with the remnants of the snowfall. The roof of the spacious, red-brick Edwardian villa opposite maintained a dusting of white too. Blake turned left and Tara followed him.

'Which road are we looking for?' she asked.

'St Mark's Street. Number eight.'

She knew it. It ran between a branch of Owlstone Road and Grantchester Street. Professor Cross could easily have found his own wife's body if he'd gone out for a walk. Paradise Nature Reserve would have been one of the first places he'd have come to.

Tara googled and found Zach Cross as they walked. 'He looks a bit older than his wife in the faculty mugshot,' she said in an undertone. It was the kind of age gap that might have got the neighbours talking. In Tara's experience, it didn't take much. She was glad her own house was so isolated. She'd hate to have people breathing down her neck, judging her behaviour.

Blake glanced at her phone screen and raised an eyebrow. 'I see what you mean.' He sighed. 'A case involving an academic always fills me with dread. One of these days I'm bound to end up interviewing someone who knows my mother. I'm glad he's a professor of History, rather than History of Art, but there's still a chance they'll have crossed paths.'

'Your mother's an academic?' Surprise made her drop her guard a little.

He put his head on one side and gave her a half smile. 'You were bound to find out sooner or later.'

'Whatever your mother's like she can't beat mine in the weird parents' stakes.' He needn't think she was going to sympathise.

'Being an actress isn't that weird.'

'Not per se.' Tara was the product of a teenage liaison between Lydia – now famous for her acting career – and Robin, who had grown into an architect. They'd both gone on to marry other people and have families that were planned in a way that Tara wasn't. When she turned up to visit them she always felt superfluous.

They turned into St Mark's Street and Tara was forced to focus her mind on what they were about to do. Breaking bad news couldn't be anyone's favourite job, and on top of making sure they gave the information in the right way – with sympathy yet total clarity, making their message gentle but unambiguous – they also had to give it whilst keeping in mind that it might not be news to Zach Cross at all. Maybe he'd killed his wife and Luke Cope too, if they'd been having an affair. She knew the thought would have gone through Blake's mind.

She realised he was looking at her.

'Ready?' he said.

She nodded, keeping her true feelings hidden.

Blake raised the brass knocker below the glass panels of the glossy red front door and rapped to get the owner's attention.

It was interesting to watch Professor Cross's face as he opened up. Tara recognised the first look of slight confusion – he'd been deep in something, she guessed, and their interruption had pulled him part way out of his thoughts. And then almost instantly, she could see he was on high alert. There was unease in his eyes – and that was a very quick reaction for someone with no reason to suspect there was anything wrong. She glanced at Blake, wondering if it was their physical appearance that had rung the professor's alarm bells. Was it obvious that they were police officers? But Blake was wearing a long, dark woollen coat she guessed might have something to do with his fashion designer sister. He wore her wares to please her. The suit trousers underneath looked like hers too. He teamed the look with an otherwise scruffy air. His hair was a bit all over the place and his tie was wonky. Nothing about him said detective. She herself was wearing a padded jacket, trousers and boots, thanks to the intense cold.

'Professor Cross?' Blake said, taking out his ID. 'I wonder if we could come inside to talk to you?'

The professor stepped back into his hallway – a wide room with polished floorboards and a dark red rug. The wall was hung with several paintings. They were mostly old-fashioned in style, with gilt frames, but one modern, abstract piece was present amongst the rest. Tara wondered if Freya Cross had bought it from the gallery where she'd worked – and if she owned any paintings by Luke Cope.

The professor still hadn't made a sound.

Tara closed the door behind them, making a noise that seemed loud in the silence.

'Is there anyone else here in the house with you?' Blake said. Cross shook his head, before Blake added: 'Is there somewhere you'd like to sit?'

The professor moved through to a drawing room with a box bay window and sank into an armchair. He filled it. He was an impressive looking man – well-built and good looking, with iron-grey hair.

'Would it be all right for us to sit here?' Blake indicated a couple more armchairs.

Zach Cross nodded.

'I'm very sorry to have to tell you that Freya – Mrs Cross – was found dead this morning in the Paradise Nature Reserve.'

There was a long pause. Tara knew there was no point in wading in with more information until the fact had had time to sink in. In the meantime, she watched the professor's reaction.

'This morning?'

His shock looked genuine. Then, within a fraction of a second, his face spoke of his pain, mixed with some kind of bereft bewilderment – as though he was trying to make sense of something. Something more than the fact that his wife was dead?

'That's right, sir,' Blake said. 'I'm afraid we don't have much firm information yet. We're waiting on reports from our medical and forensics teams, but I have to tell you that we're treating her death as murder.'

The professor's mouth was half open. He stared at Blake.

'Can I get you a glass of water, Professor?' Tara asked after a moment.

He managed to nod, and she left the room. He'd need a minute before Blake could ask much else anyway. And probably a lot longer than that before he fully assimilated what had happened. But, then again, if he had killed his wife a week ago he'd have been waiting for her body to be discovered ever since. Tara imagined him on tenterhooks, listening out for their knock. Their appearance at last could have been enough for him to look that stunned. And he'd have had plenty of time to practise faking surprise.

She opened a couple of cupboards before finding a tumbler, then went to the gleaming Belfast sink to fill the glass up with water. As she waited for it to run cold she cast her eyes around the room. The furniture looked old and valuable. A highly polished oak dresser with brass handles, and an ornate vase containing dried flowers stood out. In one corner though, standing on a low mahogany cupboard, was a modern designer lamp. It was constructed from wood, like a lot of other objects in the room, but its detailing was in stainless steel and she guessed its flat bulb was an LED. Was that Freya Cross's style creeping in, just as the modern artwork had taken a tiny foothold in the hall? The place didn't feel as though it represented two people's tastes equally. For a second, as she filled the glass, Tara tried to imagine sharing her cottage with someone else, and how she'd feel about letting them stamp their imprint on it. It wouldn't be easy, but she'd either be fair about it or avoid sharing her space altogether. Possibly the latter.

As she crossed the room, back towards the hall, she spotted a wall calendar. She could hear Blake had started to question Zach Cross in earnest, but she paused for a moment, to see what appointments the professor and Freya might have had in the last weeks. It was easy to tell whose entries were whose. One lot were written in rough capital letters and referred to lectures, faculty meetings and the like. The rest were in neat italics and included a private view at a gallery in the centre of town at the start of the previous month. There was one recent entry written in Freya's hand: *Talk to Jonny*, inked in for Monday 26 February. There was no time – it looked more like a statement of intent than an appointment. Tara sometimes added notes like that in her own diary; it was a way of shelving a decision she'd made, putting it out of her head until she could act on it. It was usually something that was making her stressed...

Back with Blake and Zach Cross, Tara put the glass on a low coffee table, inlaid with decorative tiles. The professor picked the drink up absently but didn't put it to his lips.

'So you last saw your wife a week ago last Friday,' Blake was saying, 'when she left the house. That would have been Friday the twenty-third of February. Where was she going?'

Professor Cross looked down at the rug on the floor. 'To stay with a friend,' he said at last. 'Sophie Havers. She lives in London.'

So Tara would have expected Freya to have been carrying an overnight bag at the very least. But if she had been, the killer must have taken it with them. There'd been nothing of that sort at the scene. And yet the woman's handbag and purse had still been present...

'And can you please think back and tell me what time she left the house?'

The man hesitated. His eyes were far away, and Tara could see a tear rolling down his cheek. 'Well – it was after supper. I don't know what time. Not late.'

'So you ate together?' Blake asked. Zach Cross nodded. 'What kind of meal did you have? I'm just trying to build up a picture.'

Tara could see where this was going. Stomach contents might be relevant when Agneta Larsson opened Freya Cross up.

'Steak and chips, and then chocolate fondants. We were relaxed, as it was only the two of us. If Oscar, my son, is here we have to be more careful. He has type 1 diabetes.'

The professor hadn't paused at the query. One up to Blake.

'Do you often have people over?' her DI asked.

Zach Cross nodded. 'Fairly often. Entertaining is an add-on to my academic work. One of my colleagues or a visiting scholar might come to dine with us, for instance. And as I said, my son, Oscar – Freya's stepson – is with us every so often as well.'

So his job had frequently affected Freya's lifestyle too. There could be a bit of strain there.

Tara leant forward. 'Will you be able to reach Oscar today, Professor, to break the news? Can we call him for you? We're keen to make sure close family members hear what's happened before anyone else.'

But the man shook his head, and now he spoke with more purpose. 'I understand, but I would prefer to inform him myself. He's a student, here in the city. I'll be able to reach him on his mobile.'

'We'll probably need to speak to him too, in due course,' Blake said, and Zach Cross's face registered confusion all over again. 'How about Mrs Cross's parents – and any siblings?'

Professor Cross shook his head. 'She was an only child, and her parents died in a car crash two years ago.'

She'd been very much alone then. Barring close friends, there'd been precious few people she could have confided in, if she'd had any sense that she was in danger.

'Going back to when your wife left the house,' Blake went on, 'you remained here for the rest of the evening?'

There was no sign that the professor realised he was being asked if he had an alibi for the time that his wife had probably died. 'That's right,' he said. 'I sat in the drawing room in front of the fire with a glass of port and a book I'd agreed to review. And then, after I'd made some notes, I went upstairs to bed.' He shook his head and his eyes welled with tears again. 'I was up until gone midnight. If I'd known…'

Tara passed him a box of tissues that sat on a bookshelf near the door and he took one, turned away from them and blew his nose.

'Could we have the details of the friend your wife was going to see in London please?' Blake said, once the man had had some time to compose himself.

The professor nodded slowly and got up from his chair. He moved as though gravity was having triple the normal effect on his body. Tara got up to follow him through to the hall, her notebook at the ready.

'Here.' He held an address book open at the letter H. Just one entry: a Sophie Havers in Hampstead. Tara copied down the details.

Back in the sitting room, Blake said: 'Did your wife explain why she was heading off to her friend's house so late in the day?'

More hesitation on the professor's part. 'I didn't ask her.'

'When did you expect her back?'

'She said she might be gone ten days or so. She'd been working hard; needed a break.'

He sounded less and less sure of himself as he spoke. Tara controlled the urge to look in Blake's direction. *Plenty of time to discuss all this later…* 'I understand she worked at an art gallery,' she put in. 'She'd booked leave then?' She knew what Jonny Trent had told her, but she wanted to see how Professor Cross explained it.

'It was a bit last minute,' the man said. 'I spoke to Jonny Trent, who owns the gallery, to explain.'

Which matched what Freya's boss had told her… Tara thought again of the woman's entry on the kitchen calendar. She'd been planning to catch up with Jonny Trent about something important the previous Monday, three days after her husband had last seen her. Had anyone known about her plans? Could they have killed her to prevent the meeting going ahead? It seemed far-fetched. Perhaps Freya had simply been so stressed that she'd decided to get the hell out instead of tackling her troubles head on.

'So she was out of sorts? Sufficiently tired that she hadn't prepared as she normally would if she was planning to take a break?' Blake's tone hadn't changed, but she knew him well enough to tell what he was thinking.

The man frowned. 'She was certainly preoccupied. I offered to give her a lift to the station, but she said she'd rather walk.'

'She didn't have too much to carry then?' Tara waited for the professor to sketch in the details.

'Just a smallish overnight bag,' he said.

Which was as she'd thought. The question of its whereabouts remained. As for the walk to the station, the weather would have been bitterly cold that night. Taking the shortcut through the nature reserve would have reduced the journey to around half an hour on foot... though her decision to walk at all seemed pretty strange.

The professor must have followed the same train of thought. 'I never imagined... I mean, this is a quiet district. If I'd—'

'The only person responsible for what happened to your wife is her killer, Professor Cross, and we will do everything in our power to bring that person to justice.'

On the face of it Blake was stemming the professor's words of self-reproach, but he was also laying down a promise – they were coming after whoever was guilty. No one would be discounted, least of all her husband.

Blake had kept his tone neutral but the professor swallowed. 'How did Freya die?'

'It looks like strangulation. We'll have to wait for confirmation. We made the initial identification using the photograph on her driving licence but we'll need someone to come over to Addenbrooke's to do the job officially in due course. It doesn't have to be you.'

But the man shook his head. 'I want to see her.'

The DI nodded. 'I understand. We'll arrange it as soon as we can. In the meantime, I wonder if we might have a quick look upstairs, just to get an idea of how Mrs Cross left her things. There might be something there that will give us a lead.'

Tara held her breath, wondering if the professor would object and force them to wait for a warrant, but after a moment he nodded. Not before he'd weighed up the request though, Tara reckoned.

They climbed the winding stairway to a galleried first-floor landing. Tara was especially interested to see the bathroom, which turned out to be an en suite, fitted in classic style, white with a large claw-foot bath at one side.

There were still two toothbrushes present, each in a squat glass on a shelf over the basin.

She saw the professor follow her gaze. 'Freya had a travel set that included a folding one,' he said. He walked over to the basin and bent to open a cupboard next to it. After a second he sighed. 'That's definitely what she took. It's not in its usual place.'

At that moment they were interrupted by a knock at the front door. Tara left Blake with the professor and went downstairs. Through the bay window, she could see DCs Kirsty Crowther and Evan Lewis.

Kirsty nodded a greeting as Tara let them in. 'Morning,' she said. 'DCI Fleming's assigned us as family liaison officers.'

Two. Standard practice when a family member might also be the killer. Tara wondered if Zach Cross would notice. The more he felt watched, the more he'd clam up.

Blake and the professor reappeared in the hallway and Tara introduced them all.

'DC Crowther and DC Lewis will take you to Addenbrooke's when the time comes,' Blake said. He glanced at the pair for a moment. 'Please can you go through Mrs Cross's key contacts with Professor Cross? We'll need to work out who might be able to help us with our investigation. The professor needs to inform Mrs Cross's stepson too.'

Kirsty nodded. Evan was already exchanging quiet words with their charge.

'I'll need to ask you for more information, Professor,' Blake said, 'but I'll give you a chance to take stock now. We're very sorry for your loss.'

Tara turned to shake the man's hand too, just after Blake. His grip was strong and his gaze when it met hers told her he was trying to work out what they thought. Behind all the anguish, he was wary; she could see that much.

When they left the house they turned towards the centre of Newnham, rather than the nature reserve. It was the long way round to the Lammas Land car park, but they didn't want to cross the crime scene again. The going was slow, the pavements still icy.

Tara's head was full of Zach Cross's story; *if ever a tale sounded made up...* She hadn't yet looked in Blake's direction though. It was partly because she was watching her feet; bits of the pavement were like a skating rink.

She heard him sigh. 'Are you going to tell me what you think, then?'

She paused a moment before replying. 'It'll be interesting to hear what Freya's friend in Hampstead has to say.'

For just a second she let her gaze slide sideways and her eyes met his. He looked as though he wanted to communicate something unrelated to the case, but at last he shook his head.

'I agree. I'm not sure Zach Cross did it, but he's hiding something. We need to get more background, so we know where to aim our questions. After that we'll go back in and catch him out.'

Tara took a long breath, the air so cold she could feel it deep inside her. She knew she was behaving like a kid, but seeing Babette and Blake together the night before had made her feel awkward around him. She really needed to snap out of it. She relayed what she'd seen on Freya and Zach Cross's kitchen calendar.

Blake rubbed a stubbly chin. 'Interesting…' He gave her a sidelong glance. 'You didn't go rummaging through their cupboards as well, did you?'

She shot him a withering look, but wondered fleetingly if she might have, if she'd had more time.

'I'll take that as a no,' Blake went on. 'Right. I'm going to go and call Sophie Havers. I'd better break the news, anyway, and then I can find out what light she's got to shed on all this. After that I'm going to head over to Jonny Trent's gallery. Given the calendar entry you saw it looks as though there was something up at work. It might fit in with his caginess when you rang him too. I want to watch his face as I tell him about Freya's murder.'

Tara would have liked to witness that too, but it was clear Blake had other plans for her.

'I want you to talk to Matthew Cope again,' he said. 'Once he knows Freya Cross is dead he might clam up; it depends where his loyalties lie. You've already started breaking down his defences' – he caught her eye – 'best if you carry on the good work.'

She nodded. In truth, she'd relish the challenge, and she could see Blake's logic. If Matthew Cope was prepared to protect Luke, even if he might be guilty, he was probably wishing he'd never made such a fuss about his disappearance. The last thing he'd want now was the attention of a more senior officer. He'd see Tara as an inexperienced underling who might botch the investigation and she'd play up to that. She'd aim to move him onto first-name terms before they'd finished their next discussion.

She thought again of Freya Cross's body. If the man was shielding his brother, she'd do whatever it took to get it out of him.

CHAPTER FIVE

When Tara called Matthew Cope from her car she found he'd gone back to his home, on the north-east side of the city, towards the A14. She only paused for a second to warm her numb hands by the vent of the vehicle's heater before heading off across town, through the crowded, exhaust-filled streets.

She drove on autopilot, her mind on Freya Cross. Seeing her like that, in the middle of Paradise Nature Reserve, made Tara think of Sleeping Beauty. Had the woman's death turned the fairy tale on its head? Her 'prince' might well have been responsible for her never waking up. If a lover put you on a pedestal they were just as likely to pull you down because you'd failed to live up to expectations, as to ride off with you into the sunset. Kemp, the ex-cop who'd taught her self-defence after she'd been stalked, sometimes accused her of being overly cynical, but he understood why. She'd only been sixteen when it had started and though it had gone on for eighteen months she still didn't know who'd been responsible. Every so often she dreamt of the packages they'd sent her, full of maggots, feathers and once, a pig's heart…

Out on the north-east side of the city, her journey took her into what felt like countryside – there were horses in a field to her right. But the area was mixed. Quite soon she passed an industrial estate on her left, with a tattered banner across its metal fencing advertising vacant units to rent. After that there were some newly built houses assembled from soft cream bricks that echoed the colour of the historic buildings in town. But the buildings here were a far cry from the sort that tourists would expect when visiting the ancient university city. She drove on, past a series of prefabs and more industrial units that included a car mechanic's outfit. The place looked grim under the grey sky and all around there was melting snow, discoloured by dirt to form grey slush.

After a while the road narrowed and Tara bumped her car over some potholes. Just as well it was a work vehicle; she doubted her own aging Fiat could have taken the strain. She'd left the buildings behind and now scrubby fields with overgrown hedges filled her view to left and right. The place was almost deserted, but then up ahead she saw a dark-blue Mercedes. She was instantly aware of their closing speed and gripped the wheel tightly. She steered her car tight into the side of the road as the Merc zipped past. The driver must have had their foot to the floor.

Swearing under her breath, she took a moment to steady herself. Some witless so and so with no manners – and no comprehension that they weren't the only person who counted.

A moment later, her teeth still gritted in irritation, she came to the track which, according to her satnav, would take her to Matthew Cope's place. Rounding a corner past an overgrown holly hedge, its spiky leaves now almost entirely visible thanks to the thaw, she saw a large square house – somewhat bigger than the one occupied by Luke Cope, and Victorian, she guessed, rather than Edwardian. It clearly had a lot of land around it, but whether that would be an advantage or a headache, Tara wasn't sure. She liked having plenty of space around her own cottage, out on Stourbridge Common, but it was good not to be responsible for it.

She pulled up on the rough drive and then had to move the car again when she realised she was stranded – the driver's side door was positioned over a large meltwater puddle filling a deep rut. The only other vehicle present was a BMW, which presumably must be Matthew Cope's.

As she finally extricated herself from her car, she looked up and realised that the brother of the missing man was standing at the top of the steps to his front door, watching her. His hands were clutched together, his jaw tense.

'What is it?' he asked as she got nearer. 'I heard on the news that a body's been discovered in the Paradise Nature Reserve. They didn't give any more details.' His words were clipped. 'Is it Luke?'

She shook her head. 'The body's female.'

He put a hand up over his mouth. 'Freya Cross?'

'Nothing's confirmed officially, Mr Cope. I'm just here to ask you a little bit more about your brother and his disappearance.'

The man was silent as he showed her inside, down a shadowy hallway. The place smelt slightly of damp, overlaid with cigarette smoke. At the end of the hall they went through a door that opened onto a large kitchen which an estate agent would have described as 'in need of modernisation'. All the same, it had plenty of potential, given its vast size.

Matthew Cope must have followed her gaze. 'This is my inheritance,' he said, 'left in trust until I'm forty – just the same arrangement as for Luke.'

Tara was curious about that. She ought to be able to get away with probing if she presented her questions as polite interest. She was quite sure Matthew Cope still didn't see her as the detective she actually was. Annoying, but it helped. 'Did your parents spend time in both houses? Coming here almost feels like being in the countryside.'

Cope nodded. 'It's good to get right away from the city each night. It's not all nice out here, but I'll take the smooth with the rough. There's nothing like going outside in the evening and watching the bats swoop over the grounds.'

Tara took the smooth with the rough where she lived too. The beauty and peace of the meadows more than made up for the lonely location, and the occasional antisocial behaviour out on the common around her house.

'When my father married my mother it was his second union,' Matthew Cope went on. 'He was already living in the house in town. After he divorced his first wife, she moved away from Cambridge with their daughter, Vicky, to Suffolk. He bought her out, which gave her a nice bit of money to play with, and my mother moved in.'

He made it sound like a simple financial transaction with no emotions involved. Tara wondered how he got on with his half-sister, and if she had grown up feeling resentful. As a half-sister herself, with no fewer than four half-siblings, she could well understand it if she had.

'This house was my mother's family home,' Matthew Cope went on. 'She was sentimentally attached to it so when my grandparents died my parents decided to keep it as investment rather than letting it go.'

'It's certainly quite a place.' Tumbledown, yes, but with some faded grandeur and more than enough room to swing a hundred cats. If Matthew worked long hours, getting the place renovated might not be a priority. It was the same for her; she spent so little time at home that she hadn't yet got round to much DIY, despite her cottage's shortcomings.

'Do you have to get back to work soon?' Tara asked, her mind having turned to his career.

He shook his head. 'I requested a day's leave when I heard there'd been a development. I couldn't get it out of my head that the body must be Luke's.' He closed his eyes for a moment. 'Now I know that it's not, I can't help but feel relieved. But the thought that it's Freya makes me sick to the stomach.'

'All those reactions are very understandable. As I said, there's been no formal identification yet.'

He nodded and took a short, tight breath. 'But I presume it will all come out very soon now?'

Tara tried to see where that question had come from. Was he worried that everyone would assume his brother was guilty, the moment the murder of Freya Cross went public? That might be true if most people knew they'd been lovers. But surely they'd have kept it quiet, given that Freya was married?

She nodded. 'I think so. A little later today, I imagine.'

'I can't bear all this waiting. Can I get you a coffee?' He was standing by a sink and taps that had a 1970s feel about them.

'Thank you.' The house was even colder than hers. Of course, there was a lot more of it to heat. She wondered if it was connected to the grid, or if he relied on an oil tank – and maybe a septic one for waste too.

'Please take a seat.'

She pulled a wood veneer chair, with a wipe-clean cushion, out from under a matching table and acted on the invitation. 'So your brother and Freya Cross met through Trent's art gallery?'

Matthew filled the kettle. 'That's right. My brother's art doesn't sell well, but he's had some very positive reviews. Jonny Trent – the gallery owner – was happy to stock his work; he's got plenty of space, but the paintings seldom shift. Luke probably makes a couple of hundred quid every five or six months. Trent's isn't the right platform to further his career. His work's too edgy.' He turned to put the kettle on its stand and flicked the switch.

Presumably Luke didn't have much cause to visit the gallery often then – it wasn't as though he'd be in and out, keeping track of sales and providing new artwork. Yet it seemed he'd got into a relationship with a married woman who worked there... 'Did they have any other contact with each other?'

'Not initially. But the gallery holds occasional private views – drinks parties for prospective art buyers – and Luke usually attends those.' She saw him roll his eyes as he put mugs on the table. 'He enjoys that side of things. And he always says there's a chance that he'll get talking to someone who can turn his fortunes around.'

She imagined the right contacts could make or break a career, but it was clear that Matthew didn't agree. *Time to ingratiate myself...* 'That sounds like a bit of a long shot.'

He nodded. 'I concur. It's true that lots of reputations in the arts world appear to be built on luck, but in reality you have to make your own. And there are better ways of doing it than standing about eating vol-au-vents at parties.'

Tara wondered if Luke ever got irritated by Matthew Cope thinking he had all the answers. She would, in his place.

Matthew was pouring milk into a small brown jug. 'My brother's work is every bit as good as the stuff that makes it into the top London galleries.'

Tara thought back to the strange paintings she'd seen at Luke Cope's house. They'd certainly been striking. Not what she'd want on her own walls, though. And then there was his personality, as indicated by the portrait of a woman being strangled. If he was a violent misogynist that wouldn't help him make friends and influence people...

The kettle had boiled and she watched as Matthew spooned coffee grounds into a cafetière he'd taken from a shelf and then add the water. He brought the press over to the kitchen table.

'So you were aware of Mrs Cross and your brother socialising outside work, I presume, given you suspected they were more than just friends?' With the drink-fuelled gallery parties she could start to see how an affair might have been kindled.

'Not especially. My brother and I don't live in each other's pockets. But Luke invited her and Jonny Trent to his house-warming do, and what I saw there made me think he and Freya might be having an affair.'

'House-warming?' She was confused for a moment. Surely the mansion where he lived had been in the family for years?

'Ah, yes. I should explain. Until four months ago, Luke was living in a flat on Histon Road.'

The street was one of Cambridge's main arteries, on the same side of the city as the house they were now in, but further into town. Nowhere in Cambridge was cheap, but Histon Road was more reasonable than some locations.

'He was letting the house off Trumpington Road to tenants. There are always plenty of people prepared to pay a small fortune to rent a place like that for a few months – visiting venture capitalists spending some time in Silicon Fen.'

University spin-out companies ensured there was a lot of money sloshing around the area.

'By doing that and then renting a much cheaper place himself,' Matthew went on, 'he was able to make ends meet whilst trying to further his artistic career.'

'So what changed then, to allow him to move back into the family house himself?' Tara leant forward. She wanted him to feel they were having a heart to heart, not a one-sided interrogation.

'That's what I asked myself. I double-checked the value of his paintings online to see if he'd had a breakthrough, but that wasn't it. In the end I cracked and asked him. It turned out he'd discovered one of the bits of jewellery our mother had left him was worth much more than any of us knew.'

His glance met Tara's. 'She and my father left me some nice pieces too. And we each own those things outright, so we can sell them whenever we want.' He smiled suddenly and put his shoulders back. 'I just don't need to. My work means I can afford to live in this place without extra help.'

If he'd been a bird, he'd have preened his feathers at that point. It wasn't attractive, but she managed to smile anyway. 'That's a nice position to be in, I imagine – and not that common these days.'

'Too true.'

'So Freya Cross and Jonny Trent attended your brother's party?'

He nodded. 'Freya's husband came too, in fact. He was keeping a close eye on his wife and my brother.' The man leant over his coffee and put his head in his hands for a moment. 'I could see that much. And they exchanged what are commonly known as "pleasantries", but I'm sure Zach Cross suspected things weren't as they should be.' At last he looked up at Tara. 'I suppose maybe Freya found she and her husband had less in common than she'd thought. She was a fair bit younger than him. Perhaps their priorities didn't quite match up.'

Tara kept quiet on that. She thought of Kemp. In her experience age difference was no barrier to a spark between two people. But of course, things were different when it came to a long-term relationship. Not that she'd had many of those.

'What did you think of Freya?' she asked.

Matthew shrugged. 'I never got to know her well. She seemed very passionate about her work. I got the impression she adored art and the people who create it.'

'What about the painting your brother did of Mrs Cross?' she asked quietly. 'How did you feel when you saw it?'

It was a moment before he spoke. 'I was shocked. But even though I was worried – especially when Luke just disappeared – my God, I never truly thought he'd act on his feelings. Not in my heart of hearts. The news that a body has been found brought that home to me. I thought his art was his safety valve; that doing that painting would have got his anger out of his system. It was his own welfare I was worried about when I called the police.'

There was a long silence. Through the kitchen window Tara could see crows swooping across the untidy grounds of the house.

'I'm sorry I didn't show your colleagues the painting when I first spoke to them.' His eyes met hers, more challenging than apologetic.

Tara shook her head. 'Even if you had told us, it's unlikely it would have made a difference. And we have no proof that your brother is responsible for the body that's been found.' Though things weren't looking rosy for him. She sighed. 'So what do you think's happened to your brother?'

'I'm worried he's harmed himself.'

It was possible that he had, rather than going into hiding to try and escape the consequences of what he'd done. Assuming he was guilty. 'If that were true, Mr Cope, can you think where he might have gone? Somewhere that would have given him the time and space he'd have needed?'

'Call me, Matthew, please.'

Bingo.

He shook his head slowly, his dark hair falling forward over one eye. 'I've tried, but I can't think of anywhere.'

'No place that was special to him, for instance – a childhood haunt or somewhere he liked to visit when things got tough?'

The man shook his head again. 'We used to run around the streets of Cambridge when we were little but there was nowhere quiet where he wouldn't have risked being disturbed.'

Cambridge had its secluded spots, though, and it had been days before Freya Cross had been discovered, if their assumption about the timing was right.

'Just for the record, Matthew, I need to ask where you were on the night of Friday twenty-third of February, and over that weekend too. We'll request the information from everyone we interview who knew Freya.' Tara wanted to keep the window quite wide until they'd heard more from Agneta about the time of death. She couldn't think of any reason for Matthew to want Freya dead, but it was too early to make assumptions. Even though they were conversing more easily now, she hadn't warmed to him.

He frowned, fished his mobile from his pocket and leant forward over the table as he looked at it. 'Work during the day of course, and then I just came home. My colleagues and I do sometimes get together for a drink on Fridays but looking back, that wasn't one of them. Then, the following day I went to Tesco to get some shopping in the morning, did some jobs in the afternoon, I think – and then went into town to meet Luke for our pub trip, only he didn't show. The landlord at the Snug might remember me. I suppose I was hanging round there for half an hour or so, looking at my watch and the door, and calling my brother. After that I went round to his house, knocked, got no reply, left him a note and went home again.'

'You travelled in by car?'

He nodded. 'I managed to park on Panton Street.'

It was a residential side road, just round the corner from the bar.

For a second his eyes were far away. 'It's a bit of a distance to cycle from here.'

It wouldn't make a pleasant ride home, either. Not if the speeding Mercedes she'd seen outside was a sample of the sort of driving you got down the narrow lane.

'I spent Sunday morning here – apart from nipping into Chesterton to get a newspaper – but later in the day I went back to Luke's place and let myself in to look round when I got no answer.'

'Thank you.' No useful alibis at all, then. 'I'll need to get all this written up, so you can check it and then sign it as an official statement. And under the circumstances, we'll need to get a team of investigators over to your brother's house.' Tara watched his eyes widen. 'I'm sorry. At this stage it's just a precaution, but we'll have a warrant by this afternoon. We'll need to keep everyone else out of there too.' She paused. 'Yourself included, I'm afraid. It's just so nothing's disturbed. If you like you can give me your brother's house key now. Or you're welcome to wait for the warrant.'

After a moment, Matthew shook his head. 'You can have it now. I want my brother found.' He went to a drawer and pulled out the keys to both a Yale and a mortise lock.

'Thank you.' Tara was glad – and a bit surprised – that he wasn't throwing up barriers, now that it looked as though Luke could be guilty of murder.

She stood up and Matthew did too. 'Here's my card, if anything else occurs to you. And can I please have your contact details at work, in case I need to reach you there?' If they discovered anything concrete about Luke, it might well be the sort of message she'd want to deliver to his brother in person.

Matthew Cope took out his own business card from the top pocket of his jacket and handed it over.

'I'll wait to hear,' he said, his jaw tense.

As Tara got back into her car she could hear the sound of dogs barking from somewhere nearby. And then came a man's voice: angry, swearing. The feel of the area made her glad she was leaving in a vehicle, rather than by bike or on foot. Perhaps it was another reason Matthew Cope had decided to take his car when he'd gone to meet his brother a week ago Saturday.

Thoughts of the apparent love triangle involving Freya, her husband and Luke Cope spun in Tara's head as she turned the car round in the driveway. That wasn't the only issue on her mind though. She wasn't quite convinced by the explanation for Luke Cope's move back to the grand family home in the centre of town. It must have been some jewel he'd sold, if the proceeds were enough to fund his day-to-day needs in an ongoing way, given he had almost no other income. On the one hand, Luke Cope might have just decided to live for the moment. Maybe he was the sort who got a few grand in their pocket and went wild. His brother had already implied he wasn't the most grounded of people.

But on the other hand, maybe he'd lied to Matthew about where he'd got his extra cash. What secrets had he been hiding?

Her car's wheels lost traction for a moment in the mud and slush. She'd have to put it through the carwash after her excursion or someone at the station would complain.

She was just about to join the road again, heading back towards town, when she heard a text come in.

Blake.

Off to talk to Jonny Trent at the gallery. Freya's friend Sophie Havers had no idea she was intending to visit.

CHAPTER SIX

Jonny Trent's art gallery was out along Babraham Road, close to the Gog Magog Hills and the Iron Age ring at Wandlebury. The setting felt quite rural, but it was a fairly major route down to the A11, and tourists visiting the ring would create plenty of passing traffic too, Blake guessed.

As he drove, he mentally replayed the call he'd had with Sophie Havers. She'd been shocked to hear that Freya Cross was missing, and he'd heard her swallow back a sob when he'd told her that a body had been found. Saying official news was pending formal identification had been the final straw, somehow conveying that there was no real hope, only administration to be completed. It had taken a while before Sophie had been able to answer his questions. He frowned. Although Freya hadn't arranged to stay with her friend, Sophie did say she'd been out of sorts when they'd spoken last, and that she'd said she wished she could 'escape' for a while. Apparently she hadn't wanted to elaborate. Sophie said Freya had sounded as though she was battening down her feelings, but she'd got the impression Freya had been seriously worried about something. And if she'd talked of wanting to escape, Blake could only assume it was a problem she couldn't work out how to tackle. Could it have been an affair with Luke Cope? Maybe he'd been pressing her to run away with him? Or threatening to tell her husband, in order to force her hand? But in that case, you'd expect Freya to have lashed out at Luke, yet it was she who was dead. Maybe she'd told Luke that it was over between them...

But perhaps it hadn't been relationship problems that Freya had wanted to escape. Sophie Havers had reckoned there'd been some tensions between husband and wife, but she'd thought Freya's current anxieties might have been work related. It made Blake all the more keen to talk to her employer, the gallery owner, Jonny Trent. Especially after the calendar entry Tara had spotted in Freya's kitchen, indicating her intention to speak to the man the Monday after she'd walked out of her house for the last time.

Just before he'd got in his car, Tara had called him with an update. Luke Cope's recent change of fortunes, allowing him to move back into the family home, was interesting.

The entrance to the gallery came off the road between densely planted yew trees. As the day wore on the snow was continuing to melt, dripping off their leaves. Everything looked bedraggled. As he followed the winding driveway it was like entering the illustration of one of the books of fairy tales Kitty – his-but-not-his daughter – had at home. He loved reading her those stories, but whenever they had father–daughter time together, he couldn't help thinking of that other man. The unknown guy who Babette had slept with – and who Kitty was tied to forever, without yet knowing it. She'd have to be told one day. Would that change the way she felt about Blake? He assumed she'd want to meet her biological father. If it were him, he would.

A rabbit scampered out into the driveway, causing him to slam on his brakes and return abruptly to the present. The trees surrounding the route were still dense. Over the top of them now, he could catch a glimpse of tall chimneys which must presumably belong to the gallery. They could just as well have adorned an enchanted cottage in the middle of a wood.

A little further on he could at last see the building in its entirety. He didn't know what he'd expected before he'd set out, but it wasn't this. The place looked like a large private house. Unlike most galleries it had no tall windows to let in the light and show off the artwork that must be on display. He wondered if it was where Jonny Trent lived, as well as worked.

The forecourt was gravel and currently only home to three other cars, all smart and shiny, except for their undersides, which were inevitably spattered with mud and grit, thanks to the weather. He brought his own vehicle to a halt and got out, locking it and then looking curiously through the house's windows as he made his way towards the door. The entrance was wide and wood-panelled with a fanlight over the top and a large old-fashioned-looking bell. He pressed it and heard a resounding single-tone buzz inside. As he waited, the sky darkened visibly. There'd be rain before he left again, he guessed.

The man who came to the door was dressed in a brown tweed suit with a crisp white shirt, open at the neck. He had wavy grey hair, which was slightly darker in his beard and moustache, and an engaging twinkle in his eye.

'Mr Jonathon Trent?'

At his formal words, the man's confident swagger dulled subtly, and his nod looked rather unwilling. Blake's badge accentuated the effect, but within a second the gallery owner had controlled his reactions and reinstated the twinkle. Here was a man whose default setting was 'charming'. A thick veneer over his natural character, Blake reckoned. Snap judgements ought to be avoided, obviously – except he was sure he was right.

'What can I do for you, Inspector?' Jonny Trent said. 'We have a client with us at the moment. Perhaps you'd like to come through to my office and we can speak there?'

Blake followed the man down an oak-panelled corridor. Through an open door he could see into what must have once been a drawing room. It still contained a couple of comfortable chairs and the odd side table. Other than that, it had been given over to the art on sale. The works hung on walls that were also panelled, just as the hall had been. There were stands holding prints too. A woman in a navy suit and high heels was hovering next to an elderly man with a walking stick, who was peering at one of the canvases, adjusting his round gold-rimmed glasses for a better look. Blake didn't envy the woman. The idea of having to dance attendance on all comers for the sake of a sale sounded soul destroying.

Jonny Trent walked them further down the corridor – the walls of which were also lined with art – and led Blake off to a room on the right.

'My office. I removed the panelling in here. It's a wonderfully atmospheric backdrop for displaying some of the artworks, but it does make our spaces rather dark, and I like to be able to see what I'm doing when I complete our paperwork.' His eyes met Blake's.

The news that a woman's body had been found in the Paradise Nature Reserve was already leaking out onto some of the online media sites, but Blake guessed Trent wouldn't have seen it. He'd have been busy with his customers and he didn't look like the sort to spend time glued to the internet in any case. His desk was full of ledgers that showed he tackled a lot of his work without the aid of a computer.

Yet the man had seemed agitated when he'd seen Blake's ID. Did that mean anything? Did he somehow know independently that his employee had been murdered? Or was it simply that the police seldom brought good news?

'So,' Trent motioned Blake to take a seat on an upholstered upright chair, still smiling, 'what can I do for you?' He took a seat himself, behind his leather-inlaid desk.

'I've come to ask about your gallery manager, Freya Cross.'

Trent frowned. 'Is this pertaining to the call I had from a colleague of yours yesterday? I hadn't expected to receive a visit in person.' Blake was sure his expression was meant to convey polite surprise, but he didn't buy it. Why was the man acting? Did he know something about the woman's death? Or was he expecting some other kind of trouble?

Instead of answering, Blake opted for an old gambit. 'But I expect you must know why I'm here?' It probably wouldn't get Trent to say anything he shouldn't, but it was worth a go.

The debonair man put his head on one side. 'I'm afraid I don't, Inspector.' But again Blake had the impression that he was bluffing. There was unease behind those shifty eyes.

'It seems Mrs Cross left her home just over a week ago, apparently to stay with a friend, but she never arrived.'

The frown on Jonny Trent's face deepened. 'Oh, dear me. Really?' He sat back in his chair and turned his palms upward. 'That's very worrying. As a matter of fact, I've been texting and calling her all week but she never replied.'

Blake thought of Freya Cross's mobile in the handbag found just a foot from her body; imagined it ringing, out there in the nature reserve, until its battery ran flat. If the weather hadn't been so bad a passer-by might have heard it and gone to investigate.

'I understand Professor Cross told you that his wife needed some time off at short notice? ' Blake said.

Jonny Trent nodded. 'He did indeed.'

'And yet you still tried to contact her. Why was that?'

A trace of irritation touched the man's face but it was gone in an instant. 'I was concerned for her, naturally. It wasn't at all usual for her to let me down at the last minute like that. Zach was pretty cagey about why she'd taken off as she did.'

'What explanation did he give, exactly?'

'He said she'd been suffering from stress and repeated migraines and that she needed emergency leave.'

'And when did he call to tell you this?'

'A week ago yesterday. But he didn't ring me – I rang him. Freya was two hours late.'

Interesting. 'How did he sound, when you asked where Freya was?'

Jonny Trent shrugged. 'As though he'd been thinking of something else, and had to drag his mind back to the matter in hand, if you know what I mean. But then that's academics for you. Heads in the clouds. Once he'd managed to focus he apologised and said he'd meant to ring but he'd been lecturing.'

Blake made a note to check his timetable. Had the man been making excuses? If he'd killed his wife he'd have every reason to call her employer with an excuse, to buy himself some time. But he might have been too stunned to think straight.

'He told me straight away after that that she'd gone to stay with a friend, and why,' Trent finished.

'You must have been cross, having been given no notice like that.'

Trent shrugged. 'I live here – the upstairs is converted into a flat – so I'm quite used to taking charge. And I was able to ask Monique – the lady you saw along the corridor, Freya's assistant – if she could do some extra hours. I was surprised, rather than cross.' That smile again. The man was trying to win him over. Something about him made Blake's skin crawl.

'She'd shown no signs of being under strain here, then?' Blake said.

'Not at all. We worked well together and the business is going swimmingly.'

'There were *never* any tensions? You always agreed on the way things should be run?' *That really would be unusual…*

'Oh!' Trent laughed. 'That's absolutely Freya's domain, Inspector. It's why I employ her. She's the brains of the organisation. I just show up to chat to the clients and add a bit of colour to the place.'

Blake could imagine him revelling in that side of the operation. As for the claim that it was always sweetness and light between him and Freya, he took that with a pinch of salt. Talking to her assistant, Monique, might be helpful. But not when Jonny Trent was around.

'But now you have got me worried,' Trent went on. 'Why the official visit, and all these questions?'

Blake watched him closely. 'I'm afraid I have to tell you that the body of a woman has been found in the Paradise Nature Reserve in the Newnham area of Cambridge, just round the corner from Mrs Cross's home. There's been no formal identification as yet.'

Jonny Trent raised his left hand and put it over his mouth. 'Good heavens. How awful.' He stood up, turned his back on Blake and walked over to the window. 'I just need to take a moment.'

A moment when Blake couldn't see his reactions…

It was thirty seconds or so before he turned back to face the room again – not long, but long enough to control whatever emotion he really felt at the news. Or to disguise his lack of shock if it hadn't been news at all.

'Mr Trent, we understand Freya intended to talk to you about something in particular last Monday. She'd marked it on her calendar. Can you think what that might have been?'

He was still monitoring the man's facial changes intently and swore he saw a little extra colour come to his already florid cheeks.

'How very odd to make a note of it like that,' he said after a moment. 'She could talk to me at any time. I'm always available to my staff.'

Blake wasn't quite sure he believed in the 'Britain's best boss' persona Trent was trying to convey, but he'd thought it odd himself. Maybe Freya had been trying to shelve the worry of whatever it was she needed to say, as Tara had suggested. What could have been that daunting?

'I gather you stock artwork by Luke Cope?' Blake said.

The look Trent gave Blake in response was suddenly sharp, cutting through the apparent upset traced across his features. 'That's correct.'

'Did Freya Cross know Luke well?'

The man's chest rose and fell. 'Fairly well, I think. I had the impression they met outside work sometimes. We were all at Luke's house-warming party, for instance. I wasn't quite sure…'

'Mr Trent?' Blake wasn't certain if he was pausing for effect.

'I wasn't quite sure how far their friendship went. I could tell Freya's husband was a little – shall we say – uneasy about the way they interacted.'

'And how was that?'

Trent gave a shrug. 'Luke had had a few too many drinks. He was standing very close to Freya and she didn't brush him off as quickly as she might have. After that, Zach encouraged her to leave the party. He was rather heavy-handed about it.'

'I see. Have you seen Luke recently?'

The man raised an eyebrow, then frowned. 'No. His brother called me, as a matter of fact, just over a week ago, asking me that same thing. Why do you want to know?'

He looked rattled. Blake smiled inwardly and decided not to answer his question. The more jittery he got, the better. 'When did you last meet?'

The man opened his mouth again, glanced at Blake and evidently thought better of it. Instead, he sighed, then leant to one side and opened a desk drawer. A moment later he had a leather-bound diary on his desk. He opened it and flicked back through the pages. 'He last came in three weeks ago, or thereabouts,' he said, showing Blake the entry. 'We'd sold one of his paintings and he brought a replacement to fill its place.'

'His works sell well then?' Not what the police had been told, but he was interested to see what sort of spin Trent would put on the truth.

'Not terribly, to be honest. Before that we hadn't sold one of his since October.'

'But you keep stocking his works. Why is that?'

Jonny Trent looked him straight in the eye. 'He's a good artist. A lot of what we sell is popular because it's pretty and unchalleng-ing, or derivative. I do well out of those pieces and that means I can keep stocking artists whose output is actually meaningful. It's a huge privilege.'

All very laudable. 'You haven't tried to contact Luke in the last week?'

'I haven't.' Jonny Trent ran his tongue over his lips. 'Why do you ask?'

'He's missing. His brother, Matthew, reported it just over a week ago. Do you have any idea where he might be, other than his home address?'

The gallery owner's face was a blank. 'None whatsoever,' he said. 'He was living in a flat on Histon Road before he moved into the house off Trumpington Road, but that was rented, and the landlord will have got someone new in. I can give you the address if you want it?'

Blake nodded. He took the contact details for Freya's assistant, Monique, too. He wanted to get her when she wasn't with gallery clients. A relaxed conversation was what he had in mind…

As he drove back towards town, down the wide road, past flat fields and farm shops, his mind was full of Luke Cope and Zach Cross. Possible motives for the murder of Freya Cross seemed to abound, though they were all based on speculation at the moment. He needed to talk to more people. If Luke and Freya had been having an affair someone ought to have more details. And Luke Cope must have run somewhere – unless Zach Cross had killed them both.

And then there was Jonny Trent. How did he fit into it all? He'd been happy to drop Zach Cross in it – portraying him as a jealous man – and equally happy to hint that Freya had had a fling with

Luke Cope, which would automatically make him a suspect. Yet he'd championed the man's work.

And on top of all that Blake was sure Jonny Trent had been hiding something.

CHAPTER SEVEN

Patrick Wilkins – *Detective Sergeant* Patrick Wilkins, dammit, even if he was currently suspended – was standing opposite Parkside police station, on the edge of Parker's Piece. The expansive green behind him was all but empty today, just the odd person dashing across, away from town, their heads bent against the weather. Wilkins had an umbrella with him, a decent one from Aspinal of London. He made it a rule to spend the most he could afford on both clothes and accessories, even if it meant saving up for a while. Appearances mattered; it made sense to do yourself justice when you set out in the morning.

The umbrella meant he had no need to dash into the station, out of the rain, and he certainly had no other urge to hurry.

He was bound for his third disciplinary meeting. *Third!* He remembered DCI Fleming's face from the second one. Her look had gone from patronising and firmly practical at the start to barely controlled by the end. She'd kept up appearances of course, but she'd been infuriated underneath. That had been in response to his defence of his actions. She hadn't liked him airing his grievances about Tara Thorpe, but it had been when he'd started on his DI that her cracks had really begun to show. Karen Fleming set a lot of store by Blake, Wilkins knew, but it wasn't just that. What DCI Fleming really couldn't stand was anyone questioning her as a leader. Especially not in front of the chief super… Fleming was reasonable on investigations – you could argue the toss with her about a lead you wanted to follow, for instance, and talk her round if your idea was good. But question her management style or choice of staff and fair play went out of the window. She was woefully blinkered. For a second, Wilkins tried to imagine what it would be like to work in her team again.

He couldn't.

But the options before him were stark. What would he do if he resigned, with no regular income and no glowing references? He glanced up at the umbrella over his head. No more shopping at Aspinal of London, that was for sure. And none of it was even his fault.

But he had contacts who might help him out if he decided to resign; other people who'd been 'Tara Thorped' in the past.

He glanced at his watch. It was time to go and face the panel again. Should he just turn around and walk away?

But he hadn't finished telling his side of the story yet. He was going to carry on repeating it to anyone who would listen.

CHAPTER EIGHT

Tara was on her way back to Newnham, driven by Max Dimity.

The news that it was Freya Cross's body that had been found in the Paradise Nature Reserve had started to filter out. Her stepson had been informed and the official identification of her body had taken place. At that moment Blake and DCI Fleming were giving a statement to the press.

Tara had had a quick look at *Not Now* magazine's website earlier, to see if Shona Kennedy had been ahead of the pack of newshounds. It wouldn't be the first time she'd managed to squeeze privileged information out of a contact on the force. But in fact, all they'd reported so far was that the police were attending a 'serious incident' at the nature reserve. She glanced down at her screen again now and watched as 'Breaking News' scrolled across the publication's website.

Body found at Paradise Nature Reserve is wife of local professor.

Tara flung the phone back into her bag. Five years earlier, when she'd worked at *Not Now*, she'd have made damn sure the report referred to Freya as a 'local gallery manager', not just someone's wife.

'What is it?'

Tara took a deep breath. 'Nothing important compared to the case – just frustration at my erstwhile colleagues at *Not Now*.'

'Ah. Say no more.' Max gave her a fleeting smile, then indicated to turn into the Crosses' road.

Not many people on the force had much time for *Not Now*.
The exception had been Tara's now-suspended boss, DS Patrick
Wilkins. It transpired that he'd had a whole load of time for the
reporter Shona Kennedy, in particular, both in the bedroom and
outside it. He'd indulged in pillow talk and also leaked information
directly to *Not Now*'s editor, Giles Troy.

The weather outside matched Tara's mood. Although the
temperature had struggled up to a few degrees above freezing, the
sky had been darkening all day and the rain had started just after
they'd set off from the station. Max had got the wipers going at
maximum speed now, and still the water ran in rivulets over the
windscreen faster than it was pushed away.

Tara glanced sideways at Max. 'How was Shona this morning?
You and Blake managed to send her packing pretty quickly.' She
was still wondering what had been said.

Max shrugged. 'Just her usual poisonous self.'

He didn't want to go into details, she could see that – but she
found she really wanted to know. It was like picking off a scab – you
knew it would probably hurt, but it was irresistible. 'Blake looked
cross when he came back into the nature reserve.'

'Just irritated by her interference, I guess.' Max's voice was
calm as usual. 'That and the fact that he had to take his overalls
off and put them back on again thanks to her. You know how he
hates fiddling about when there's something important going on.'
He'd paused next to a tight-looking space between two other cars
parked on the road: a Jaguar and a BMW. Not many of Cambridge's
Victorian houses had garages.

Blake's impatience rang true, but she bet there was more to it
than that. 'Did Shona say anything about me?'

Max pulled a face before glancing over his shoulder to judge
the angle he needed to reverse into the parking space. 'Why would
you take any notice of what she says? I didn't.'

That was a yes then. 'But just out of interest…'

'Really?' He cocked an eyebrow and his look was sympathetic. 'You know what she's like. She just said the first thing she could think of to stick the knife in.'

'Which was…?'

He sighed. 'That it was touching that DI Blake was so protective of you. She implied he was keeping you out of sight on purpose and running the gauntlet of the press himself, out of gallantry.'

And from a liking for Tara too, she was willing to bet. Max wasn't spelling it out, but Shona probably had. No wonder Blake had been tight-lipped. Shona had tried to imply there was something going on between them when she'd written that last foul article in December too. She'd paid no attention to the lack of facts, or to Blake's wife and daughter's feelings. It would be all the worse if she went for the same angle again now Babette was so obviously pregnant. Maybe Shona hoped members of the public would start abusing Tara in the street if she spread enough rumours. *Nice…*

She longed to reassure Max that nothing had ever happened between her and their boss. But it was no good; it would look as though she was protesting too much. And of course Max had seen Blake holding her when she'd narrowly escaped death at the tail end of last year. A natural reaction from the head of a team perhaps, but Max might have noticed her clinging to him too. In the heat of the moment she'd reacted on instinct. If he'd noticed at all, she guessed he probably had a good idea of her feelings; he was sensitive to that sort of thing. His perceptive nature was one of the many reasons she liked him, but it was a bit of a double-edged sword…

As if to prove her right he turned to her now and gave her a smile. 'Don't take it to heart. We all know what Shona and Giles are like.'

She took in his friendly brown eyes – no judgement there. For a second she felt her nose itching – a sure-fire warning of oncoming emotion. She'd been a loner for so long. Working with Max made her realise you didn't have to keep everyone at arm's length. For one second, she wondered what might have happened if she'd met him under other circumstances. Circumstances where Blake didn't exist… They got on well together, and objectively she knew Max was good-looking.

'Thanks.' Time to move the conversation swiftly on. 'Bloody hell, I can't believe you managed to get the car into this space.'

He grinned. 'You don't spend years in this job in central Cambridge without learning to park like a demon.'

They were going door to door. At mid-afternoon on a Tuesday they might not find many people in, but Tara was reasonably hopeful. The neighbourhood was moneyed, and the residents would probably include several people who'd retired, as well as some that were senior enough to work from home when they felt like it.

They were going to get wet, that was for sure. The volume of water running down the street and into the drains was increased by the remaining meltwater from the snow. Up above, the grey slates on the street's roofs were awash with rain that streamed into the gutters.

Max made short work of some final straightening up and a moment later he and Tara were out on the street. Tara turned up her collar and shivered as she fumbled with her umbrella.

They started from the villa next to the Crosses' house, with no luck, but two doors down they got a reply.

When they showed their IDs, the woman with iron-grey hair who'd opened up nodded. 'You're here about Freya Cross, I presume? The item's just come up on the local section of the BBC News site. You'd better come in.'

Max glanced at Tara and they followed the woman past her smartly painted red front door and into a corridor lined with bookshelves.

'I'm Cindy Musgrove,' the woman said, turning to them part way down the hall, which was long, leading right through to a back door at the end. 'Emeritus Professor of English. I don't have much contact with Zach Cross in the academic world – different departments, and we're attached to different colleges – but you know how it is with neighbours, one builds quite a bond over time.'

She didn't look like a Cindy somehow. She was dressed in jeans and a loose-fitting blue denim top. Her grey hair was close cropped and she wore large dangly earrings decorated with multicoloured beads. Her fingers were adorned with several silver rings.

'Come through here, into the kitchen,' she said. 'Coffee?'

Tara and Max both thanked her but said no. Tara didn't want to get to the point when she had to knock on doors primarily to ask to use the occupant's loo.

'How can I help you?' Cindy Musgrove said. 'You want to know when I last saw Freya?'

Tara had the urge to take back control. Though, in fairness, it was a reasonable place to start. 'That would be useful.'

Cindy Musgrove frowned. 'I saw her very briefly in the street about a week and a half ago. I'm sorry – I can't be precise about the date. She was getting into her car and, I assume, going off to work. But the last time I met her properly, to talk to, was on Saturday tenth of February at a drinks party in Owlstone Road. It was in celebration of an anniversary and the couple there, Moira and Tony, had invited a wide group of people locally. Wine, sherry, nibbles – all that sort of thing. Early evening.'

'Did she seem happy, when you saw her?' Tara asked. Not that you'd probably give much away at that sort of do – but Cindy Musgrove seemed incisive, and if there was anything to spot, Tara guessed she'd have noticed.

Once again, the emeritus professor frowned with concentration. 'She was perfectly sociable. I remember that she made her way round the room, talking to most of the people there. She was the public face of that gallery she worked for, so she was used to networking, I suppose. I spoke to her myself for a while.'

'Can you remember what you talked about?'

'I asked her about her job – she said the gallery was doing well, but she didn't elaborate. Thinking back, she said it rather quickly, possibly to shut the topic down. And then we moved onto the plans for redevelopment around Mill Lane and Silver Street. Everyone's worried about the effect it will have on Coe Fen. It's so rare to have such a rural spot in the centre of the city and the extra visitors will surely change the character of the place. There's precious little opportunity for peace and quiet anywhere these days.' Then she paused. 'I still can't take it in that Freya's dead. And killed in such a beautiful, tranquil spot.' She took a deep breath and then sat up straight suddenly. 'But this isn't helping.'

'What you've told us about the drinks party is useful background information,' Max said.

The woman's account fitted with the suggestion Blake had relayed to Tara back at the station, that Freya Cross might have had problems at work. 'Was there anything else you noticed?' she asked.

Cindy Musgrove chewed her lip. She looked as though she was going through some kind of inner battle. At last she said: 'I'm sure it's not relevant, but it struck me that she and Zach didn't interact at the party. Not until the end, when they left together. But up until that point it occurred to me that a stranger wouldn't have known they were husband and wife.'

'Was that unusual?' Tara said.

The professor put her head on one side and frowned. 'Well, they were certainly very attentive towards each other in the beginning. I suppose it's natural for things to become less intense as a marriage wears on, but they'd only been together for a couple of years, and it was marked enough for me to notice it.'

'How long have you known them both?' Max put in.

'Zach, for years – I was already living on this street when he moved in with his first wife and their son, Oscar. Oscar was a small boy then – around six or seven perhaps? – and he must be twenty or twenty-one by now. He's most of the way through his degree.'

'So you must have seen that relationship come apart,' Tara said. 'I wonder if you could tell us the background?'

For a moment the woman hesitated.

'It's probably not relevant, but we want to know as much as possible about the context of Mrs Cross's life.'

Cindy nodded. 'I rather think Zach had taken up with Freya before things were over with Eliza – his first wife. Hard on Oscar, of course. Freya moved in very soon after Eliza moved out.' She shook her head. 'And then later on there was the wedding – Freya and Zach's I mean. Eliza didn't come – unsurprisingly – but Oscar was there, under sufferance by the look on his face. I've never seen such a scowl. He'd just finished his A levels, I remember, so all the upheaval must have been going on whilst he was still studying for them. I overheard someone who didn't know them well asking if Oscar was Freya's brother. There were only eight or nine years between them in age. Oscar was angry – I could see that. And although Freya was radiant that day, I couldn't help feeling…' Suddenly she seemed to realise she was speaking rather freely about her neighbour and paused.

'Professor Musgrove?'

The woman sighed sharply. 'I just wondered how long it would last. I felt the odds were stacked against them, because she'd hardly lived life yet and he was already so settled. And Oscar looked full of ire, and – oh I'm just being cynical. I like them both – *liked* I should say in Freya's case – I liked them a lot. Zach's first wife was the wronged woman, of course – but my goodness she was difficult. She made lots of enemies in the neighbourhood – physically beautiful but the personality of a viper. And as I say, Zach and Freya looked like the perfect couple, the day they married.'

But two years could be a long time in a relationship.

After they'd left the professor's house, Max said: 'It'll be interesting to hear what Oscar Cross has to say.'

'You're right there.' Tara wondered just how many people had a potential motive for killing his stepmother.

Most of the other doors they knocked on went unanswered, or were opened by people who couldn't expand on what they already knew, but an hour into proceedings they struck lucky. Diana Johnson hadn't yet heard the news about Freya. Unlike Cindy Musgrove, who'd been sad but matter-of-fact, Ms Johnson went pale and shaky. Tara and Max followed her inside, and Max made her some tea.

'I saw her not long ago, out in the street,' the woman said. 'I was taking Henry, my dachshund, out for his final walk before bed. It was bitterly cold, so I didn't go far. But I saw Freya across the road. I shouted "hello" or "good evening" or something like that, but she barely replied, which was unlike her. I actually wondered if she was upset. She was looking down at the ground, almost as though she didn't want me to see her face.'

'Can you remember when this was?' Tara asked.

The woman put her hand to her head. 'I can't think. A week ago maybe? Hang on a minute.' She frowned. 'When did the snow start?'

'A week ago last Thursday, I think,' Max said.

Ms Johnson nodded. 'Then I think it was the Friday. I remember how treacherous the pavements were. The day before, after the first fall, they hadn't been too bad. I'd put on my boots and crunched my way round the block. But on the Friday the snow had got compacted and frozen hard. I remember stopping even sooner than I'd meant to because it was so slippery.' She nodded now, slowly. 'Of course, yes, that's right. Because then, on the Saturday, I took the car out and drove Henry over to Fen Ditton, so I could take him out for a proper airing on the meadows. It was so much easier to walk across the fields without falling over.'

Tara made a note. 'So a week ago Friday was when you last saw Freya Cross. That would have been the twenty-third of February. That's very useful, Ms Johnson. And you're confident of the date now?' If she was, she might have been the last person to see Mrs Cross alive. Apart from her killer, of course.

'I'm sure, now that I've remembered the sequence of events.' She was still very pale but her tone was firm.

Tara nodded. 'Thank you. And did you notice anything else about Mrs Cross that night? How she was dressed, for instance? Or what she had with her?'

Ms Johnson frowned. 'She must have been wearing what you'd expect, I suppose – dressed for the weather, I mean.' For a second, her eyes were far away. 'She was walking under one of the street-lights. Yes, that's right – she had her coat pulled around her quite tightly, as though she was holding it in place, and maybe hadn't yet done it up, and as I say, looking down.'

'So she used her hands to hold her coat closed,' Tara said. If she hadn't done it up, it sounded as though she'd left in a hurry. 'She must have had anything she was carrying slung over her shoulder, presumably?'

To her surprise, Ms Johnson nodded. 'Yes, of course. That's right. She did have some kind of holdall. I didn't think too much about it at the time, but I suppose it struck me as a little odd that she was setting out on foot with luggage at that time of night. I'd almost forgotten in the interim – none of my business. But it's coming back to me now.' She sniffed. 'I can't believe she's dead. I wish I'd asked her what was wrong, but it would have felt like interfering.'

*

Back in Max's car, Tara looked at her fellow DC.

'I didn't expect that. Professor Cross *said* she'd taken an overnight bag but I didn't believe him. Why would the killer take that and not her handbag? And why did the friend she was supposedly visiting know nothing about her plans?' She thought hard. 'Maybe she was genuinely going away but not with the friend, and Zach Cross believed the line she spun him? Perhaps she was really heading off with Luke Cope instead – and he killed her. Or Zach Cross saw through her story, followed her out and did for her and Luke Cope too? But either way, why the hell would Luke and Freya arrange to meet in the nature reserve? If you were planning to go away somewhere it's not exactly the logical place to start.'

Max rubbed his chin. 'True. It's more somewhere for doing something secret.' He turned the key in the ignition.

Tara frowned. He was right. It was the sort of place where a low-level drug dealer might conduct a quick transaction, or teenagers might head, intent on an illicit fumble. What did that tell them?

She pushed her seatbelt home and glanced at her watch. 'Blake ought to have finished at the post-mortem by now. And we should get straight back anyway.' The briefing meeting at the station had been scheduled for five thirty. 'I really want to know what Freya Cross's mobile shows us – if anything.' She was hoping for some nice, revealing texts. But of course if there were any, the killer would have taken the phone with them. That presumably meant their perpetrator was happy for them to have all the information it held, which might be a clue in itself.

CHAPTER NINE

DS Patrick Wilkins' skin crawled as he left the meeting room and walked down a corridor that smelt of carpet cleaner. Each of his disciplinary hearings had been worse than the last. No one was in any mood to listen to him. Not that he should be surprised; they were fools, the lot of them. Today had been especially galling as he could see DCI Fleming's attention had been wandering. He'd caught the breaking news about the body in the Paradise Nature Reserve on his phone, just before he'd entered the station. She was probably eager to catch up with her remaining team; Wilkins simply wasn't a priority. And so she, and the other powers that be, would miss what was under their noses. He shook his head.

But the upside of the incident out in Newnham was that most of his closest colleagues were absent. He didn't have to run the risk of coming face to—

He'd rejoiced too soon. DC Megan Maloney was standing there right in front of him. On the way to the coffee machine or wasting time in some other way probably. She saw him in an instant and blushed. No one knew what to say to him; they were embarrassed for him, for what he'd done. Adrenaline shot round his system. How could they be so blinkered?

'Afternoon, Megan,' he said, hiding what he really thought of her with a smile.

'Afternoon, sir.' Very formal, but he was pleased she was still acknowledging him as her superior. And maybe their meeting had some benefit after all. It suddenly occurred to him that what he had said in his disciplinary meetings wouldn't have reached the wider staff.

Down the corridor to their right he could see that there were no other officers currently standing by the coffee machine. 'If you're going for a quick shot of caffeine I might join you before I head off?'

She nodded and turned in the direction of the drinks station. 'Of course.'

Once she'd got her coffee from the dispenser she turned to him. 'What can I get you?'

'Black coffee as well. Thank you.' Maybe Maloney would be more receptive than Fleming. She'd had to deal with Tara Thorpe joining the team too – she'd be aware of how bossy the woman was. And how much she was given her head; she counted herself as more accomplished than the others, and Fleming and Blake seemed to believe the hype. If Maloney had any sense – a moot point – she might feel the same resentment that he did.

'How are things in the team?' he asked, taking his drink from the DC.

'Busy.'

That was a non-committal answer if ever he'd heard one. And her tone was still cool. She was avoiding his eyes. There was an awkward pause.

'Listen, Megan, I know everyone was furious with me before Christmas, and I can understand why. I overstepped the mark.'

He was disappointed and surprised to note the woman's look in response. She clearly thought his words were an understatement.

'When I come back' – *well, if, but it was better for his cause if Maloney thought of it as 'when'* – 'when I come back, I'd like my colleagues,' he avoided the word subordinates, even though it was what he was thinking, 'to understand why I acted as I did. That way, even if they feel I made an error of judgement, they can at least understand why that was.'

He barely had the patience to make his case. Part of him felt it simply wasn't worth his time and effort. But he owed it to himself – and to people who had been under his direction, for God's sake – to set the record straight. And if it robbed DI Blake and Tara Thorpe of an easy ride, that was all to the good.

Maloney didn't respond, but she met his eyes, waiting for him to carry on. Her decision not to encourage him or sympathise in any way made him feel hot under his jacket. She was being bold. She might have called him 'sir' just now, but the balance of power between them had still changed. After his downfall she felt herself to be pretty much his equal. Maybe even better than he was. His sweat now was brought on by anger. If he was going to use this opportunity he'd better make it count.

'I'm afraid I was frustrated by the way certain elements of the team were working,' he said at last. 'Now, you might be perfectly happy with how things have been since Tara Thorpe joined us.' He took a deep breath to counteract the anger coursing through his system and held up a hand when she threatened to interject. 'If you are, then that's fine. But one thing: I'd suggest you keep a very close eye on DI Blake and DC Thorpe – the way they work together, I mean, their body language, any preferential treatment Thorpe might get, any odd decisions you think DI Blake might have made, under her influence. You see, I saw the two of them together once, and their feelings… Well, let's just say their feelings for each other won't necessarily benefit the team as a whole.'

He left out the fact that the occasion he was referring to had been nearly five years ago now, when Blake had been separated from his wife – and that Tara Thorpe had been receiving artificial respiration from another officer at the time, having almost drowned. He'd never forgotten the look of anguish on his boss's face. He'd known immediately that his feelings for Tara Thorpe were something out of the ordinary. The pair of them had each been investigating the same murder – she as a journalist, he as a detective – and Tara had shared some of her information with Blake and the police. Their cosy chats must have had an effect.

Blake might have decided to give his marriage another go, but Wilkins was in no doubt that his feelings for Tara Thorpe remained. And Wilkins dated his own problems at work to when she'd joined their team and started to question his judgement.

His eyes met Megan Maloney's again. 'If you don't notice anything untoward you can put this conversation out of your head,' he said. 'But it's best you're alert to the possibility. I wouldn't want the way you and Max are treated – for instance – to be affected by their relationship.

'Anyway,' he swigged the bitter dregs of his coffee, 'I'll see you soon.' He turned and walked back towards the exit. He had no evidence at all of any 'relationship' between Blake and Thorpe, in fact, as DCI Fleming had pointed out, furiously, her eyes flicking to the detective chief superintendent. But it was as well to sow the seeds of doubt in Megan Maloney's mind. It was for her sake – hers and Max's. He'd been their boss and they needed to know he'd got their backs. His own feelings didn't come into it.

As he let the station door swing shut behind him he unfurled his umbrella with a sharp, angry movement, scaring a pigeon that had been sitting on the paving just outside. It flapped away noisily. *Idiot bird.* The whole world was full of idiots.

CHAPTER TEN

Blake dashed into the incident room slightly late for the briefing. He'd come straight from Addenbrooke's and witnessing Freya Cross's post-mortem. It wasn't an experience he'd ever get used to – and he'd worry if he did. He tried to banish the dead woman's pale flesh from his mind. *Fat chance.*

As he entered the room he saw Tara and Max at the front, near the display boards, talking to DCI Fleming, who glanced over and met his eye as he approached. His boss looked as though she'd got something on her mind – more than just the murder. No doubt she'd offload on him sooner or later. Behind them, Blake could see photos of Freya Cross in life and death, as well as one of a Byronic figure. He walked closer to the board.

'That's Luke Cope?'

Tara nodded.

The man looked every bit the impassioned artist – full, sensitive lips and a slightly wild spark in his eye. He'd be easy to recognise once they did catch up with him.

'Let's make a start now,' DCI Fleming said, achieving instant hush. She'd had her hair done two weeks earlier and Blake couldn't get used to it. The jet-black dye was still in place, but the spikes had gone. She'd had the whole arrangement slicked down into a sleek pixie crop.

He took a seat in a chair next to Kirsty Crowther and glanced across at Tara, wondering what she'd been passing on to Fleming. He took in her red-gold hair, her neat frame and the look of challenge in her eyes. In an instant his mind ran back to when he'd sat opposite her, flirting in a pub, yet still resolutely turned back to a wife who'd betrayed him to try to save his marriage. What the hell had he been thinking?

'What's the news from Agneta?' Fleming asked, pulling Blake out of his thoughts.

'The conditions outside over the past week mean it's hard to be absolutely precise over her time of death, but Freya Cross's stomach contents indicate her last meal was the one she had with her husband on Friday twenty-third February, so I think we can assume she died at the Paradise Nature Reserve that night. There's no sign of intercourse before she was killed, and her death was suffocation caused by strangulation. There were strands of her scarf embedded in her skin.'

Fleming nodded.

'What we didn't expect was that she'd also had a blow to the head. The wound was to the side of her skull, but the snow banked up around her meant we missed it when she was lying on the ground. It might be that the killer wanted to subdue her before finishing the job. It would have given them the chance to tighten the scarf round her neck without so much resistance.'

'It begs the question, why not just finish the job by bludgeoning her to death?' Fleming said.

Ever practical, the DCI. 'The killer might simply have got squeamish.' It seemed highly hypocritical to Blake that murderers might find some methods more palatable than others, but it appeared to be the case. 'Or perhaps whatever they used for the initial blow wasn't suitable. Agneta said it could have been something like a stone. If the killing was in anger, on the spur of the moment, they might have lashed out with that first, but realised it wasn't big enough to smash through her skull at speed.'

'Back to Luke Cope,' Fleming said, 'what's being done?'

'The warrant came through to enter his house. The CSIs have been checking for less obvious signs of trouble that might have been missed. If a third party killed both Luke and Freya they could have murdered Luke at his home. They're searching for traces of blood, or anything that's been disturbed, but there's nothing doing as yet. We've put his number plate through all the usual systems too. The last time his car was picked up was when he drove past a camera on the ring road, the night before Freya's death.'

'Other than Luke, who do we have as suspects for Mrs Cross's murder?'

'Most obviously, the husband, Zach.' Blake pictured the large, powerful man, sitting in his beautifully ordered Cambridge home. 'His explanation of his wife's plan to go away was vague at best, and he looked as though he was improvising. Meanwhile, the woman he says Freya was intending to stay with wasn't expecting her. Freya's employer, Jonny Trent, of Trent's art gallery, says he called Freya's home number when she didn't come in for work. He spoke to Professor Cross who gave him the same story he told us – that she'd gone for a last-minute break having felt under pressure recently. If Zach Cross really believed that, he probably assumed Freya had told Jonny Trent herself that she wouldn't be in, but everything about his story seems flaky. There are rumours that the marriage was under strain. That said, if he did kill his wife, then I'd like to know why he didn't call Trent pre-emptively to make excuses for her absence.'

Fleming nodded and turned to Tara. 'I think you and Max have information to contribute there?'

Tara relayed the conversation she and her fellow DC had had with another professor on the Crosses' street, Cindy Musgrove, and how distant Freya and her husband had seemed at a recent drinks party. 'And another neighbour, Diana Johnson, said she saw Freya walking towards Paradise Nature Reserve on Friday twenty-third and that she was carrying a holdall.'

That put a new spin on things. He'd have sworn the professor had been lying about what his wife had taken with her.

Tara glanced round at Blake, and her eyes held his for a moment before she spoke. 'I've been trying to work out why the killer would have removed that luggage from the crime scene, and yet left her handbag next to her body.'

Blake nodded. 'A very interesting question.'

'The first woman,' Tara went on, 'Cindy Musgrove, mentioned how resentful Oscar Cross, Freya's stepson, was about his father remarrying. Apparently he's only eight or nine years younger than Freya was.'

'We should add him to our list of people of interest,' said Blake. He glanced at Megan Maloney. 'Megan, we'll want to arrange an interview. And can you check his, Luke's and the professor's names for any previous trouble?'

The woman nodded. 'You might want to keep one of Luke Cope's contacts in mind too, for possible involvement in some way.'

Blake knew she'd been re-examining the list of the missing man's acquaintances, as provided by his brother, Matthew. He raised an eyebrow. 'Go ahead.'

'A Dr Imogen Field,' the DC supplied. 'She's an ex of Luke's apparently. They were together for three years, and the timing means it might be Freya Cross who superseded her. She says she hasn't seen Luke and has no idea where we might find him.'

'Useful knowledge. Thanks, Megan.' Blake faced the room as a whole again.

Before he could speak, Fleming butted in. 'Certainly, a top priority has to be to find Luke Cope.'

No, really? 'I agree, ma'am,' he said, trying to relax his knotted shoulder muscles. 'I'm not clear yet whether he's our killer or a third party has murdered him and Freya too. Zach Cross has a motive for wiping them both out, but I'm not so sure about his son. Unless

Oscar found the pair of them playing around. If he already blames Freya for breaking his family apart, finding her being unfaithful to his father might be enough to make him lose control.' It didn't seem likely though. Managing to kill them both, one by one, then move Luke Cope's body, would have been no mean feat.

As for Dr Imogen Field – she sounded interesting…

Kirsty Crowther, the family liaison officer, lifted her hand and Fleming nodded for her speak. 'Oscar Cross came with his father to identify Freya's body,' she said. 'In spite of the horrific circumstances he didn't show much sympathy for his dad's upset. But Professor Cross's shock and sorrow seemed genuine, as far as I could tell.'

'I've also got my eye on Jonny Trent, the gallery owner,' Blake said.

'For what reason?' Fleming looked at him from under her new un-Fleming-like fringe.

'As well as employing Freya Cross he stocked Luke Cope's artwork, so there's a connection there.' He gave them the background. 'And for a moment, when I first showed my ID, Trent looked alarmed – though that could just be habitual. I appreciate no one relaxes when they're visited by a detective. But throughout our conversation I got the impression he was trying to butter me up. And he claimed there were no tensions at all at the gallery, whereas the friend of Freya Cross's in London said she thought Freya was having trouble at work.'

'The neighbour, Cindy Musgrove, said she didn't seem to want to talk about her job when she last saw her, too,' Tara said. 'And of course Freya was planning to tackle Jonny Trent about something the Monday after she was killed.'

Blake nodded. 'Trent claims not to know what her problem was.'

'On top of all that he was definitely cagey when I called to ask to speak to Freya, before her body was found,' Tara finished.

'Interesting,' Fleming said.

'Not strong as evidence goes, I grant you.' Blake knew what his boss was thinking, and he'd rather spell it out than pussyfoot around. 'But Trent's reaction to hearing the news about Freya Cross was odd as well. He turned away and walked across the room. He didn't want me to judge his response. And when I mentioned that Luke Cope was missing too, he went pale. There's something off about that man. I'm just not sure what it is yet.'

Fleming nodded. 'What do we have from Freya Cross's phone?'

Blake glanced down at the list he'd been given by the tech team. 'Jonny Trent's been texting her repeatedly since she went missing.' For a second he remembered Trent claiming he'd tried to reach her because he'd been concerned. 'The messages are each more impatient than the last. The first says: "We can sort this out, just give me a call. Everything will be fine." Which does imply there were tensions at work. They carry on in a similar vein. The final one reads, "Where the hell are you? Call me".'

Fleming's dark eyes met his. 'He could still have killed her and then sent the texts afterwards to make his claims seem more plausible.'

'He could have,' Blake replied. 'Though in that case you'd think he'd have made the messages match the "concerned employer" persona he was trying to portray when I spoke to him. But it's possible. He could even have predicted this conversation we're having now.'

'Anything else?' Fleming said.

Blake nodded. 'Two very interesting facts. One, Zach Cross didn't text or call his wife for the entire time he supposedly thought she was away, visiting her friend. He said himself that she was troubled. You'd think he'd have at least tried to check in with her.'

'And the second?'

'There's a text from Luke Cope's number, earlier in the evening on the night Freya Cross died. It reads: "Please, Freya, meet me. Usual place. Nine tonight. Give me a chance and we can start again."'

'What kind of car does Luke Cope drive?' Tara asked.

Megan Maloney answered. 'A dark red Volvo.'

Fleming raised her eyebrows. 'Why do you ask?'

Blake watched frown lines trace their way across Tara's expressive face. 'When I went to talk to Matthew Cope at his home earlier a dark blue Mercedes came at me at speed from the direction of his house – I assumed from somewhere further up the road. I thought back to it just now and looked on Google Maps. There isn't anything beyond Matthew Cope's place – just some fields. The road peters out. So, if they were visiting Matthew, I wonder what they could have been doing there. The more I think about it, the more convinced I am they were very keen to make themselves scarce.'

CHAPTER ELEVEN

Jonny Trent watched Freya Cross's second-in-command, Monique, teeter down the gallery driveway towards her Mini Cooper. How could she afford such a stylish little runaround? He must be paying her too much. She was faffing around with her handbag now, must have mislaid her keys. She was good with the customers, especially the male ones, but not the brightest of specimens. Of course, in many ways that was a blessing. He hadn't told her about Freya's death. After all – he excused himself – the detective inspector had said the news was pending a formal identification of the body. And if Monique was going to spend a couple of hours or so blubbing, he'd rather she did it in her own time... She'd hear the details on the news, soon enough.

Hurry up. Hurry up, woman!

At last she reached down deep inside an inner pocket and found what she was looking for. Before she'd started her engine, Jonny was fetching his own car keys and locking up. For a second he stood looking up at one of Luke Cope's paintings, so dramatic and so hard to sell. It was of a church somewhere out in the Fens: bleak and atmospheric. The sky was stormy, and behind one of the windows of the building Luke had added a streak of blood-red paint. Jonny had always felt the man was only a whisker away from violence. The trouble was, he wanted to make some kind of dramatic mark on history. *Don't we all, to begin with?* But most people reached some kind of acceptance at some stage of the game. Jonny had. But Luke was still waiting for it to happen, and the lack of it seemed to fill him with a desperate kind of rage. And of course he was talented, that was the ironic thing.

Jonny shook his head. *What have you done, Luke? And who are you going to drag down with you?* If only he hadn't had a fussy brother to highlight his absence to the police.

Peering out through the window he saw that Monique was out of sight now. He set the alarm system, then left the building and went to unlock his Range Rover. Within five minutes he was sitting in traffic on the ring road, bound for the A10. How long would it take him to reach his destination in the ludicrous Cambridge rush-hour? He was shaking now, his hands quivering on the wheel. But he needed to make the journey. He'd been texting and calling Luke all day, ever since that scruffy-smart policeman had been to visit. But he'd got no reply.

CHAPTER TWELVE

Blake had been about to head home, but Fleming called him into her office. He'd had a feeling she would. He remembered the look in her eye as he'd entered the incident room.

She nodded him into the seat opposite her desk. They'd already discussed the plan of campaign the following day, so it couldn't be to do with that. Tara was going to get straight round to Luke Cope's house with Megan and Max to gut the place and search for any possible lead on where the missing artist might have headed. Meanwhile, Blake was going to talk to Monique – the woman who'd worked as Freya Cross's assistant – to see what secrets might have passed between them. And he wanted to talk to Zach Cross again too – to find out what he said under a bit of gentle pressure. So Fleming's desire for an extra conversation was a mystery.

'Ma'am?'

'Megan's promotion to DS is official.' She smiled at him. They both approved of the move, Fleming especially so. She and Megan were on the same wavelength. Blake still missed his old DS, Emma, whom Megan would replace. She'd had a relaxed positivity that Megan lacked. But still, Maloney was efficient and had the right priorities – she was a world away from Patrick Wilkins.

'I'm delighted for her, of course,' Fleming said. She gave him a look. 'I thought I'd let Patrick know about the move. As a courtesy, so that he's in the picture when he returns to work.'

Blake raised an eyebrow and his boss gave him an innocent smile. 'He won't like it, of course. If he comes back, I'll be very careful to pick and choose the cases he can work on, and what information he has access to. Megan will have a far freer hand than he will. That and respect.'

'You're hoping the news of her promotion might put him off returning to work?'

Fleming opened her eyes wide. 'What an extraordinary thing to suggest, Blake!'

He allowed a smile to surface.

'Speaking of which, if Patrick doesn't come back, we'll have another vacancy at DS level,' his boss added.

'Max,' Blake said. His DC had let his career stagnate since his wife was killed in a car accident. She'd been so young. Blake got the impression Max had clung to the job he knew because he couldn't cope with anything more, emotionally. But in the last year he'd started to come back out of his shell. He'd already taken the necessary exams.

'Max indeed.' Fleming leant forward, her elbows on the desk, her new sleek hair gleaming darkly under the overhead lights. 'You put him with Tara today, for the door to doors.'

She made it sound like an accusation.

'Tara's excellent at interviews and observation. She complements Max. You know what he's like; he'll drink everything in without the interviewee even noticing. And then between the two of them they come up with some interesting ideas.'

Fleming nodded. 'All well and good. I'm aware worming information out of the unwary is Tara's forte. But I feel it would be better to get her and Max working separately.' She put her head on one side. 'We still need to finish assessing him for the core competencies. At this stage, he needs someone who'll nudge him onto centre stage. He's a good copper, Blake.'

He didn't need Fleming to tell him that. Blake had been the one who'd championed Max's cause when he'd been going through hell. He opened his mouth, but Fleming held up a hand.

'I know I was tough on him in the early days, soon after his wife died. I sympathised with him, truly, but he was unreliable back then and jeopardising the team. That doesn't mean I ever doubted his abilities; I just wanted him to take more compassionate leave if he wasn't up to the job. He's on top form now.

'But I bet it was Tara who took the lead today when they went out together,' Fleming went on. 'She's a huge asset to the team, but she's not backward in coming forward. Max needs to be given the chance to develop. Meanwhile Megan, in her new role, needs experience of managing other staff. I'd like you to pair them together for now, and task Megan with giving Max the extra push he needs.

'You can take Tara along with you instead. She's interviewed Matthew Cope twice now, and quizzed the gallery manager over the phone. She's ended up with a lot of background that you could make use of. And you're well-matched personality-wise – you can wade in if Tara oversteps the mark, tell her to be a team player.'

It was something Fleming had had to remind him of before and by the twinkle in her eye he could see she thought Tara would give him a run for his money.

Blake sought a way to undermine her argument, but in about half a second he realised that she was right. Having Tara there to snoop round the gallery whilst he'd interviewed Jonny Trent, for instance – that would have worked. She could have intercepted Monique downstairs as soon as the gallery client had left too. He'd been unable to catch her alone himself; by the time he'd finished talking to Trent, the first potential buyer had left and been replaced by another. *Damn.* And he'd half thought of taking her with him too. But he'd held off. Deep down, he knew why that was. Too much time with Tara, day in, day out, was a problem. When they were together there was a spark.

He glanced up at Fleming. Had she guessed the truth? Or did she just think he was being a control freak, heading out on his own?

She'd had another one of Patrick Wilkins' disciplinary meetings that morning and it had been Wilkins who'd spread rumours about him and Tara. It might have focused her mind on the possibility that Blake's feelings for Tara could be affecting the way he ran his team.

'You could pair Max with Megan tomorrow, for the search of Luke Cope's house and interviewing the neighbours. Good plan?'

Blake nodded. 'Ma'am.'

'Right,' Fleming said, swiping her fringe to one side with her right hand. 'You'd better get off.'

He'd go out and talk to Tara; have a rethink about the plans for the following day and pull her out of the house search. He couldn't run away from the situation he was in, and they were both quite capable of being professional. He wanted to talk to her about that car she'd seen too, making a dash away from Matthew Cope's place.

But when Blake left Fleming's office, his DC was already gone.

CHAPTER THIRTEEN

Tara had sat in her car in the dark, outside Parkside police station, for some time, thinking about the Mercedes that had sped past her that morning when she'd been to visit Matthew Cope.

Just because Luke drove a dark-red Volvo, didn't mean it hadn't been him. If he'd killed Freya Cross, he'd hardly take his own car if he needed to travel.

Luke could have left the car out in the lane to avoid anyone associating the unfamiliar vehicle with his brother. Maybe he'd been after help; someone to support him in his attempts to get away. If so, had he already been in to talk to Matthew before she'd turned up? Or had he been forced to abandon the idea because she'd arrived? Matthew Cope had been on edge when he'd greeted her, but he'd naturally be a bundle of nerves under the circumstances. It didn't tell her anything one way or the other.

If the driver of the blue Mercedes *hadn't* been Luke, then could it have been someone else connected with the case? Someone who had their own reasons for wanting to find the missing artist before the police?

Either way, it made her want to talk to Matthew Cope again. He must be anxious – possibly close to breaking point. If he was protecting Luke, she reckoned she might be able to coax the information out of him: convince him that it was in his brother's best interests to hand himself in – and make him see his own role clearly. She could ensure he'd sweat over his part in hiding the bastard who'd killed Freya Cross.

She thought again of the text Luke had sent to Freya, the night she'd died. *Please, Freya, meet me. Usual place. Nine tonight. Give me a chance and we can start again.* She'd noted it down. The message fitted with the assertion that they'd been lovers. They'd quarrelled and Luke had painted the chilling scene of his hands around Freya's neck. And then what had happened?

There was still the possibility that someone else had found out about Freya and Luke's planned meet-up and killed them both. Zach Cross could have seen the text on his wife's phone.

But if Luke was guilty the text could have been a callous bluff, to lure Freya out into the night. Or alternatively he could have meant what he'd said at the time he'd sent the message. Perhaps they'd argued again in the nature reserve and he'd lashed out.

Freya had been struck with an object before she'd been strangled. Maybe that spoke of a spur of the moment act. And yet there weren't many large stones in the nature reserve. If you were after a weapon, you'd have to search to find a suitable one.

How had Freya felt when she'd got Luke's text? Had her heart leapt at the thought of making up with her lover? Or had she been nervous and full of doubt as she'd headed off on the night of Friday twenty-third of February? Tara imagined her, waiting in the silent, frigid night air, listening for Luke, seeing him come closer, her anticipation mounting, then cowering in confusion and fear as he raised his hand, smashing down the rock he'd used to stun her.

She rammed her key home and activated the ignition. She was going to go to talk to Matthew Cope again that night, before she went home. If he was hiding something, getting to him quickly was crucial. If Blake were there he'd probably decide to go instead of her. As she swung the car round in the car park she acknowledged that – officially – she ought to give him the chance. But her plans were the result of her own detective work. She'd been the one to notice that the Merc had been on a road to nowhere. And besides, there was no time. She reckoned Blake would be a while. DCI Fleming had had that look on her face – the one that spelled a heart to heart with her favourite employee.

She wasn't worried about going it alone. Thanks to Paul Kemp, the ex-police officer who'd taught her self-defence, she knew how to take care of herself. For a second, as she pulled out of the car park, she smiled into the darkness. Just before Christmas, Kemp had come to visit her unexpectedly – taken her by surprise, out on Stourbridge Common at night. He'd mock-attacked her as a joke (testing her skills, he'd said). And she'd had him on the ground, groaning, before she'd even realised who he was. He wouldn't do that again in a hurry.

Driving along Matthew Cope's lane after dark was a different prospect to approaching his house during the day. Even that morning the area had put her on her guard. Now, she saw additional signs that made her watchful. A large fire, burning next to what looked like a derelict building on her left-hand side. It was raining hard, yet still they'd managed to keep it going, such was its size. Were there people sheltering inside the building? There must be. She heard dogs barking as she had earlier, and an angry shout. She'd reduced her speed to cope with the potholes – her Fiat wasn't in its first flush of youth – but instinct made her want to put her foot down.

She was just rounding a bend when something flew out of a hedge and hit the rear of her car. *Hell.* Someone had thrown a stone. Maybe people round here felt so disenfranchised they'd lash out at any stranger on their territory. Matthew Cope's house might be large, with massive grounds, but it wasn't in an area Tara would have chosen. Not that he'd chosen it, of course. Luke had certainly got the better deal when it came to the family houses they'd inherited.

She was relieved that Matthew's place was further out still; in this instance, leaving the populated areas felt like a plus. At last she turned into the man's driveway, but the house was in darkness, and the BMW she'd seen earlier in the day was missing.

She exited her car, closing its door as quietly as she could. Out there in the rain-washed night, in the countryside with no visible moon, it was hard to see much. She turned up her collar against the weather and surveyed her surroundings first, checking for any sign of movement amongst the dark holly bushes and shrubs that bordered the grounds. The place seemed quiet, but she rescanned everything in her line of sight as her eyes adjusted to the light levels.

She went to knock on the door, just to be sure, but the missing car made her certain she'd had a wasted trip. There was no sign of life when she peered through one of the windows.

Where had Matthew Cope gone? The state he'd been in that morning hadn't led her to suppose he'd be up for an evening out. What if he was missing because he was already off somewhere, helping Luke?

She put a hand in her bag and felt for her mobile but before she found it she registered a noise. There was a car approaching up the lane. She could hear its engine, and the sound of its wheels against the loose surface of the road. She was up by the house still, but her car was sitting there in the driveway for all to see. Was it Matthew Cope returning home? She glanced at her watch. It was early yet, if he'd gone out for the evening. She stood there, tensed. Even if it was Matthew, it wasn't impossible that he was coming home with a killer in his passenger seat. How far would he go to protect his brother? They clearly had a close bond. Matthew had been desperate for the police to take Luke's disappearance seriously. Tara remembered his irritation at his brother's unworldliness but also his sense that he knew what was best for him. Maybe he was in the habit of taking charge…

The sound of the engine was getting louder. She could shut herself in her own car, ready to make her escape – but if the incoming vehicle saw her and blocked the exit she'd be more vulnerable than if she stayed hidden. At least this way she could escape through a hedge into the neighbouring fields if she needed to. *In theory…* She didn't like the look of that holly. Thank goodness for the thick winter coat she still wore.

She could see the car's lights now, at the head of the driveway. They swung round to face the house full on – the dual beams dazzling her.

She stood absolutely still at the side of the building. She was half hidden, yet able to peer round to view who got out of the vehicle. But the driver left their headlights on. Although she could see a figure emerge from the car – on the driver's side – she couldn't tell if it was Matthew Cope. The person was a little shorter, she thought, and broader in the shoulders too. They moved behind their own car and towards hers, peering in at the windows, trying the door. Which she'd left unlocked…

They'd taken out a phone to use as a torch. And now they shone it at the house, sweeping the beam over its frontage.

Tara ducked back and held her breath as they walked towards the building.

Damn the torch. If it wasn't in her eyes she'd be able to see who was carrying it. Adrenaline coursed round her body. She was ready for them if she needed to put up a fight. At least it seemed they were alone.

She was poised to spring, when the torchlight was suddenly switched off. 'Come out, come out, wherever you are!'

Right.

She stepped forward. 'Evening, boss. What brings you here?'

She could just see Blake's eyes glint. She knew that look. When he answered, his voice was calm, but that didn't fool her. 'Same as you, I imagine. Your observations earlier made me think it was worth coming to check that Matthew Cope was safely tucked up in bed. I was going to suggest we made the trip together, especially given it's off the back of your intelligence. But by the time Fleming finally let me go you'd disappeared.'

Tara was glad he'd acknowledged her work, but she could hear the edge to his voice.

'What the hell did you mean by coming over here on your own? Worse, without letting anyone at the station know what you were up to?'

His sharp words were accentuated in the still, wet night, and were all the more annoying because he had a point. Trying to justify herself wasn't a viable option. She stayed silent instead. She couldn't bring herself to argue or explain.

She heard him sigh; saw his breath in the cold night air. 'You're not a journalist any more, Tara. Policing means working as a team. If you put yourself and a case at risk everyone's affected.'

She knew this was where she should apologise. And that her anger was for a multitude of complicated reasons, mostly unrelated to why she'd been outside on her own, preparing to deal with a man who might be shielding a killer.

At last she saw Blake's shoulders go down. 'What were you about to do, before I showed up?' he asked, his voice quieter now.

'Call Matthew Cope's mobile. If there's any chance he's helping his brother that might be what he's up to right now.' *Whilst we stand here, and you treat me like a schoolchild. And I behave like one…*

'Agreed.' He nodded towards the phone she'd now dragged out of her trouser pocket. 'Get on with it, then.'

Tara dialled. It took Matthew Cope several rings to pick up. *What are you up to?*

'*Matthew Cope,*' the disembodied voice announced.

'It's Tara, Matthew, Tara Thorpe,' she said, earning a raised eyebrow from Blake. He ought to be pleased. No one unbuttoned when you were constantly rubbing your job title in their faces.

There was a momentary pause. *'You've got news about Luke?'*

In the background, she could hear multiple noises: glasses clinking, laughter, several voices and pop music. Unless he'd taken his brother to a pub, Tara guessed her and Blake's fears had been groundless after all. And his voice was still taut with worry.

'Not yet, I'm afraid,' she said. 'Perhaps we'll get a lead at your brother's house tomorrow. Our CSI colleagues have already had a first look.'

'Have they found…?' He let the question trail off.

'If there's anything concrete, we'll let you know. Matthew, we came to find you at home, but when I saw you were out I thought I'd better call.' She left a faint questioning note in her voice.

'I was sitting there at my place and the tension was just building and building. I felt as though I was going crazy, with all the images spinning round in my head. I wanted to do something constructive.' Unlike *you*, his tone seemed to say. The background noise receded. She guessed he'd taken his phone outside. *'I'm at a place called the Flag and Diamond. My brother mentioned coming here a few times. I wanted to chat to the regulars – see if they know anything.'*

'Don't put yourself at risk, Matthew. We still don't know what we're dealing with here.' She heard his sharp sigh, imagined his irritation at her comment – a young woman taking it upon herself to advise him. 'I can understand why you wanted to get out. It must be a terrible strain for you.' She paused for a second, wishing she could see his face. 'Have you managed to glean anything useful?'

'Nothing. I don't think they like outsiders here. They don't even admit to knowing Luke.'

Tara wondered what kind of a place the Flag and Diamond was, for everyone to be so tight-lipped. Then again, she couldn't imagine Matthew Cope being subtle in his approach. He was too short-tempered to exercise the patience and subterfuge required.

'Please let us know immediately if anyone does tell you anything useful. Whatever time of night it is. You've got my number.'

'I'd hardly keep information to myself.'

Tara remained silent. She'd rather he knew she wasn't going to take everything he said on blind trust.

After a pause Matthew Cope spoke again. *'Do you want me to come back home now, to speak to you?'*

Tara still wanted to ask him about the blue Mercedes she'd seen racing away from his house that morning, of course, and she'd rather do it face to face. But after a moment's thought she dismissed pushing for a meet-up that evening. 'No, it's okay. But I'll be over at your brother's house first thing tomorrow. Could you manage to drop in on your way to work? We could have a quick word then.' She'd seen from his business card that his office was on the south side of the city. It would be on his way, even if it did mean an unnecessary detour into the town centre during rush hour.

'All right,' he said. She could hear his frown. *'I'll be there at eight fifteen.'*

'Perfect.' She hung up and relayed the result to Blake.

'So what do you reckon?' he said.

'That he's telling the truth about where he is, though my belt and braces instinct makes me want to go and check he isn't there with his brother. There's a chance we could catch him out, only he'd recognise me if I went barging into the Flag and Diamond.'

'The name of the pub rings bells. North-west of here, isn't it, on the city's outskirts?'

Tara nodded. 'I think so. I drove past it once.'

Blake met her eye. 'Near where Max lives, in fact.'

'That's a point.' Max would be glad to follow up the lead, too. Tara reckoned he'd finally got the policing bug back in the last few months. He no longer wanted to work all hours solely because he couldn't face his empty house and the memories of his wife; he needed to get his fix.

'I'll send him Matthew Cope's work mugshot,' Blake said, getting busy with his phone. A moment later he made the call to Max.

Tara could just hear the DC's responses from where she stood, close to Blake.

She looked at his broad shoulders, his head bent down against the rain, dark hair blowing in the wind, and wished she could switch off the automatic response the sight of him always triggered. *Talk about conflicting feelings…*

She turned her mind back to his over-familiar behaviour towards her, when his wife had been newly pregnant. That ought to be enough to bring her to her senses.

CHAPTER FOURTEEN

Twenty minutes later, Tara had parked her car on Stanley Road, the Victorian-terrace-lined street that led down to Riverside. It was round the corner from where she lived. There was no vehicular access to her own house – unless there was an emergency that warranted opening the wide gate onto Stourbridge Common. Her tiny Victorian cottage was on a bit of no-man's-land, surrounded by the meadows, close to the River Cam and the Green Dragon Bridge that led to the village of Chesterton. Not that it was a village these days really; it had become absorbed into Cambridge itself.

Her location meant reaching home involved walking or cycling – through a pedestrian gate or across a cattle grid. Red poll bullocks grazed the common in the spring and summer.

Tara reached Riverside and turned right, passing a short row of houses facing the river before pushing open the creaky swing gate. It was still raining and the common appeared darker than usual under the cloudy night sky. There were periodic lamps on the main pathways across the grass, but the light they emitted was diffused by the drizzle.

As she began to cross the dark space, Tara's mind, which had been on Megan Maloney's promotion to DS – news that Blake had passed on before they'd parted – shifted back to the case. She shivered. What had happened to Freya Cross brought home the dangers of walking in an isolated spot at night. It wasn't late now, only eight, but thanks to the weather Stourbridge Common was deserted. Automatically she checked over her shoulder and then glanced up at the trees that bordered the meadow, straining to catch any movement. It seemed she really was alone, but still she quickened her pace slightly. She liked being out in the middle of nowhere: having her own space, keeping other people at arm's length. But nearly five years earlier she'd had a killer on her trail. One who'd watched her on that very common, and who'd taken the life of one of his victims there too. She hadn't been intimidated into moving away then, and she wasn't going to let that sort of worry affect her now, either. She could take care of herself. But she was always wary. Thank God for Kemp. He'd given her the tools to regain control.

With one last glance over her shoulder, she walked past the low brick wall which was all that separated her tiny front garden from the common, then let herself inside her house, pushing the door shut behind her.

She picked up the pile of post that had arrived whilst she'd been out. *Bill. Bill. Letter from a charity, asking for cash.* She shuffled through them in her hands before she took off her coat, and finally came to one that wasn't pre-printed. Her heart sank as she took in the telltale signs: her address completed in ink, in a copperplate script that she recognised. The sender was Robin – her father, though in name only. Why the hell was he writing to her?

The house was cold – as usual. The heating would have come on at six but the aging boiler struggled to match the temperature she'd set the thermostat to. She kept her coat on and went to dump the post on the kitchen table before heading upstairs to find a couple of extra jumpers. She made the switch from coat to woollen layers as quickly as possible, then went to put a bottle of red wine in a washing up bowl of warm water.

Only after that did she sit down to open her post. Robin's envelope contained an invitation.

In order to ignore it for a while longer she went to the fridge and pulled out some leftover arrabbiata pasta bake. She'd put enough chilli in it to warm her up the night before and she was more than keen to tuck into the second half now. But as it heated in the microwave, she couldn't help letting Robin and his wife's twenty-fifth wedding anniversary party filter into her mind. She couldn't think of anything more ridiculous than them inviting her. Tara knew from an argument she'd overheard as a child that Robin had wanted her mother, Lydia, to terminate the pregnancy. If it had been up to him, she wouldn't be sitting there today. *But hey, as you're still around, let's be inclusive and invite you along to a family do.* Talk about adding insult to injury. The argument she'd witnessed had involved Lydia complaining how difficult it was, bringing up a small child. (Even though she'd mostly off-loaded the job onto her cousin Bea anyway.) After which Robin had pointed out that she'd brought it on herself. If she'd taken his advice and had an abortion she would still be young and free.

Tara had never forgotten overhearing them. She wasn't one to forgive easily, even at the best of times.

She took her microwaved food and a large glass of red over to the table. Robin's invitation included a note scrawled on the back of the card: *We are hoping to see your mother, Benedict, Harry and Bea at the party too.*

Her stepfather and half-brother into the bargain, eh? To say nothing of Robin and Melissa's kids – yet more half-siblings. Bea would be the saving grace – *if* Tara decided to attend.

She could see where the invitation stemmed from. Her mother had thrown a party the year before, to celebrate her and Benedict's twentieth anniversary. It had been a glamorous affair: full of film stars and other celebrities. Tara's mother wasn't one to hang onto the past. She would have invited all her friends without giving it much thought; even including her teenage lover and his family. (*The more the merrier*, she'd have said to herself. *It'll be a hoot.*) But to Robin – and especially to his wife Melissa, who was the defensive, sensitive sort – it might well have seemed that Lydia was rubbing their noses in her successful, moneyed, jet-set lifestyle. Robin's architecture firm was prosperous too, but for glitz, it wasn't in the same league.

So maybe Melissa was behind the invitation to *their* anniversary do. Perhaps she was determined to show she could hold her own.

At that moment Tara's mobile rang. She pulled it out of her trouser pocket and picked up. Kemp.

'This is a pleasant surprise.'

The sound of an aggrieved sigh came down the phone. *'You say that as though you think I'm up to something.'*

'Well, aren't you?'

There was a pause. *'I was just wondering how you were – that's all.'*

'You didn't, by any chance, see any news items that have led you to call?' The brutal murder of the wife of a Cambridge professor was the kind of thing that might have reached the nationals. As usual, Tara found it frustrating that it would be Freya's association with her husband and his institution that made her more newsworthy, despite her own successful career. A link with the university added a certain mystique that journalists loved.

'I might have happened to notice something.' She heard the sound of Kemp swigging a drink. Beer no doubt. He'd probably sorted himself out with refreshments before calling, as others might take popcorn into the cinema. As an ex-cop he relished hearing her gossip – even though he'd left the force under a cloud. Officially, he had no truck with his former colleagues. *'You on the case then?'*

'Yup.'

'And?'

'I can't discuss it with you. Not beyond what's already in the public domain, anyway.'

'Plenty of suspects?'

'Yes, thank you.'

He groaned. *'Mean-spirited, I call it. Does our past mean nothing to you?'*

He'd saved her sanity back when she was a teenager. No one else had realised how damaging the attentions of her stalker had been. And, much later on, their relationship had moved on a step. Now, they were good friends who'd once been lovers. Kemp would never imply she owed him anything for that.

He sounded so comically morose that she laughed. 'Our past means plenty, but given my boss is currently under suspension for leaking information, I'm not about to make the same mistake.'

She heard him chuckle quietly. *'Dear old DS Wilkins. What's the news on him?'*

Kemp had provided the evidence required to put her boss on a disciplinary. He'd been staying at the boarding house that Bea ran, just before Christmas and – at a loose end – he'd decided to do some unpaid investigative work into the man who had been proving to be a thorn in Tara's side. After a few days he'd got photos of Wilkins making out with Shona Kennedy from *Not Now* magazine, and chatting cosily to the publication's editor, Giles Troy, in a local pub. But it was the recording he'd managed to secure of their conversation that had sealed Wilkins' fate.

'I haven't heard anything, but thanks to you the professional charges are pleasingly serious.'

'There'll be fun and games if you ever do work on the same team again.'

'Yes, thanks for that. It had crossed my mind.' The images it conjured up weren't pleasant. They'd been at daggers drawn even before Kemp had got Wilkins into trouble. She wouldn't be able to stomach so much as speaking to her DS after what he'd done.

'I'm coming down at the weekend by the way,' Kemp said. *'Staying at Bea's. She's got one of the suites free so I'm going to give her a hand, sprucing it up.'*

He'd helped with another one of the guest rooms when he'd stayed just before Christmas, too. For a second Tara felt an odd twist of something that she refused to call jealousy. That would be crazy – and show her in a terrible light. It was just that Kemp had once been *her* special friend – one of the people she was closest to. That was still true, but his bond with Bea was becoming every bit as strong.

But she was glad of that, of course. Bea had had a horrible year – losing her husband, fighting grief, coping with running her business alone. If ever someone needed support it was her. It just felt a tiny bit odd that Bea and Kemp were arranging visits where she was only involved as an afterthought.

You are so childish. Like a toddler, clamouring for attention. She needed to get a grip; stand on her own two feet. Kemp and Blake were moving on, and she wasn't. She took a swig of wine.

'*You're a bit quiet,*' Kemp said. '*Are you out of sorts?*'

'Sorry.' She strove for inspiration and Megan Maloney's promotion came to mind. The woman was a world away from Wilkins, and her move to DS was expected, but the change still made Tara uneasy. They'd never be on the same wavelength – not that that should matter. She relayed it all to Kemp.

'*Sure you're not just jealous?*' he said, unhelpfully.

'Quite sure.'

He laughed, making Tara grit her teeth. Once again she tried to move the conversation on. Her eyes fell on her father's invitation. 'The post today put me in a bad mood, too.' Which was true – though shaming to admit, given the horrors of the morning. The party was such a trivial thing. She filled Kemp in on the details.

'I'm going to call him and say I'm not going,' Tara said. 'They don't want me there anyway.' Her tone sounded whiny, even to herself.

'*In that case you should definitely go,*' Kemp said. '*Where's your fighting spirit? Don't make it easy for them. Show up. Drink their drink; eat their food.*'

'That's not compensation enough.'

'Well, you'd have to really go for it, obviously. Start by taking more than your fair share of all the most expensive stuff. Then make an effort to talk to their stuck-up friends and explain exactly who you are. Then smile. Make a nuisance of yourself. That's what I'd do.'

She snorted. 'That I can believe. Well, taking your advice in the past has stood me in good stead. But on this one, I'm not sure.' She'd have to think about it.

Two minutes later, she'd rung off and resolved not to dwell on Robin and Melissa any more. Or on her mother. Allowing them to prey on her mind, one way or another, meant they'd won, and Kemp was right: she shouldn't let them quash her spirit. Instead, she focused on Luke Cope.

Where was he? Somewhere close at hand, watching the police scurry round after finding Freya's body? Or long gone? Abroad maybe? Or was he also dead?

But even if he'd met a violent end like Freya, he'd still imagined killing her. His painting proved that. If he was a victim, he couldn't be an innocent one.

She opened up her laptop and googled him. There were multiple hits, including various sites offering punters the chance to buy his art. On two, his work was reduced, in one case as part of a pre-Christmas sale. The owner of the site clearly hadn't bothered to update the page. The reviews of Luke's paintings were the most interesting. One lengthy piece in an online arts magazine had heralded him as the next big thing – predicted he'd be a household name like Damien Hirst before the year was out. Tara glanced at the date. It had been written eight years previously. He must have been sick of waiting for success.

Yet he'd still had people who were prepared to champion his work. His brother thought it could sell if marketed properly, and Jonny Trent had displayed his paintings in his gallery. Two people who didn't appear overburdened with sentimentality – so presumably their judgement counted for something. But neither of them had helped Luke Cope achieve his dreams. You'd think Trent, who had a business to run, would have given the project up as a bad job by now.

The more Tara considered it, the odder it seemed that he hadn't.

CHAPTER FIFTEEN

Jonny Trent had finally made it to the other side of Cambridge. Now he was driving north-east, out into the Fens. The rain was lashing down, flooding the Range Rover's windscreen as fast as the wipers could whisk it away. The sky was completely dark already. That was the thing driving eastwards, and in poor weather too. You lost the light all the more quickly. Though for his mission, darkness might be no bad thing.

As he turned his vehicle down the lane he needed he felt the wind buffet his car side on. The land was flat, bleak and exposed. He missed the rolling countryside he'd enjoyed as a child over in the Cotswolds. The time was coming when he'd finish up in the east and relocate, back to his roots. He'd been thinking about it for a while anyway. Now he wished he'd already made the move. The news of Freya's death and bloody Luke being missing too had left him feeling as though an abyss was opening under his feet; something he couldn't control.

Up ahead he saw it at last: the mill. Its sails had stopped turning years ago. One of them had chunks missing; it had been damaged in a storm apparently. In the dark the place looked menacing, looming there before him. He pulled into the driveway that went round the back of the building, and after a moment he saw Luke's Volvo, parked out of sight of the road, slewed across the gravel. It was at an odd angle, but then tidy parking wasn't something that tended to trouble Luke. It might not mean anything. He didn't go towards the car – he went straight to the door of the mill and knocked.

It was hard to make a decent noise with his fist on the thick wood. He could barely hear his knocks himself above the howling of the wind. Rain trickled down his hair and dripped under his coat collar, making him shiver and curse.

'Luke!' he yelled, but his voice was carried off on the wind. And if the artist was inside, and heard Jonny shouting, would he feel inclined to come and answer? Jonny wasn't sure how things stood. 'Luke?' he bellowed again, before walking back and looking up at the dark, blank windows.

He might have gone out, if he'd had a lift in someone else's car. Was he thinking clearly? That was the question. If he'd done a runner in another vehicle, and anyone found this place… He should get inside – check for himself, make damn sure. He needed to talk to Luke, but this was even more imperative. He rattled at the door, then looked around for somewhere where the artist might have hidden a key, but he found nothing. There were no low windows – nothing he could reach without a ladder. Breaking in wasn't an option. He could come back with the right equipment, but was it worth the risk? It all depended. If Luke was still on top of things, it might be okay, but if not… if not, Jonny's whole world could come crashing down.

CHAPTER SIXTEEN

Kitty was in her pyjamas when Blake arrived home. She trotted down the stairs whilst he was asking Babette about her day and he bent down to hug her. She was warm from already having been tucked up in bed. He felt her hair shifting against his cheek as he cuddled her close. She smelt of shampoo – the same baby brand they'd always bought for her – but these last few months Blake had suddenly been conscious of how grown-up she was getting. Being in year two at school with a new teacher had made a difference.

'What did you do today, Daddy?' she asked, her voice alert. Blake could tell his arrival had got her stirred up again when she had been drowsy. He gave Babette an apologetic look over Kitty's shoulder but she shook her head.

'Work, work, work, Kitty,' Blake said. 'I wanted to come home much sooner than this.'

'But what were you actually *do-ing*?' She drew the word out for emphasis.

He swung her up into his arms so he could cuddle her properly without wrecking his back. Babette's eyes were on his. She knew about Freya Cross's murder. 'Well, I've been asking people a lot of questions. And I went to see Agneta to talk to her too.' Kitty liked Agneta and was fascinated by her and her husband's baby, Elise.

'Why did you have to ask them all questions?'

'Because when you're a detective you have find out the truth about what's happened, so you can help people who are in trouble.'

'And stop the baddies?' Kitty asked. She was repeating back what he'd told her before.

'That's right.' Whenever he thought about asking questions to find out the truth, he thought of Kitty's natural father – and the fact that he still didn't know his identity. It ate away at him. He pushed the question away now and looked into his daughter's brown eyes. Eyes that – when she'd been a baby – he'd assumed she'd inherited from him.

'Okay then,' Kitty said, suddenly seeming satisfied. Perhaps she was getting sleepy again after all.

'Shall I come and tuck you in?' Blake said.

She nodded. 'Will you read me a story?'

Blake knew it was late for her – especially on a school night. 'I'll read you a poem,' he said, 'whilst you close your eyes.'

'"The Owl and the Pussycat"?'

He nodded. He could say that one in his sleep. Backwards. It had been a favourite since Kitty was three years old.

Ten minutes later, he pulled the door to Kitty's bedroom almost closed. She liked to have a chink left, so that light carried through from the landing.

Downstairs, Babette had taken a casserole dish out of the oven and was spooning out a sizeable helping of coq au vin.

'Let me,' he said. It was partly guilt for being an absentee husband, but partly, he knew, because he didn't want to be beholden to her. Being in her debt – even in a small way – made him feel ever more powerless. It chipped away at his treasured place on the moral high ground, he supposed, which didn't show him in a good light. Somehow, he felt he wanted to shore up his justifications for resentment. It was insurance, in case one day he decided to throw in the towel. At that point he'd need to explain his many reasons for leaving her.

But in reality, that wasn't going to happen. He'd always been loath to put distance between him and Kitty. Her being another man's child left Blake out on a limb. If he left Babette, and she and her erstwhile lover reunited, what kind of place would Blake have in Kitty's future?

And now Babette was expecting a baby that was genuinely his – as far as he knew. He thought again of her claim that she'd forgotten to take her pill. Instead of owning up to it, when she'd found she was pregnant, she'd started to broach the subject of having another child to get Blake used to the idea, as though it wasn't already a fait accompli. Babette's attitude to the truth was fast and loose. Blake couldn't call what she did lying exactly, but sometimes it seemed even worse. When he tried to call her out on it, the facts disappeared like mist. He took a deep breath. His father had left his mother when he'd been a baby. And now, his overall impression of his dad was coloured by what his mother had told him, early on. Everything his father said he processed through the filter she'd created. He didn't want that to happen with Kitty – or with the new baby. But still, he felt trapped. In another life... For a second Tara's unflinching green-eyed stare filled his consciousness. He closed his eyes and shut out the thought.

As Blake ate, Babette left him to it and he was grateful for that. She knew him well enough to understand that he'd benefit from fifteen minutes' peace after a day filled with horrific images. He'd got himself a bottle of Leffe from the fridge, and as he worked his way down it and the plate of food his mind ran over the murder scene and the post-mortem. How did Agneta do it, day in, day out? He wondered what Max might have found out at the Flag and Diamond too. Not much, he guessed, or his DC would have been in touch. Still, he was glad he'd sent him. It fitted with Fleming's desire to give him more of his own work and increase his independence.

Five minutes later he no longer felt hollow from hunger. It might be time to try to address other things that were bothering him. After he'd put his plate in the dishwasher, he took the rest of his beer over to the sofa and sat down next to Babette.

'How are you feeling?' he asked.

She looked at him and smiled. 'Good.' And then she took his hand and placed it on her stomach. Her bump was quite pronounced now. 'This little one's been very active all day. The movements feel quite strong.'

She was right. He felt a ripple under the palm of his hand and experienced a sudden hot rush of affection for a person he'd yet to meet. But when his eyes found Babette's he still came up against the same barrier. How to connect with *her*, as well as with their unborn baby?

'You still find it hard, don't you?' she said. 'It's been years now, Garstin.' Her eyes registered irritation she'd no right to feel and his heart rate increased.

'Yes.' How were you supposed to get past something like what she'd done? 'I think…' What did he think, really? Could anything solve this? He started again: 'I think it doesn't help that you've never told me more about Kitty's real father. I can't put the subject to bed, because I'm always wondering. And even if you never tell me the whole truth, you're going to have to tell her one day.'

Babette looked down. 'Do you think so? I wondered if it was better for her simply not to know. Less worrying. I'd hate to unsettle her.'

He tightened his fists so hard that his nails dug into the palms of his hands. Did she really think it was that simple? 'She's got a right to know about her heritage, Babs.' He took a deep breath. 'Her genetics too. And what if her father comes looking for her, later in life? How the hell do you think she'd feel then, if it was a bolt from the blue?' He strove to keep his voice down, but he could feel the anger building up inside him.

'Let's cross that bridge later, Garstin. She's too young to understand properly at the moment anyway. We can talk about it again when she's older.'

Never tackle today what you can put off until tomorrow... He tried to steady his breathing. When Babette finally told Kitty who her real father was – and he'd insist that she did, eventually – Blake would be the only one not to know the secret. It was unthinkable. 'I want you to tell me his name, Babs. And I want you to tell me what really happened when you left me and took Kitty to Australia.'

She'd given him the bald facts before, of course: told him she'd realised quickly that she'd made a mistake and Kitty's true parentage wasn't as important as the relationship both she and Kitty had with Blake. But he was increasingly sure that wasn't the whole truth. And each time she recounted events there was a chance she'd let something extra slip, or say something contradictory that would hint at what she'd left unsaid.

He was using his detective tactics on his wife. He'd never imagined being in such a situation the night, eight and a half years ago now, when they'd got engaged, on a sunny evening over a bottle of fizz and a picnic out on Ditton Meadows, by the river.

'For God's sake, Garstin! I told you what happened in Australia. From the moment we arrived, he started to sideline Kitty. Within days it was quite clear that it wasn't the genetics that counted. He didn't care for her like you do – and his claim as her father was the only reason I finally decided to go with him. It was always you that I loved. I made a terrible mistake by having a very brief fling. I don't want to go on paying for it for the rest of my life. I can totally understand why you were angry, and why you still hurt. But what more can I say?'

'You can tell me his name.'

'He was just a guy, Garstin. What difference does it make what he's called? And he emigrated to Australia anyway.'

He looked at her steadily, waiting for her to realise he meant what he said – finally. He hadn't pushed it before but suddenly he realised it was something he needed.

'Okay. All right. If it makes you happy, his name was Matt Smith.'

'Matt Smith? Like the old *Doctor Who* actor?'

She raised an eyebrow. 'Exactly like. But not him.'

No kidding.

Later that evening, in the bathroom as he washed his face, Blake thought through what Babette had said. Would anyone really arrange to emigrate to Australia with a lover they'd only known fleetingly – even if the affair had resulted in a child? And then come all the way back again after trying out the new relationship for just a couple of weeks, for the reasons Babette had told him?

And if this 'Matt Smith' had put that much pressure on Babette to let him be with his natural child, why had he left them entirely alone ever since, never approaching her to try to get access to Kitty?

It didn't make sense.

And as for the name… Well, it might really be what the man was called. But it was convenient that Matt Smith was such a common combination it would prove nigh on impossible for Blake to track him down. If he googled, he'd just get page after page of hits about the actor…

CHAPTER SEVENTEEN

Tara had arranged to meet Blake, Max and Megan round at Luke Cope's house on Wednesday morning. Blake had had a change of heart about how they should arrange the day. Megan's promotion to DS seemed to have made a difference already. She might have known.

The plan now was for Max and Megan to interview Luke's neighbours before they left the street to start the working day. Tara and Blake would talk to Matthew Cope when he dropped in as planned. After that, she and the DI would head off to catch Monique, Freya Cross's assistant at the gallery. Max and Megan would carry on the search of the house. Being in on the main action was what she'd wanted, of course, but she was also conscious that she'd been split up from Max. Fleming and Blake must think he'd work better with Megan…

Tara glanced up at the sky through her car windscreen as she pulled up once again on the quiet, elegant street where the missing man lived. It was weird to think of how much had happened since she'd first visited, two days earlier.

It was still raining – she didn't think it had stopped all night. Each time she'd woken she'd heard it battering against her cottage windows. The heavens were leaden and the wind strong, blowing the cold torrential downpour into her face as she got out of her vehicle and made her way to the villa's grand entrance. She nipped up the short flight of steps to the glossily painted black front door with its brass lion's-head knocker. It had a sort of iron canopy jutting out from over the fanlight, which she appreciated as she stood there, waiting for someone to let her in. She'd given Blake the keys Matthew had entrusted to her the day before.

It was Megan herself who appeared. Her dark, curly hair was still dripping. 'Come in.' She stood back. 'The DI and Max have just arrived too. Max has got an update.'

'That's good. Congratulations on your promotion, by the way.' She seemed to be congratulating everyone at the moment, what with Megan and her job news and Blake and the baby.

The new DS glanced at Tara over her shoulder for a split second. 'Thanks.'

Tara followed her through to the kitchen, where Max had opened a flask of coffee and was pouring it out into plastic cups he'd brought with him.

She met his questioning look as she entered. 'Yes, please.'

Blake was already raising a coffee to his lips. They were all aware he needed several cups each morning before the tetchy creases round his eyes smoothed out. But it was Max who'd thought to act on the fact. He was one in a million, Tara reckoned. And *she* thought they worked well together.

Max handed a cup to her and, as she thanked him, Megan went back to one she already had, lined up on the worktop.

'So what happened at the Flag and Diamond last night?' Blake asked.

Max screwed the lid back on the Thermos. 'Our man Matthew Cope was there all right. He was chatting to a couple of young guys. One had arms full of tattoos and the other had those ear-stretching ring things.'

'God – those always make me feel sick,' Megan said, with a shudder.

Tara could believe that. Megan was a conventional dresser.

'It's a rough old place, the Flag and Diamond,' Max said. 'The mates he'd picked up fitted the venue.'

Blake put his empty coffee cup down. 'What were the dynamics like? Were the regulars hostile? Did Cope seem intimidated?'

Max frowned. 'I wouldn't have said so, on either count. But both Cope and the locals looked as though they were finding their feet in the conversation, if you know what I mean. I couldn't get close enough to hear what was being said, unfortunately. Cope stayed on for twenty minutes or so after I got there, then raised his hand to the landlord and off he went. The two guys he'd been with stayed at their table for another pint and then they left too.'

'How did you manage to blend in?' Megan asked.

Max shrugged. 'I know the pub's reputation, so I dressed for the occasion. It's the kind of haunt where the regulars are probably taught to smell coppers from infanthood, but nobody gave me a second glance.'

'Well done,' Blake said. 'So what do we think about Luke Cope being a regular at a pub like that? An artist from a wealthy background who liked to frequent private views in central Cambridge…'

'And who used to meet his brother in the Snug.' Tara remembered that detail. The trendy city bar would be a far cry from somewhere like the Flag and Diamond.

'You think Matthew Cope was lying about it being a haunt of Luke's?' Megan said.

Blake shrugged. 'I can think of other reasons he might want to visit the place, if he is trying to help his brother. I'd be interested to know if they do any other business there, beyond selling booze. If Matthew Cope had wanted to pick up a fake passport, for instance…'

'It might be the perfect place to go,' Max agreed. 'And that would fit with the sort of discussion they seemed to be having, just as neatly as if he'd been trying to get information on his brother's whereabouts. Want me to go back in there and try to find out more later?'

Blake nodded. 'Sounds like a plan. It would be worth doing some background checks, too. But be careful – and let me know what you find.' He turned to his new DS. 'Anything useful from the database checks yesterday, Megan?'

She shook her head. 'It doesn't look as though we've crossed paths with Luke Cope, Professor Cross or his son Oscar in the past.'

'Ah well. Thanks for trying, anyway.' Blake glanced at his watch. 'Matthew Cope's due here in five minutes. Tara – we'll tackle him when he arrives. You can lead, as you're already on first name terms.' His tone was wry. Out of the corner of her eye, Tara thought she caught a look from Megan, but it was gone before she could analyse it.

'Megan, you and Max had better head straight off to talk to the neighbours. Keep your heads down if you see Matthew Cope arrive – I don't want him recognising Max. Follow your noses, but in particular, find out Luke's habits: whether he was sociable, how often he went out and if anyone knows where to.'

They nodded in agreement and left via the back door. Within minutes there was a knock at the front.

Matthew Cope's face was pale and taut, but there was something else in his expression too, Tara reckoned. Haughtiness? After all, he was coming into his childhood home – he probably felt he ought to be in charge. In reality, he was anything but, and he must know that. He wasn't the sort of man to find the situation easy. Knowing the CSIs had been crawling all over the place, sifting through his brother's things, was bound to feel like an invasion of privacy. But was he also worried about what they might discover, and where it might lead them? Things had spiralled out of Matthew Cope's control. Maybe that was why he looked so twitchy.

Blake glanced at Tara, handing her the reins.

'Thanks for coming,' she said. 'We'll find somewhere quiet to talk. Where would you prefer?' That ought to give the man some feeling of influence.

'We should go to the study,' he said immediately, leading the way down a short corridor that led right, from the front entrance. He opened a door to the left, revealing a room with a window facing onto the side garden. It was he who motioned them to take seats too – round a large desk inlaid with a leather top. He was certainly happy to take charge. The trick now was to let him keep believing he was in control whilst quietly extracting the details they needed.

'We were sorry to miss you last night,' she said. 'I can well understand you wanting to get out to help pass the time. It's horrible to have to wait with no news.' She leant forward and looked down for a moment. 'I always find pubs difficult if I'm on my own.' A worthwhile lie. She'd leave it at that to start with. She didn't want to put him on high alert if she could possibly avoid it. Instead she just raised her eyes to his and waited for him to fill the gap in conversation.

'I don't find it a problem,' Matthew said after a moment. 'Though the Flag and Diamond wouldn't be my choice of place to drink. It helped that I had a mission.'

Tara nodded. 'That makes sense. How did it go after I called you? Did you get any useful information?'

It sounded as though he'd been chatting to the men Max saw for some time. Surely that wouldn't have been the case if they'd just given him the brush-off, as he'd claimed?

Matthew met her eyes and smiled for a second. 'There were a couple of young guys who'd had a few drinks. They weren't able to help, but they seemed to regard me as a bit of a curiosity, so they settled down to talk. I left once it was clear that I'd got myself companions for the night. It made approaching other people difficult.'

If he had been trying to make useful contacts on Luke's behalf he'd certainly got his story straight. But then he'd naturally be prepared.

'It does sound awkward.' She made a sympathetic grimace. 'What on earth did they find to chat about?'

'They wanted to know where I usually drank and what had made me venture into the Flag and Diamond.'

All well and good, but that conversation wouldn't have lasted for twenty minutes. 'Did they ask you more about your brother when you mentioned him?'

Cope nodded. 'But they didn't give me any information in return.' He leant forward. 'I'm still desperate to find him. If I had a lead I'd want your help in pursuing it.'

She wasn't getting anywhere. It was time to change tack. 'Matthew, who was it who visited you just before I arrived at your house yesterday?' Switching from gentle to direct questioning might achieve something. It was fair enough to pretend she knew he'd had visitors. Where else could the dark-blue Mercedes have been coming from?

Matthew Cope frowned. 'I don't…' he began, but then stopped. 'What visitor?'

'The one driving the Mercedes.'

The frown was still present. 'What makes you think they were coming to see me? Did you see them coming out of my drive?'

She couldn't carry on the bluff any longer. 'They drove at speed from the direction of your house – and there isn't anything beyond, so I assumed they must have called to see you.'

'Really?' His shoulders relaxed. 'I'm afraid the area where I live has its drawbacks, Tara. I love the sense of space – beyond me the landscape really is just countryside until you come to the A14. But that remoteness also means you get a certain amount of laddish behaviour. People sometimes use the road as a race track.'

She could imagine that, but… 'I was just surprised that boy racers would have such a nice car.' Though it could have been stolen for all she knew; she hadn't managed to get its number, so she couldn't check.

Matthew shrugged. 'I've heard people say that drug dealers tend to have classy cars. Could that be a possibility? The area does have that sort of reputation.'

'It could.' She caught Blake's look. He was probably thinking the same as her – that you wouldn't expect dealers to be racing around the country lanes for kicks. They tended to be hard-nosed business people, focused on the bottom line.

'All the same, Matthew,' Tara said, 'it's just possible they were close to your place for a reason. If you see a dark-blue Mercedes near your house – or outside your work for that matter – please let us know.'

He looked edgy. 'If you think it's important, I will.'

'Thank you – and thanks for your time. We'd better let you get on to your office now.'

As they walked him to the door, Matthew Cope blinked a couple of times. 'I don't know how the hell I'm going to concentrate. I meant what I said about finding Luke. Whatever he's done, it's too late to change it. I just want to know what's happened to him – the uncertainty's horrible.'

After they'd closed the door behind him, Blake's dark eyes met Tara's. 'What do you think?'

'I'm surprised it took him twenty minutes to ask his questions and extricate himself from the conversation with the guys Max saw. I think we should keep an open mind as to what he's up to. And I'm still not happy about the Mercedes. If it wasn't Luke driving a hired car, or a contact Matthew had approached to try to help Luke, then could it have been someone who's looking for him – just like we are?'

Matthew Cope's house would be a logical place to start.

CHAPTER EIGHTEEN

Max and Megan were between interviews, walking up the street with its grand four-storey townhouses. It was a far cry from the estate where Max lived. Still, he'd been happy there when he'd first been married. He and Susie hadn't wanted anything but each other. For a second his mind spun back to the knock he'd had at the door of that very house to tell him his wife had been killed. How could life be so cruel? She'd only been twenty-five. For the first year the memory had brought tears with it, each and every time. Now, five years on, he could control his reactions. Inside, the thought still felt like a raw stab in the gut. People tended to assume he was well over the loss by now…

He felt Megan's eyes on him and thought for a moment that he'd let his feelings show, but within a second she'd glanced away again. Two beats after that, her gaze was back on him. She half opened her mouth, shut it again and once more faced away. It suddenly occurred to him that it might be she who'd got something on her mind.

'You all right, boss?'

He saw her blush for a moment at the way he'd started to address her since yesterday's news. The look of embarrassment – mingled with pleasure – was gone as quickly as it had come. He saw her swallow as she paused. 'Yeah.' Then she shook her head.

'A problem shared is a problem dumped on someone else, so you can feel better. Feel free to go for it.'

She laughed for a moment, but it faded too quickly for his liking. 'I bumped into Wilkins yesterday at the station. You know, when he came in for one of his disciplinary meetings.'

'Ah, I see. You have my sympathy.' No wonder she was looking fed-up. A run-in with Wilkins wasn't anyone's idea of fun. It must have been when he and Tara were out of the building. He was glad of that.

Megan nodded. 'It wasn't pleasant. But even though we all know he's a shit' – Max wondered what was coming – 'there was something he said that's been niggling at me.' She gave him a look. 'I'm sure it shouldn't. But, well, it got me thinking.'

'Unusual for him to say anything that's worthy of proper consideration.' Max felt odd, saying things he would have uttered without a thought two days previously. The way Megan was hesitating, he guessed she was suffering from the same, new-found reticence. Her promotion made a difference to their relationship. Still, he was curious. 'What on earth did he come out with?'

Megan relayed how the disgraced DS had advised her to keep an eye on Blake and Tara, and the way they behaved together. It was clear he'd as good as told her they were having an affair. Max felt an adrenaline rush as Megan said Wilkins had implied he'd only spoken out of concern for Max and Megan's welfare; he was worried Tara would get preferential treatment, and they'd be left out in the cold.

He took a deep breath. Wilkins' stirring comments shouldn't come as a surprise after the rumours he'd spread just before Christmas, but trying to use his poison to drive a wedge in the team was new.

'I'll tell you one thing for free,' he said to Megan. 'I'd take Blake as a leader over Patrick Wilkins any day of the week. Wilkins doesn't give a toss about anyone else, whatever he says.' He turned to Megan and grinned at her through the rain. 'And he used to call me "Max Dim" behind my back. Thinks I don't know. Funnily enough, some of the guys at school used to shorten my surname in exactly the same way, so he's not as original as he thinks.' Megan's expression hadn't lightened. 'He was the one who walked all over us when he was on the team. Do you remember, Megan?'

After a moment, she nodded. 'I do. And he's funny about women. Doesn't ever see them as equals. But even with all that, it doesn't mean he's wrong about everything.'

'He's wrong about this, that much I'm sure of.'

Her eyes were fixed on his. 'So you've never suspected any kind of special feeling between the boss and Tara?'

As she scrutinised his reaction, Max tried not to think of his DI holding his fellow DC, just after she'd escaped burning to death before Christmas. It was a perfectly natural reaction. Max was in no doubt that his boss would have been torn apart by emotion if Max had been the one whose life had been at risk. But he also knew what he'd seen in the DI's eyes.

'You're too nice, Max,' Megan said, nodding. 'You deal with so many bad guys in your work, but you still see the best in your colleagues.'

Max cursed inwardly. Wilkins' bile-filled words had had their effect.

'I don't think they're having an affair.' He really didn't. He'd pick up on that, surely? And the DI was one of the good ones. He didn't reckon Tara would do it, either. 'And as for anything else, the important thing is, would either Blake or Tara let their feelings affect their judgement and the way they treat others? I've got no doubts in that direction.'

Blake had stuck by him when things were as rough as they could get, fighting his corner with DCI Fleming. And he liked Tara.

But for all his heartfelt words, he could see Megan remained to be convinced.

There might be trouble ahead.

CHAPTER NINETEEN

Tara was standing in Luke Cope's bedroom. She and Blake had a short while before they were due to meet Monique over at the gallery, so they were giving the place a once-over. Max and Megan were still out interviewing the neighbours.

The sheets on Luke's king-sized bed were flung back, humped and dishevelled. It was eerie, looking at the abandoned room in the grey morning light, the rain lashing at the window. His sleeping quarters matched the studio for their untidiness and lack of order. There were clothes strewn over a chair next to the wardrobe, and books piled on a bedside table. Tara glanced at the top paperback, which was about art. In fact – she scanned the spines of the entire pile – they all were. Illustrated, critical volumes. Luke Cope was clearly dedicated to his specialist subject. There were books about art therapy too; painting to heal the soul.

She tried to imagine having copies of Blackstone's police manuals on her bedside table, but failed. She was keen enough, but bedtime was for relaxing.

To one side of the room was a chaise longue. *Very fancy.* But its velvet cushion was covered with belongings, including an overnight bag, a pair of jeans (half inside-out) and a couple of newspapers, which were several weeks old.

For a second she wondered about the overnight bag. Was there any connection with the holdall that Freya had supposedly been carrying the night she'd disappeared? But when she went to examine this one, she could see it contained a couple of pairs of boxer shorts and a business card in an inner see-through pocket with Luke

Cope's name on it, together with an address on Histon Road. It must have been the place he'd rented before he moved back to the family home; Tara remembered Matthew mentioning it.

She heard Blake's heavy footsteps just behind her, making the old floorboards creak. 'Anything interesting?'

She explained, turning towards him, and he nodded.

'I'll get Max and Megan to give this room a more thorough going-over,' he said. 'But I want you to show me the studio now.'

She led him downstairs, quickening her pace.

'Where was the picture of Freya Cross, when Matthew Cope showed it to you?' Blake asked.

Tara walked over to the stack of small paintings that had included the portrait of the dead woman. 'Here.'

The CSIs had bagged the work itself the day before, as evidence, but now Blake took out his phone to look again at the photograph of it they'd put on record. He went absolutely still, and Tara felt the chill that had swept over her two days earlier take hold again. Logic told her this was a sign of Luke Cope channelling his passionate anger with Freya Cross into his work. Matthew had said he'd thought his brother would have used the act as a safety valve, to let out his feelings. And yet there was something so calculated about the picture too.

'He planned the composition,' Blake said, echoing her thoughts. 'He considered how this would look to anyone viewing the artwork.'

Of course. Blake had said his mother was an art historian. He was probably better placed to judge than most DIs.

'It's the colours he's chosen, as well as the angles,' Blake added. 'Blonde hair on a scarlet cushion.' His eyes met hers. 'This is someone who thinks of art as more important than anything else. His desire to make something pleasing to his own eye trumps other values.' He paused for a second and shook his head.

Tara nodded. 'I wonder what your mother would say.'

He frowned as he put his phone back in his pocket. 'I might bring her in as a consultant.'

At that moment, there was a knock at the door. Tara went and found Max and Megan, shivering on the top step. The hems of Max's trousers were damp. Megan didn't meet her eye, she noticed; she was sure she wasn't imagining things. They followed her back through to join Blake in the studio.

'Anything?' their DI asked.

Max nodded. 'Well worth the walk in the rain. Spoke to an elderly gent next door who was very helpful. He's around a lot of the time so he tends to see the comings and goings, from what I can gather. Apparently, Luke Cope didn't mix much with the neighbours in general, though this guy – Montague Cavendish – remembers him and Matthew from when they were kids, and he knew their parents fairly well.'

Blake raised an eyebrow.

'Says the Copes senior had very particular ideas about how to bring up their boys. Leaving them each a house in trust was their way of ensuring they would make their own way in life rather than just relying on their inheritance. But with reference to Luke's current lifestyle, he said he sometimes disappears off for the day. And recently, on occasion, overnight, too. He usually takes a bag with him – and often his art equipment, as well.'

The fact that he occasionally went off overnight fitted with what Matthew had told Tara, back when she'd first interviewed him. But the news that he took his art equipment made her pause for thought. That implied pre-planning, and the intention to achieve something whilst he was away. It wasn't what she'd imagined when she'd spoken to his brother – at that point the periodic disappearances had sounded random and dysfunctional.

'Unless he has close friends his brother isn't aware of,' Megan said, 'then perhaps he has some kind of bolthole where he goes alone.'

Blake nodded. 'Thanks, both – that's definitely food for thought. Right – let's carry on searching the house now. We'll start with this room. It looks as though his heart and soul is here. I think it's our best bet for a lead.'

Tara followed Max to near where the painting of Freya Cross had been stored, and Blake and Megan started work opposite them.

She and Max each picked a stack of paintings to look through. Her collection leant against the wall, just to the left of an old fireplace. As she looked through the artworks she kept thinking of Matthew's assertion that his brother was talented and that, under the right circumstances, he could place his work in the top London galleries. She didn't know much about the art world, but the paintings were haunting. The one of Freya had been shocking, of course, but all of them, even the ones of the sea, or a moonlit night, had the ability to hit you in the gut. They got an emotional response from her, though generally not a pleasant one.

She paused for a second, looking at an oil painting of an old mill. Luke Cope had shown it by moonlight. The surrounding landscape made her think it was out in the fens. Silhouetted reeds appeared behind the imposing bulk of the building. You could almost feel the wind that had probably rustled through them on the night he'd depicted. Suddenly she realised Max was standing next to her.

'They're eerie, aren't they?' he said. 'I'm not sure I'd want one on my wall.'

Maybe that was Luke Cope's problem. To be commercially successful in a small way – selling lots of mid-priced paintings to members of the public – perhaps you had to make your creations easy to live with. Maybe Luke Cope's work was more akin to the stuff fashion designers put on the catwalk: Joe Public wouldn't be likely to adopt it as it was, but it could influence a whole generation if it was spotted by the right people. And at that point the really big buyers would invest their megabucks in it.

At that moment Megan's voice brought Tara out of her thoughts. 'This is weird…'

The DS was standing in the opposite corner of the room from her and Max. Tara watched. The woman's eyes were fixed on a large canvas, wrapped round a deep frame, standing in a stack on the floor, just as the ones she'd been viewing were. As they looked on, Megan knocked the painting against the wall, then peered again at its reverse side.

'What?' Blake was next to her now, with Tara and Max close behind.

Megan was frowning. 'There's something jammed into the back of this canvas.' She glanced around her, spotted a palette knife on a window sill and picked it up. In a moment, she was using it to drive between the back of the frame and the board they could all see had been wedged into it.

The knife was a bit flexible for the job, but after some work, as Tara watched, the extra panel came free. And so did another slim board, behind it. Two paintings, both deliberately hidden – even the CSIs had missed them.

'Oh my God.' Megan took a step back, allowing the works to fall against the wall.

Blake adjusted them, so that they could all see the compositions.

Tara moved in to photograph the pictures. One showed a young woman hanging from a noose. The room she was in was unfamiliar – a window behind her showing nothing but a dull cloudy sky. She wasn't yet dead in the picture, but her hands were at her throat, fingers desperately trying to get under the rope, a look of unbridled panic on her choking face.

The other was of a man in late middle-age: his body splayed out at the bottom of a flight of stairs. Tara recognised the scene this time; it showed the house they were now standing in.

CHAPTER TWENTY

'We'll need to talk to Matthew Cope again,' Blake said, his eyes on the road ahead. 'Find out if he knows who the hell those people in the paintings are. And if the subjects are really dead or not.'

The car's heating was on, but the icy shock that had taken hold of Tara when she'd seen the pictures hadn't loosened its grip. The second of the paintings was at the forefront of her mind. 'Matthew Cope said his father died falling down stairs,' she said.

Blake's eyes met hers for just a second. 'God.'

For a moment there was silence and she guessed they were both wondering how old Matthew and Luke had been when that had happened – and if Luke had been in the vicinity. If he'd been a child and he'd witnessed the fall or just seen the body afterwards, Tara could imagine he might want to paint it out of his system. Occasionally, if she saw something horrific on the news, she'd carry on watching, even if the coverage got repetitive, just to try to come to terms with the information.

'Luke can't be tied to both the deaths, surely?' Blake said. 'The bloke at the bottom of the stairs is one thing, but the hanging? If there was the thinnest connection between him and an unsolved murder I think we'd be aware of it. Even if his name never made it as far as the official records it would have been mentioned at the station.'

They'd left Max and Megan still trawling through the contents of Luke's house, meticulously searching for clues to where the man might have gone. Tara knew Max would do a good job – his calm determination ensured it. Megan was thorough too, she had to admit, but Tara still wished she could be in two places at once. Finding the key to Luke Cope's location was a tempting prize.

They were nearing Jonny Trent's gallery now. Tara watched the uneven hedge of trees and shrubs skim past on one side. To her right, beyond Blake's hands on the steering wheel, she could see flat fields. It was only mid-morning but everything looked almost colourless under the dark clouds, through the sheets of torrential rain.

Blake had arranged for them to see Monique, Freya's assistant, in her break.

'Though from what she said on the phone she doesn't get a breather as a rule,' Blake said, his eyes on the road. 'She had to put me on hold for a moment when I asked for a time, and it was a good two minutes before I got her back again. I'm not sure Trent would make an ideal boss.'

'Granted. And I guess it must go further than general mean-spiritedness if Freya wanted to "escape" work troubles. Though I suppose she might have been running for multiple reasons.'

Blake nodded. He swung into a wide drive lined with overgrown yew trees – dark and forbidding-looking. It didn't help that they reminded Tara of almost every graveyard she'd ever visited.

'Whatever the truth is,' Blake said, making her snap back to the here and now, 'I don't trust our Jonny. The whole time I spoke to him yesterday I had the impression he was putting on an act. He's hiding something, that's for sure. When we get in there, I want you to tackle Monique whilst I talk to him again.'

Tara hadn't realised that was the plan. She liked the idea of having a free hand with Freya's assistant – and the woman would probably open up more that way too – but she couldn't help wondering if she was being sidelined. 'What line will you take with Trent?'

He smiled for a moment. 'No line. I'm just going to make small talk. And if he's got a customer with him, I'll hover in the background and observe. I imagine he'll spend the entire time trying to work out what I'm after. Hopefully it'll unsettle him enough to make a mistake.' He drew up in front of the imposing building at the end of the drive. 'But my main aim is simply to keep him occupied whilst you talk to Monique. I'm hoping she'll deliver something really useful. She and Freya must have talked a lot to coordinate their work. I hope to God they chatted about more than just sales and tax.' He glanced at Tara. 'I'm guessing Monique won't unbutton if she thinks Jonny Trent is listening at the keyhole – and if I didn't act as minder, I'm quite sure he would be.'

Five minutes later, Tara was installed in the gallery's administration office with the door firmly closed. There had been no customers on site when they'd arrived, and she'd had the chance to cast her eyes over the paintings in the front room of the building as she'd walked through. She didn't have to be told which of the works was by Luke Cope; she recognised his style. His large framed canvas was diagonally opposite the room's doorway and showed a bleak fenland scene with lowering clouds and black peat soil. The artist had looked down on endless, barren winter fields, the only distinguishing features being a water-filled drainage ditch and, in the distance, a church with a distinctive spire. It looked faintly familiar – probably from her childhood days. The family house her mother had inherited was out in the Fens.

She'd been introduced to Jonny Trent in the building's hallway and watched as he'd cast his eyes anxiously in her and Monique Courville's direction. He'd looked very reluctant as Blake herded him off into that large, front gallery room.

Monique was an elegant woman with sleek, chestnut-brown hair that reached below her shoulders. She wore knee-length chocolate-coloured boots and a navy suit with a crisp white shirt underneath, unbuttoned at the neck revealing a simple gold necklace.

'Thanks for talking to me, Monique,' Tara said. 'We're trying to speak to everyone who knew Freya, to get an idea of what life was like for her in the run-up to her death.'

The woman nodded. 'I saw the detective you arrived with here yesterday. He spoke to Jonny, but I had no idea who he was.'

Tara nodded. 'DI Blake wasn't able to say much at that stage. He had to wait until Freya's next of kin had been informed.'

Something crossed Monique's expression. 'Of course,' she said after a moment. 'I was upset that Jonny hadn't told me what had happened whilst I was at work, but that will have been why.'

Bloody hell – by the end of the day the man could have let on. It had been all over the news by then. Judging by the way Blake had described the gallery owner's reaction she found it hard to believe he hadn't been checking for updates. It was interesting that Monique was ready to make excuses for her boss's inconsiderate behaviour. Perhaps she didn't like confrontation. That was something to bear in mind when listening to her evidence. Tara needed to make sure the woman relaxed. *Easy questions first…*

'So what's the set-up here?' she asked, noting the two work stations in the room in which they sat. 'I gather Mr Trent asked you to do extra hours to cover for Freya when she didn't turn up as expected last week?'

Monique Courville nodded. 'I'm normally only here in the mornings. I've been working full-time since Freya… since we…' Her eyes were glistening and she let the sentence hang.

'It must have been awkward to have to drop everything to help Mr Trent out,' Tara said. 'It was a lot to expect.'

But Monique shook her head, then raised her hands to cover her eyes for a moment. 'To be truthful, I was very glad of the extra money, what with the price of rent here in Cambridge, and repayments on my car.' She looked up again. 'I feel terrible admitting that, now I know the real reason she didn't come in to work.'

So Monique needed her income then. It wasn't some part-time job to bring in a bit of extra pocket money. She'd be all the more reluctant to rock the boat.

'It was a totally natural reaction,' Tara said. 'You mustn't feel guilty. Did Mr Trent tell you why he thought Freya was absent?'

Monique nodded, and gave a story that backed up her boss's version of events – that Trent had called Freya's home number when she didn't show up, and had been given the story of emergency leave due to stress by Professor Cross.

'You didn't try to call her at all, during the week?' Tara asked.

Monique looked even more miserable as she shook her head. 'I was concerned, as you can imagine – but I only have Freya's work mobile number. It didn't seem appropriate to bother her if she'd taken sick leave.'

'I understand. I'd have thought the same.'

Monique gave her a grateful look.

'So how was the work divided up here?' Tara hoped by getting her to talk about general topics, she might find an anomaly that she could focus on. And then when their conversation was flowing, she'd ask more about Freya's relations with Luke Cope and Jonny Trent himself.

'Freya was the linchpin,' Monique said. 'She was here full-time, and she and I were in charge of the two main galleries at the front of the building which house our most valuable works. We sell the paintings on commission, and then restock with more from the artists that sell well.'

Once again, Tara thought of how Luke didn't fit into that category. But she'd get onto him later…

'You say the two main galleries? There are more then?'

Monique nodded. 'Well – one more. The back gallery. It's housed in an extension at the rear of the building, and it's Jonny's pet project.' She smiled. 'He leaves us in total charge of the main rooms, but he's still very hands-on – an enthusiast. He has lower value works out at the back – ones he's taken a chance on, based on gut instinct. He picks up the pieces at small sales, via dealers or occasionally from the artists direct, and buys them outright. Then he aims to sell them at a profit. He's always delighted when his instinct pays off and occasionally he does really well.'

Tara could see him getting a powerful rush from that; it was a form of informed gambling, after all. 'I can imagine.'

She nodded. 'He's always on an up if it happens. He sometimes invites us into his office for a glass of celebratory sherry afterwards.'

High rewards. 'And what about all the financial management, and legal stuff?'

'Oh, Freya and I deal with that. We cover our side of the business digitally of course. Everything's inputted on the desktops here.' She indicated the two computers in the room. 'But Jonny's approach is' – she lowered her voice – 'out of the ark, to be honest.'

Tara raised an eyebrow.

'He uses an old-fashioned ledger to record the details of his sales.' She gave an indulgent smile. 'Freya and I did try to convince him to use a computer, but he wasn't having any of it. And, in fact, I think his customers find it charming.' She sighed. 'He's always saying how everything was better in the old days. Given what happened to Freya, maybe he's right. You'd think it would be safe to walk around Newnham in the evenings. But nowadays, with drug dealers and the like…'

Tara didn't bother telling the woman that they suspected good old-fashioned lust or jealousy might be behind her colleague's murder. 'I gather the gallery stocks Luke Cope's work.'

Monique's face went a shade paler. 'Jonny said he's missing.'

'That's right,' Tara admitted. 'Did Mr Trent ever stock his paintings in the back gallery?'

The woman frowned. 'No.'

'It surprised you?' It surprised Tara, given that most of the lower-value stuff was sold as part of Jonny Trent's pet project. But maybe Luke Cope hadn't been prepared to sell his work outright for a sufficiently low price.

Monique shrugged. 'I remember Freya being taken aback. She'd brokered the first meeting between Luke and Jonny, knowing Luke was looking for an outlet. I think they'd all met at a drinks event at another gallery in town. The morning Luke turned up for his and Jonny's one-to-one, Freya was on edge. I remember she thought Jonny would probably turn Luke down altogether. But they must have got on. Their meeting went on for an hour or so, and in the event, Jonny decided Luke's paintings would fit with the main gallery collections.'

It was interesting that Freya had been worried about Luke's success – or otherwise – even back then. Had she already been fond of him? 'How long ago was this, do you remember?' she asked.

'Around eighteen months back, I think.'

'I see. And did you meet Luke, that first day he came in?'

Monique nodded. 'Just when he was on his way out. He was pleased of course, as you'd expect. And when he and Jonny shook hands before he left, Jonny looked just as delighted too.'

It sounded as though they'd built up quite a rapport in a short space of time. And although Freya had been in charge of the front galleries, officially, it was clearly Jonny Trent who decided whose work ended up there.

'I understand Freya and Luke were close too,' Tara said.

Monique's eyes met hers, her expression searching. 'I got that impression as well,' she said at last, 'but Freya didn't confide in me. We got on with each other, but it was a working relationship.'

Tara nodded. 'Monique, we know Freya was having trouble here at the gallery.' Well, Sophie Havers had thought so, anyway. *Good enough.* 'You won't be breaking any confidences if you tell me more about it.'

There was no denial from Freya's assistant, but she didn't reply.

'She'd been planning to have a serious talk with Mr Trent on Monday of last week, too,' Tara went on. 'So I assume the trouble was a disagreement between them.'

But now Monique Courville shook her head. 'She had been short with him just recently perhaps. But on the whole he kept himself to himself, and let us do the same. If there was a problem then I don't think it stemmed from Jonny.'

'Really?'

'No.' The woman's cheeks coloured and she looked down at the desk in front of her for a moment. 'I think it was something to do with Luke. The last time he was here – around three weeks ago maybe – I heard them quarrelling.'

'Where were they?'

'In the back gallery.'

'And was Jonny in there with them?'

She frowned. 'I don't think so – but he can't have been far away.'

Listening at keyholes?

'Monique, this might be significant.' Tara leant forward. 'For Freya's sake, did you overhear anything that was said?'

The woman frowned and closed her eyes for a moment. 'I didn't hear much. I was still sitting here in this room. I think I heard her say "how could you?" or something like that.'

'What was she like in general? Was it usual for her to lose her temper?'

Monique's eyes were shocked, as though the very idea was laughable. 'Not at all. She was a true professional.' There was a long pause but then suddenly her eyes opened wider and she said: 'No, wait, I remember what she said to Luke now. "How could you be so stupid?" That was it.'

Tara didn't manage to get much else out of Monique Courville – her relationship with Freya Cross had clearly been formal – but the insights into the gallery workings had been interesting. What had Luke Cope done that Freya regarded as so foolhardy?

After they'd spoken, she asked Monique to show her the back gallery. It was a pleasing room – cosy, with dark red walls. There were several artworks hanging up, lit by the warm glow from individual picture lights, but the majority were unframed prints and canvases stacked upright in racks that meant buyers could flick them back and forth to gauge what was on offer. Not being able to see what the room contained at a glance led to a feeling of anticipation. You didn't know if you might find a gem, somewhere amongst the collection. She was just getting the measure of the stock, some of which she quite fancied herself, including a pen and ink drawing of Great St Mary's, the university church in town, when Blake appeared at her elbow.

'We need to go.' There was a meaningful look in his eye.

After they'd said goodbye to Monique (who looked tearful) and Jonny (who looked worried), they both got into the car and Blake turned the key in the ignition.

'Something new on our agenda?' Tara asked.

'Back to Professor Cross.' He manoeuvred the car to face down the drive. 'I directed a couple of constables to carry on going door to door, to try to mop up his neighbours who were out when you and Max started the job yesterday.' He signalled right at the end of the driveway and waited for a gap in the stream of traffic which splashed through the deep puddles at the side of the road. 'Turns out the professor's next-door neighbour heard him and Freya having a noisy row, the night she left the house for the last time. They bumped into the professor in the street a couple of days later and asked after her. Apparently they were a bit worried. And when the professor said she'd gone off to see a friend, they guessed she'd maybe walked out.'

He pulled onto the far carriageway and put his foot down.

'They're now wishing they'd called us, instead of talking to him…'

CHAPTER TWENTY-ONE

If Professor Cross had looked wary last time they'd left him, it was nothing to how he appeared now, Blake thought. The trauma of discussing the discovery of his wife's body – whether or not he'd been responsible – would have abated a little. Maybe now his own place in their investigation was sinking in.

Blake planned to make the most of it – for the greater good. Before Tara had even sat down, and as soon as the professor sank into the same chair he'd occupied on their previous visit, Blake got stuck in.

'We have a witness who says you and your wife argued immediately before Mrs Cross left the house on the twenty-third of February. A row so loud it could be heard from the street.'

The colour came to the professor's cheeks almost instantly. Not that Blake had doubted the neighbour's word.

'Why didn't you tell us about this when we spoke yesterday? It's relevant information.' But of course, it didn't take a genius to work that one out; whether he was guilty or not, it didn't look great. Whilst Zach Cross was still thinking about how to frame his answer, Blake went in again. 'Why were you yelling at your wife?' He wanted Cross so flustered that he'd fail to lie convincingly.

The professor sat forward in his chair, his hands clasped together, knuckles white. Then suddenly he fell back against the cushions and put his palms over his face.

'We already have several witnesses who say your marriage was in trouble.' The guy was bereaved, but he might be a killer too. Blake couldn't let him off the hook. 'As well as rumours that Freya was having an affair. Was that why you were so furious?'

At last the professor's hands fell to his lap and he nodded. 'I'd got no proof,' he said. His eyes were open wide now, his jaw slack. 'I might have been wrong.'

Was this guilt at having killed his wife over what had only been a suspicion? Or horror at Freya having walked out to her death, on the back of upset he'd caused?

'What triggered the argument that particular night?'

'She wanted to go for a walk. It was a filthy evening – it seemed like a pretty odd time to take the air. When I said I'd go with her, she told me she wanted to be on her own "to think".' He took a tissue from his trouser pocket and blew his nose before carrying on. 'But I suspected her of going to meet someone, and I told her so.'

'And you believed that to be Luke Cope? You faced her with it?'

The professor paused for a moment, tense again in his chair, but at last he nodded.

'What made you think they were having an affair?'

'You only had to hear Freya talk about him to know he'd cast a spell on her!' His voice was angry now, and several times the volume it had been. Blake was starting to see how the neighbours had overheard him, the night of the argument. The man took a deep breath and Blake watched his powerful chest rise and fall. 'You have to understand, Inspector, that Freya lived for her work. Art was her life. And here was a man she regarded as a troubled, undiscovered genius. Each time she spoke about him it was clear she was captivated. And when I saw them together the connection they felt was obvious.'

'You were suspicious about their feelings for one another when you attended Luke Cope's house-warming party?'

He nodded. 'There were at least fifty people in that makeshift studio of his, but when I watched them it was as though they were the only two in the room, sidestepping round everyone else, performing their own private dance.'

For a second Blake thought of Tara. It sounded as though the pull between Luke and Freya had been intense. Relationships like that could lead to trouble. It made him think of Romeo and Juliet. *These violent delights have violent ends...* What had happened to make Luke so angry that he'd painted her dead? And maybe made the image a reality? Zach Cross had said Freya thought the artist was troubled. And Freya had asked Luke how he could have been so stupid, when *they* had argued. Tara had filled him in on their way over in the car.

'What was your wife's reaction, when you confronted her?'

'She was angry, but she didn't answer my accusation directly. She said she—' He stopped abruptly and then restarted. 'She said she felt constrained.'

Blake wondered exactly how she'd put it. He guessed the professor's pride wouldn't let him echo her precise words. *Trapped? Like a pet on a leash?* He'd have been better off being explicit, rather than letting Blake's imagination run wild. 'And then?'

'She told me not to come near her. She was crying by that stage. And she went out as she'd planned.'

'Why did you lie to us about her taking overnight things?'

'I stayed up until half past midnight, waiting for Freya to come back. I assumed at first that she was taking her time to teach me a lesson. But gradually it dawned on me that if she *had* gone to meet Luke, she'd probably decided to go off with him. If I didn't trust her anyway, where was the benefit of meekly coming home and playing the loyal wife? So I went to bed, but I couldn't sleep. The very next morning people started to ask where she was.'

'Jonny Trent at the gallery?'

Cross nodded. 'Even though I'd concluded that Freya had walked out on me, I hoped she'd realise how foolish she was being and come back, once she'd had the chance to think. I certainly expected her to go into work. Luke Cope lives here in Cambridge too – there would be no barrier to her carrying on other aspects of her life as normal. Trent's call, telling me she was absent, came as a shock but I'd already decided what to tell anyone who asked. I couldn't face the gossip if I admitted we'd had a row, so I just kept repeating the same excuse to everyone: that she was taking some time out.'

'Repeating a lie to your friends and colleagues is one thing,' Blake said. 'Giving it as part of a statement in a murder enquiry is on an entirely different level.' He knew his anger was showing and he let it.

'I didn't kill my wife, Inspector,' Zach Cross said. 'It was for that reason that I wasn't worried about glossing over why she walked out that night. I guessed someone would mention Luke Cope's name sooner rather than later. You didn't need me to put you onto him by washing our dirty linen in public.'

But Blake was still incredulous. 'I'd have thought your fury at the man you suspected of killing your wife would have overridden all that.'

'Nothing I could do would bring her back. And I still have to live in this road, and work in a claustrophobic environment at my university department. If I once admitted to the row, people would always blame me for Freya having walked out into danger – at best. At worst they'd suspect me of killing her myself. That's not a smear I want to live with, given my position.'

But Blake still wondered. The professor would have every reason to lie if he was guilty of his wife's murder, too.

'So as far as you're aware she didn't take overnight kit with her,' Blake went on. 'Are you sure there's nothing missing? You'd notice if pyjamas had gone, or make-up? Anything like that?'

'I don't keep an inventory of Freya's things.' The professor spat the words out, but then he sighed. 'I didn't see her packing anything of that sort, and I'm fairly certain nothing's missing.'

'Yet we have a witness who said she was carrying a holdall, as well as her handbag, when she left home.'

'Dear God,' the professor said, 'what a street I live in; full of spies. Yes, she was carrying a holdall.'

'Can you remember, did she fetch it after your row?'

The question clearly wasn't what he'd expected and he frowned for some moments. 'No,' he said at last. 'She must have had it downstairs already. She grabbed it just before she left, along with her handbag, and walked straight out.'

Five minutes later, Blake and Tara were in the car again, on their way back to join Max and Megan. Blake had suggested they pick up some sandwiches to keep them all going. He wasn't looking forward to returning to the artist's empty house; he found the gloomy atmosphere oppressive. The weather wasn't helping, either. It was still raining and the sides of the streets were awash with water.

'So, we know Freya Cross had a text from Luke, asking her to go and meet him the night she left home,' Tara said. 'The professor was right; she wasn't just after time to herself. And whatever she was up to involved carrying something to their meet-up – but likely not overnight gear.'

Blake nodded as he upped the speed of the windscreen wipers. 'Right. And someone – we assume her killer – removed her holdall. It might have contained something valuable, or something the killer didn't want found.' He swore. 'There's something I'm not getting here. I can't work out how it all ties together.'

'Zach Cross could have followed Freya if he was jealous and suspected her of seeing Luke. It would have been perfectly natural.'

'Agreed.'

'He could have found them together, stunned Freya with the stone Agneta thinks was used and then killed Luke, before finishing the job with his wife. He'd be big enough to move Luke's body without all that much trouble.'

Blake nodded. 'He could have taken his car round to the Lammas Land side of the nature reserve and picked up Luke's body from there, then gone and dumped it somewhere, hoping we'd assume that Luke had killed Freya, then done a runner.' He sighed. 'What are the chances of Fleming letting us apply to get his car checked over, based on our clever speculation?'

Tara give him a sidelong glance. 'Slim.'

She was slightly more optimistic than he was, clearly. For a moment they drove on in silence, but then Blake heard Tara curse under her breath.

'What?'

'Breaking news on *Not Now*'s website. *Cambridge artist and rumoured lover of murder victim, Freya Cross, sought by police.*'

Blake swore harder than she had. With Patrick Wilkins on suspension he'd thought they'd have put a stop to this sort of leak. Clearly not. If he ever found out who'd passed the information on this time he'd be tempted to break the law himself, in the course of meting out justice.

He'd been planning to run a statement and appeal for information on the man's whereabouts once he'd spoken to Fleming, but he'd wanted to manage the news carefully, not have it come out in this haphazard way. Publicising the unsubstantiated rumour of his relationship with Freya Cross could cause them problems on several counts.

'Ask Max to ring them,' he said. 'I'd like him to press them on their source.'

There was a pause, during which he guessed Tara was considering arguing that she should be the one to tackle her old employer, but then thinking better of it. 'Okay. I'll call him.'

As she exchanged news with Max, Blake mused on who could have contacted *Not Now*. It might not be one of their own, of course. If Luke Cope was innocent perhaps the leak had come anonymously from the guilty party, to make sure everyone's attention was focused elsewhere.

He was pulled out of his thoughts by Tara, who'd ended the call.

'Max is going to call Shona f-word Kennedy and ask her,' she said. 'He had another update too. There was a painting of a windmill he and I both spotted when we were back at Luke Cope's place. It looked like a fenland scene.'

'Yes?'

'He and Megan have found three more drawings of what appears to be the same mill.'

He glanced at her for a second.

'Max wondered if it's an area Luke Cope visits regularly. They've asked for advice, but I gather they're having trouble pinpointing the location. The backdrops in the compositions don't give much away. They're going to keep searching.'

'Good,' Blake said. He pulled the car up outside a sandwich bar on Hills Road. 'Any special requests?'

'Something big.'

He found himself grinning. 'Noted.'

He'd just undone his safety belt and opened the car door when Tara let out an exclamation.

'What?'

'The painting of Luke Cope's at the gallery. Did you see it?'

He nodded. 'The fenland scene that looked a bit post-apocalyptic?'

'That's the one. I've just remembered: the angle meant you could see into some kind of channel of water below. He was looking down on the scene.'

He frowned for a moment but then the penny dropped. Where had the man been when he'd painted it? 'There aren't many high vantage points in the Fens…'

'Very few,' Tara agreed. 'And those that there are, are man-made. I wonder if Luke Cope could have been sitting high up in a windmill when he painted that scene.'

CHAPTER TWENTY-TWO

'What can you remember about the painting in the gallery?' Blake asked.

Tara was trying to conjure up the image. 'I wish I could look at it again.'

'I don't want Jonny Trent to get wind of our suspicions. I don't trust him.'

'Nor me. He was watching and waiting this morning, I reckon. Hang on.' She called up the website for Trent's gallery. 'His approach to business might be old-fashioned, but it sounds as though Freya was on the ball – and Monique too. With any luck…' She found a selection of images of the current artworks on sale. 'Yes. Here's Luke's painting.' She noticed the church again – a small black silhouette against the skyline, with that very tall tower…

Blake was craning over to see too, his head an inch from hers. 'It's familiar to you?' he said, turning to meet her eye.

'Yes. I'm just trying to think where from.' She cast her mind back to childhood days, out in the countryside. The bus to primary school in a nearby village, cycle rides to isolated spots in summer where she could do her own thing without anyone hassling her, and then later—

'Wait. When I got as far as secondary school I used to go into Cambridge. I spent half my time living with Bea anyway, so it made sense. But when I was travelling in from my mother's house there was a bus route…' She called up Google Maps on her phone, pinpointing her mother's place and scanning the villages she used to have to travel past. She relived the route in her mind's eye. Suddenly she had it. 'The spire of St Peter and St Paul's, on the outskirts of Whitwell.'

'So where would Luke Cope have painted that picture from?' Blake's voice was urgent.

She frowned for a moment. 'I'm not sure. I would have viewed it end on from the north, but it was out on the edge of the modern-day settlement, so I reckon you'd be able to see it from other directions too. If I could just work out what that waterway is… but there are so many rivers and dykes in the Fens.'

Blake was already keying the location of the church into the satnav. 'Let's get straight over there,' he said. 'We can look around and see if we can see a mill. I don't want to risk going back to the house to get Max and Megan. Us going in and out might be how *Not Now* picked up on our interest in Luke Cope in the first place. If they're keeping an eye on the place I wouldn't put it past Shona Kennedy to follow us and foul up our operation.' He gave her a sidelong glance. 'If we find the place we can call Max and Megan to follow us. Sorry about the sandwiches – but there are some emergency rations in the glove compartment. Why don't you eat whilst I drive? If Luke Cope's hiding out there, we'll need to be on our toes.'

It was already well after what most people would call lunchtime and Tara felt cold and hollow. She was slightly surprised to find four fruit and nut chocolate bars when she looked for the food he'd suggested. He didn't have the physique of a man who had a snacking habit. Maybe they were for Babette – after all, she was eating for two…

'Thanks.' She took one. 'Probably makes sense to keep well-fuelled.' But as Blake pulled the car into a hasty U-turn she paused her unwrapping for a moment as a shiver of anticipation tickled her stomach.

*

By the time they reached the Fens the sky had darkened still further. Tara scanned the road signs for Whitwell with her breath held. When at last they reached the turning, adrenaline was pumping round her system. *Crazy.* They didn't even know if Luke Cope was still in the locality, let alone if he was guilty. But then she thought of the paintings they'd seen in his studio. Whatever his story, he'd want careful handling.

Blake was totally focused on the road, and covering the distance at high speed. Neither of them spoke.

At last Blake made the turn towards the village, driving through quiet, wet byways, past thatched cottages, until he reached Church Lane. As they ground to a halt in the gravel car park, the spire of St Peter and St Paul's towered above them, slate grey against an even darker sky.

She was out of the car before her DI, striding along the pathway which sloped upwards slightly as it reached the church doors and would give the best vantage point. She was looking in the direction she'd used to travel to school now. No mill. She shook her head at Blake, then walked round the perimeter of the church, scanning the skyline.

She needn't have worried about missing it. As she rounded the corner to face south it rose up from the horizon. It was still small at this distance, but Tara couldn't quell the feeling of unease the building gave her. It stood solid against the angry sky, the chunks out of its sails like missing teeth.

Blake was at her side as she worked with her phone, trying to see where the mill was marked on the map. She couldn't find it.

'It's all right,' he said. 'It's around a mile from here. I'll take a bearing.'

She gave him a quick look. 'A bearing? Were you a boy scout or something?'

Blake gave a half-smile. 'No, but I have my skills. You tackle the enemy by breaking their fingers, whereas I, well, I reference stuff. With my brain and your brawn, we make a crack team.'

'Ha ha.' It was unfair of him to bring up the broken finger incident. If she hadn't thought the journalist she'd injured had been intent on doing her harm she'd never have attacked him in such an efficient way.

He glanced at her for a moment from under his untidy fringe, which was dripping with rainwater. 'I'm only partly joking. It's handy that you have such excellent skills at your disposal should the need arise.'

Tara saw from his expression that he meant it. She hoped she could perform as well as required if she was called upon. She'd certainly got enough adrenaline going round her system to power her. That and the chocolate…

She tried not to react to his dark eyes as they met hers. It was a relief when he finished the work he'd started with a compass app on his phone and strode back towards the car. Tara put her map away.

'Want me to drive whilst you eat now?' she asked, walking after him but keeping her distance. She'd appreciate it if he was fully fuelled too.

'Thanks. I'll take you up on that. I'll call Max and Megan as well. Get them to follow us over.'

But Tara couldn't see either her or Blake waiting for their arrival before investigating further. She felt as though the mill, still within sight now, was drawing her to it. She wanted to know the truth, whatever it cost; to find the person who'd killed Freya.

Blake's instinct for distance and direction were good. Within minutes he'd sent her to the correct road. The mill was up ahead; imposing now that it was near.

'What do you say to a surreptitious scout around before the others get here?'

She nodded and found a bank where she could pull up safely without landing the car in a ditch. They'd be able to approach from a distance on foot, but it wouldn't stop them being seen if

Luke Cope happened to be watching. The mill's windows faced in multiple directions and there was no cover. Quietly, she let herself out of the vehicle and locked up once Blake had done the same. Not that anyone would be likely to steal it out here; the place was deserted. Whitwell must be the nearest village. To their left as they walked was a drain, high with water, the rain making patterns on its surface. Her hair quickly became sodden and she pushed it away from her face. Blake's shoulders were hunched against the weather under his dark wool coat.

She wondered what awaited them. This could be a complete wild goose chase, but her gut told her not. Her insides felt taut as a drum.

At last they crossed over the road to the mill, the wind whipping at their faces; the ground was so flat, there was nothing to slow its progress. There was a large area surrounding the building, covered with shingle. And slewed across it – you couldn't really call it parked – was a dark-red Volvo. Luke Cope's car. Tara felt her pulse quicken. She double-checked the number plate, but it was just a formality – a way of trying to steady herself by following procedure.

She raised her eyebrows at Blake. The car looked as though it had been abandoned – left without a second thought. The action of a man who'd just killed a woman and was intending to go to ground? Or someone who had a second vehicle waiting and only cared for his getaway car? Maybe the Volvo had served its purpose.

The day was as dark as they came. If you were doing anything indoors you'd want a light on. But Tara had had her eyes trained on the building the whole way up the lane and she hadn't seen one. 'Reckon he came here to get sorted out, and then did a runner?' she whispered.

Blake frowned. 'It's certainly possible, but we sure as hell can't rely on it.'

She hadn't been planning to. Together they edged round the forecourt, peering up at the mill's blank windows. Even the lowest ones were well above their eye level; there was no way of telling who might be inside.

At last, Blake raised his fist and thumped at the knockerless door. After that he stood back and shouted up at the windows.

'Luke Cope? Police! We want to talk to you.'

Tara kept her eyes on the upper storeys. There was no sign of movement. But even if the artist were there, she wasn't sure he'd hear them. The mill wasn't in a great state of repair. She tried to imagine being inside, with the wind making the ancient sails creak and rattling at the windows.

Blake thumped at the door again, but Tara's eye had been caught by a notice, close to the entrance to the forecourt. She hadn't seen it before, she'd been so preoccupied with the building itself.

'What is it?' Blake asked.

She hadn't got to the point where she could answer that yet… 'Details of the agency that lets the place out,' she shouted a moment later, yelling to make herself heard above the storm.

Blake was at her side now, keying the number into his phone. A moment later she strained to hear his half of the conversation. He'd cupped his hand round his mouth and the microphone.

'Detective Inspector Blake, Cambridgeshire Constabulary. I'm trying to reach a Luke Cope in connection with an enquiry. Is it right that he rents,' he paused for a moment, scanning the notice board again, 'the Great Whitwell Mill from you?'

A pause.

'I see. When did he move in?'

Another moment's silence.

'We're right outside now, but there's no reply. I'm concerned for his welfare. Is there a spare key? I see. Yes, yes, carry on.' He rolled his eyes at Tara.

She could see why. They could be anyone, but the person on the end of the phone was clearly quite happy to let them walk right in. Even though they were on the level, they'd normally need a warrant to enter the place, too. It was only their intention to arrest Luke for Freya's murder that gave them a free hand.

Blake strode back towards the mill and beyond it.

Tara was hard on his heels.

'Third from the left?' He approached a post – one of the ones that marked the edge of the driveway, its white paint peeling. 'At the bottom and behind? Okay.' He crouched down and reached to the rear of the stake, into the thick, evergreen hedge that brushed against it. A moment later he had a small red and green plastic tub in his hand. He frowned as he shook it. 'It's empty.'

There was another pause. 'Yes please, that would be helpful.' He put the tub back where he'd found it, jammed his phone between his shoulder and ear and took out a pen and notebook from his pocket, scribbling down some details.

He hung up and looked at Tara. 'The guy I spoke to said there was a spare key in the box when they let the place to Cope three months back. Apparently people are always locking themselves out and it's inconvenient because the mill is so remote, hence the back-up provision. Maybe Luke Cope forgot to put the key back or…'

'Or maybe he wanted to make damn sure no one else could get inside without breaking down the door?'

'That is one alternative. But if so, he's been foiled by a woman called Mrs Bolt, who lives in the next village. She's got emergency keys for this place and a couple of other "character properties" let out by the same agency.'

Tara glanced up at the mill. It had character all right; much like her own home out on Stourbridge Common. What *kind* of character was another matter. She could see how the situation would have inspired Luke Cope's wild compositions though.

'Shall we pay Mrs Bolt a visit?' she said, walking back towards the road.

'You go. Straight ahead for two miles and she's in the white thatched cottage on your right. First place you'll come to, apparently.' He glanced up at the mill. 'The letting agency are going to ring to let her know she should expect a visit. I'll stay here. Just in case.'

Their eyes met. She didn't actually know what Blake's self-defence was like. 'Okay.'

As she drove up the road like the wind, she tried to tell herself it was fear of missing out, not fear for Blake, that was causing her to ignore the speed limit.

CHAPTER TWENTY-THREE

Blake kept his eyes on the mill's windows, blinking the rain away. Everything was quiet. He could hear from the wheels of their car that Tara was going to make short work of her mission, but the minutes still seemed to drag. He'd walked all round the building now. There was no back way out. If Luke Cope *had* seen them turn up, he couldn't have done a runner without crossing their line of sight. What preparations might he be making for their entrance, if he was inside?

When Tara returned she left the car parked on the verge again. It made sense. They'd want to preserve any evidence there might be on site. There were indents in the shingle on the forecourt that might indicate there had been another car present at one point. *A getaway vehicle for Luke Cope?*

He watched as Tara walked closer, holding the keys up in front of her.

'Fast work.'

'I thought time might be of the essence.' Her green eyes showed a mixture of anxiety and excitement. She turned towards the door to the mill, put the keys in and released the lock.

Blake pulled on gloves from a bag in his pocket and Tara did the same.

They were standing inside the mill's ground floor. The central upright shaft, a solid iron pole that disappeared through the raised floor above them, was still in place. They could see signs of Luke Cope's presence; there were canvases stacked against the rough plaster of the curved walls. Other than that, the place was bare. It was odd to think back to when this would have been the miller's main control room, allowing them to adjust the whole operation, to dictate the fineness of the flour and the amount of grain that was fed into the millstones. Now the space was still and eerie in the gloomy light that filtered through from a small window, high up in the room.

The route to the next level was via some steep wooden steps – not quite a ladder but almost. Whoever was letting the place hadn't done much to make the living space more practical. He imagined the agent would present it as 'old world charm'.

He and Tara stood still, listening. There was nothing to hear except the creaks a building makes when its innards are connected to sails being buffeted by the wind. It was intensely cold.

'Heating can't be on,' Tara whispered.

He was surprised any kind of system had been installed, given the state of the place, but there was an ancient radiator in the room.

'If you were going to make a run for it from a rented place, would you bother to switch it off?'

Blake shook his head. 'Perhaps it was never on in the first place. Maybe he only stopped here to pick up a hire car he'd had delivered.' He made for the ladder-cum-steps, glancing at her over his shoulder. 'Ready?'

Of course she is. He'd only just beaten her to the bottom step.

Cautiously, he raised his head above the level of the next floor. Through the murky half-light he could see that one of the millstones was still present. Another sign that the conversion for residential use had been minimal. The room was also home to a day bed, covered by a couple of blankets, one emerald green and one dark purple. They didn't look anywhere near enough to keep out the cold in this place, even if the heating had been on. He climbed the rest of the steps and straightened up in the deserted room. As well as the day bed and the millstone, there was an array of artist-quality sketchpads and several pencils strewn across the floor.

Once again, the route to the next storey was via a set of wooden steps. Tara *was* there before him this time, climbing up steadily, cautious but controlled.

But then suddenly she missed her footing. He was so close behind her that for a second it was his physical presence that prevented her from falling.

That sound. What the hell had caused it?

And then, in that moment, something large and black flew straight at them. Tara and he both flinched, leaning away from the ladder to avoid being struck. Tara was flung back against him as the crow flapped down into the room below.

Tara swore. If Luke Cope was in the mill he'd know they'd managed to get inside. But that had already been the case, he guessed. It was impossible to move without making the floorboards or the steps creak.

Suddenly he realised he was still holding Tara rather more tightly than was necessary. For a second she leant against him and he could feel her heart thump. It was nothing to what his was doing. The crow had started the effect, but…

He felt her pull away from him sharply and move back close to the ladder.

For a split second she turned her head to look at him. 'I forget sometimes,' she said, 'just for a moment.' Her voice was tight. 'It's like it was back when we were both working on the Seabrook case, when you were single. But you've got more reason to remember than me – not so long until the birth of your second child now.'

Her words made him catch his breath. He had imagined that he had always hidden how he felt around her, so it was a shock to hear her refer to it so directly. *And Tara had clearly felt something too…* Her words stung: like someone rubbing vinegar into a cut.

He thought of that old excuse, *my wife doesn't understand me*. But in reality it was he who didn't understand Babette. He sighed. Whatever the case, Tara was right. If he was going to stick by a woman he knew was lying to him, he needed to bury his feelings towards Tara and bury them deep. He fought the urge to explain; doing that might bring them closer again, but it would also make things more complicated.

'How the hell did the bird get in, anyway?' Tara said, snapping her head back round towards the floor above. The edge was still there in her voice.

And now that she'd refocused his mind, Blake began to wonder about the way the air shifted in the old mill. Yes, you'd expect a building like this to creak in the wind, and for there to be draughts aplenty, but the gusts blowing down from above were more than he would have expected.

Tara glanced back at him. 'There must be a window open up there.'

He nodded. 'Either that or a big hole in the roof.'

They stepped up onto the third storey, walking past a rudimentary kitchen which would suffice so long as your expectations didn't go beyond beans on toast. There was some kind of cupboard Blake reckoned might have been adapted from an old grain bin. Beneath his feet he could see an ancient trapdoor through which the cereals would once have been hauled to the top of the mill. They were almost at the highest point in the building now. There could only be one more floor, surely, before they reached the roof?

Tara was at the stairs again. That didn't surprise him. She'd be smarting at being startled by the crow. He watched her from behind, her red hair still damp, as she raised her head above the level of the final floor.

And then she stopped.

He heard her gasp for breath, and it was a full two seconds before she turned to look at him over her shoulder.

'He's here,' she said. He saw her swallow – knew that look. 'He's dead.'

Tara called Max and Megan to update them. They were very close by, now. And then she rang Agneta Larsson and the station to request the presence of the pathologist and CSIs.

As she spoke, her eyes ran over the situation in front of her. She'd managed to control the feeling of nausea that had risen in her throat when she'd first looked into the room, but it was an ongoing effort. Luke Cope was slumped in an armchair, a syringe still sticking out of his arm, a tourniquet a little way above it. One of the man's eyeballs was a mess. Her mind turned to the crow… She didn't envy Agneta for her job at the best of times, but working on Luke Cope's body was going to be stomach churning.

A window facing away from the mill's forecourt had been left wide open. They hadn't been able to see it from below, standing as close to the mill as they were. For a second, she wondered if it was the cause of the low temperature, rather than a lack of heating, but she'd touched the old-fashioned radiator with the back of her gloved hand and it was stone cold. It seemed it really had been switched off.

As well as the chair occupied by Luke Cope's body and a second armchair, this upper room was home to an easel, a work in oils sitting on it, half complete. There were a few other paintings standing against the walls, a sink in a curved stand, and a set of paints still open on a table next to the easel. The artworks were landscapes: views from the mill in all directions.

Through one of the windows she could see the scene that hung in Jonny Trent's gallery.

Matthew Cope's worries for his brother's safety had been right. She was going to have to break the news to him.

The tableau rounded off the story neatly. Luke had killed Freya Cross, then driven straight here, abandoned his car on the drive and come up to the mill's old dust floor to kill himself. But there were too many oddities for her to take the scene at face value. If Luke had travelled here solely to commit suicide, then okay, he wouldn't have bothered to fire up the heating, but why open the window too? It was bitterly cold and wet even now, but on the night Freya had been killed the Fens would have been thick with snow. If he'd wanted to do something precise, like injecting a drug, why make it so that his hands would have gone numb within half a minute?

She wanted to chew it all over immediately, but they'd have to nail down the facts first. If Luke had been dead a week they'd already lost the advantage of getting the evidence fresh, but they'd have to work with what they'd got. Surely the mill, or Luke's Volvo, would tell the CSIs something?

And besides, it made sense to leave any intense discussions until they were in a larger group. Heat rushed over her at the thought of how frank she'd been about her feelings when she'd fallen against Blake on the steps. It was the first time she'd put anything into words.

At last, she and her DI withdrew from the scene to avoid disturbing things further. Neither of them spoke. At the door of the mill, they came face to face with Max and Megan. Tara's mind was still full of what she'd just seen, her stomach turning at the mental snapshot of Luke Cope's pecked eye, which she'd now hold in her memory forever.

And yet Megan's look, which took in both her and Blake, distracted her. What was on her mind?

'You went ahead without us then,' she said, unnecessarily.

Tara saw Max give the woman a sharp glance as Blake replied. 'We did, though as it turned out, there was no urgency after all.' Tara saw his shoulders twitch for a second. He was probably reliving the scene on the dust floor too. 'Luke Cope isn't going anywhere.'

CHAPTER TWENTY-FOUR

Tara drove back to Cambridge along grey lanes, past the saturated peat-black fields, through a landscape that was even more water-logged than usual. She skirted round the edge of the city to reach the firm where Matthew Cope worked. According to the card he'd given her he was responsible for 'New Business'. So, an expert in sales and promotion, she guessed, able to influence the thinking of prospective customers. It fitted with the market-savvy way he'd talked about his brother's paintings.

She swung her car into a wide driveway that led up to a large old manor house that had been converted into offices. The company specialised in medical devices and from what she understood, their software, sales, marketing, design and admin teams were all based here. The pale stone façade of the building was impressive. Elegant pillars rose up to a portico jutting out above the wide main entrance.

Her stomach clenched as she exited the car and locked up. Better get it over with. She needed to ask Matthew Cope more questions, too. Time mattered, after so much enforced delay.

She pressed the intercom and was admitted to a spacious recep-tion area, modern-looking with a sweeping glass-fronted desk. She wouldn't have fancied sitting there. There was no privacy at all. The only part of the receptionist that wasn't visible was the bit hidden behind her computer. Tara showed her ID. 'I'd like to speak to Matthew Cope please. Is it possible you could find us somewhere private?'

The receptionist nodded, her eyes were full of questions and speculation. *Understandable, but unbecoming all the same…*

As the woman dialled a number on her desk phone, Tara realised there was someone standing next to her.

'Excuse me.' It was a middle-aged man with tanned skin and a perfectly cut charcoal-grey suit. He'd had some winter sun by the look of it. *All right for some.* 'Did I hear you ask for Matthew, Detective…?'

He must have seen her warrant card. 'Detective Constable Thorpe,' Tara said, taking the hand the man proffered.

'I'm Edward Armstrong, CEO of this place.' He gestured round the reception area. 'This is about Luke, I suppose.' He must have seen her face and held up a hand before she spoke. 'I understand. You can't comment – of course you can't. But the Copes are old family friends. My father was at boarding school with their father. Luke and Matthew are products of their father's second marriage, so they're somewhat younger than I am.'

Tara pieced it all together in her mind. And now Matthew was working for Edward. Was this the old-boy network coming into play, then? 'How long has Matthew been with you?'

'Oh, since a few years after he graduated from university. He spent a little while working out what he wanted to do, and I offered him a place here.'

'I see. And he's in charge of new business, I gather.' Tara was determined to keep the conversation on neutral territory.

Edward Armstrong's features moved into an easy smile, but there was something emotional in his eyes. 'That's his role. One of the new business team.' He put his shoulders back. 'He's an excellent salesman. If I needed to offload oranges onto the people of Valencia, it's him I'd send. He ought to run his own business really. And then Luke is a first-rate artist too.' There was something paternal about the way he referred to the two men, in spite of them being the same generation. Perhaps it was the age gap.

Armstrong sighed. 'Luke never has been an easy person, Detective, for all his talent. Just recently I noticed Matthew was trying to build bridges with his brother, but Luke didn't want anyone's help, least of all Matthew's. That said, they'd become better friends of late and that was down to Matthew's efforts. Matthew confided in me, to a degree. I'm devastated to think that Luke has somehow gone off on the wrong path.'

'Detective Constable.' It was the receptionist who'd interrupted them. 'I've asked Matthew Cope to meet you in the Peterson Room. If you'd like to come with me…'

'I will show Constable Thorpe the way, Fiona,' Edward Armstrong said, and ushered Tara through some glass double doors.

Matthew Cope was already sitting at a highly polished table when Mr Armstrong opened the meeting room door for her. He looked up, his eyes hollow, cheeks pale. She could see the tension in his expression. There was a very slight delay before the CEO left them alone. Tara wasn't sure if he was desperate to know what had happened, or just anxious for his employee.

At last he retreated, and they had some privacy.

'Matthew,' she said, walking over quickly to take a seat alongside him. 'I'm so sorry.' He knew the moment she said that, of course – she could see from his face – but she was obliged to spell it out. 'DI Blake and I found your brother's body earlier this afternoon. We're not sure how he died yet – we'll need to wait for the pathologist's report – but there are signs it might have been an overdose.'

Matthew Cope's voice was tight and controlled. 'I felt in my gut that he'd done something terrible.' His eyes met Tara's. 'We knew each other so well, you see. Not because we were especially close in adulthood, but because we spent our entire childhood together. We could often predict each other's behaviour.'

She nodded.

'Where did you find him?' Matthew asked, his tone still wooden. It was as though shock had stiffened his features. 'I can't believe no one had stumbled across his body before.'

'He wasn't out in the open,' Tara said. Though immediately she thought of the open window and the crow that had flown in from the Fens.

'What are you trying to tell me?' Matthew's eyes were on hers.

'It seems he'd rented a property to the north of Cambridge, out in the Fens.'

The man's brother shook his head. 'Why would he do that, in secret? Why wouldn't he have told me?'

'Maybe he just wanted a bolthole where he could go for complete solitude,' she said. That was one bit of Luke Cope's behaviour that she *could* understand.

Matthew was facing the table again. 'Maybe.'

'You never got any hint that he had somewhere regular to stay overnight? Perhaps he had an extra set of keys on him that you couldn't identify?'

'I never noticed any – and if I had, I suppose I'd have assumed they were simply a spare lot, and not paid any attention.'

'What will happen to Luke's house now, Matthew? We'll need to talk to his solicitors anyway, given we've got an ongoing presence there, but it would be useful to know.'

Matthew blinked. 'Yes, yes. It's a good point. If Luke died before he came into full possession of the house it was to go to Vicky – Vicky Cope that is, my father's daughter by his first marriage. She's around seven years older than us.'

Tara remembered he'd mentioned her, that day when she'd visited him at his home and he'd explained his family background.

Matthew gave her a look. 'My father and his first wife weren't together for that long. He moved on quite quickly from Vicky's mother to mine. Vicky lived in the house off Trumpington Road when she was a small child. She might have missed it, I suppose, after her mother took her off to Suffolk – it's odd to think of her moving back in after all these years.'

'Had your father provided for her in any other way?'

Matthew nodded. 'Oh yes. She inherited his business. Vicky will be able to sell the house if she likes and plough the proceeds back into the family firm. I think they imagined she'd make sensible use of any inheritance – and she had that old connection with the house. But of course, my parents could never have anticipated the situation we're currently in.'

'No, no – of course not. Do you know Vicky well?'

'Not terribly.' His eyes met hers for a moment. 'Her mother allowed us to be introduced, but I'm sure she never forgave my father for being unfaithful. Maybe it was guilt that made him put the clause in his will that would allow the central Cambridge home to go straight to Vicky if Luke predeceased her.'

Tara would be curious to meet the woman; she hoped she'd be the one who got to interview her. 'Is she local still?' Suffolk wasn't any great distance away.

Matthew nodded. 'My father ran a patent law firm; it fed off the new innovations that come out of the university spin-out companies here, so he set it up in the city centre. Vicky's in and out of Cambridge all the time.'

A potentially resentful sibling who'd been pushed out of her home and was on the spot. Right… She switched topic. 'Matthew, I'm afraid I need to ask you about some more paintings we found at your brother's house, too. Are you up to it now?'

He gave a quick nod. 'Of course. I won't get any peace until I understand how all this could have happened.'

Tara took out her phone. 'You alerted us to the painting your brother had done of Freya Cross,' she said. 'Were you also aware that he'd painted other scenes showing people who were dead or near death?'

Matthew opened his eyes wider. 'You've got photographs?' he said, glancing at her phone. 'Show me. I'd rather know.'

She scrolled between the images of the two paintings Megan Maloney had found in Luke Cope's studio.

Matthew went completely still, and it was a moment before he spoke. 'I believe' – he paused again and closed his eyes – 'I believe the man who is dead at the foot of the stairs is meant to be my father.' His eyes met Tara's. 'Luke wasn't in the house when my father fell. There's no question of him being involved.' The words came quickly. 'The second picture is of Dr Imogen Field.'

The name brought back a memory. Luke Cope's ex; the one he'd seemingly abandoned for Freya Cross, judging by the timing.

Matthew's eyes were on hers. 'You already know about her?'

She nodded. He didn't miss anything.

'Imogen's very much alive. I saw her at a gathering in town only two weeks ago.'

Freya Cross had been alive back then, too. But Megan had spoken to Dr Field more recently, when she was running through Luke's contacts. A chill ran down Tara's spine; what part might she have played in recent events? A woman who'd been painted dead in Luke Cope's imagination, and seemingly superseded by Freya Cross in the artist's affections.

CHAPTER TWENTY-FIVE

Shona Kennedy had agreed to meet Patrick Wilkins for a drink at the Grain and Hop Store. Patrick had had to accept Shona's choice of venue, which overlooked Parker's Piece, the large square green in front of Parkside police station. He couldn't quell his irritation when she kept glancing over his shoulder at his place of work and squinting.

'I'm glad the view's so fascinating,' he said at last, when he realised she was still concentrating on the comings and goings of his erstwhile colleagues rather than his account of his most recent disciplinary meeting. 'Is anything actually happening?' He and Shona had been sleeping together for over a year, but he was starting to wonder if their relationship would last, now that he was no longer in a position to share the titbits of privileged police information that he used to put her way. *Was the woman really that shallow?*

'Nothing much,' Shona said, sighing.

He'd intended his words to make her remember herself and focus on him. Clearly, the subtle approach hadn't worked.

'I'm worried I've missed something,' his girlfriend said, picking up her glass of chilled Sauvignon Blanc and taking a sip, her eyes still fixed on the station. 'After we got the tip-off about the police going after Luke Cope for Freya Cross's murder, I was sure things were about to kick off.'

'Who gave you the information? One of us?' Had she already managed to sweet talk someone at the station into handing over the secrets he'd once shared with her?

Now Shona faced him properly. 'Not as far as I know. Your lot didn't believe me when I told them, but it genuinely was an anonymous tip-off. I was curious, so I checked the caller number and it turns out someone used one of the phone boxes next to Great St Mary's in town. I can't imagine who would have made the call.' She laughed suddenly. 'Giles says maybe I've got a secret admirer, intent on helping me out.'

Patrick decided not to feed her ego by replying.

'Anyway,' Shona went on, 'as soon as I got the tip-off I went straight round to that gorgeous townhouse Luke Cope owns and the information was clearly true. I saw DI Blake go into the house himself. But after a while he went off again and eventually the rest of the team did too. No one seemed in a major hurry, but now, I don't know…'

'Was Blake with Tara Thorpe?'

'What?' Shona frowned.

'When he left this Luke Cope's house, was Blake with Tara?' Shona disliked their mutual former colleague almost as much as he did. Patrick just needed to get her mind on the right train of thought. Currently, he was more interested in bringing his old adversary down than who had killed some Newnham housewife. *Bloody artists. Unstable lot.* The Luke guy was probably guilty.

'Oh.' Shona nodded, tucking her sleek, golden-brown hair behind one ear with a well-manicured hand. 'Yes, he was. I'd say she'll step right into your shoes before long, Patrick.'

He shook his head. 'Hasn't got enough experience to go for DS yet. Dim Dimity and Moany Maloney have a lot more under their belts.'

'I'm not sure she'll be held back by her rank. Your DI already treats her as an equal. How long before you get back to work and remind her who's boss?'

Her words made his stomach knot. She might be on his side, but she knew just how to twist the knife in his wound. He could well believe Blake preferred having Tara at his side and Wilkins himself out of the picture. He didn't want to make it easy for the man, and yet…

'I'm thinking of resigning, Shona.' That would be a true test of his girlfriend's affections. Had she just been hanging onto the relationship in the hope that one day soon she'd be able to go back to getting inside information from him?

Shona put her head on one side. 'Really?' She leant in close and reached one red-nailed hand up to his cheek. 'It's not like you to give up, Patrick. Don't let the bastards get you down, remember?'

'Sad to be losing your source?' He looked for the self-interest in her eyes. It would take her a while to find another informant. Or so he hoped. But did she seriously imagine that he, Patrick, was still a viable option? That he'd be allowed back into a position where he had access to information that really mattered? Whatever poxy job they graciously allowed him to perform, it would be away from case-critical material and inside knowledge.

Her smile only took a moment to arrive, as sweet as syrup. 'Of course not. But you're such a great detective; it would be an awful waste if you resigned.'

'I've got my pride. If I go back I want to go back on my terms, and that's not going to happen.'

Shona raised her glass to him. 'I admire your spirit.' Then she lowered her voice and her tone became husky. 'But darling, how will you get even with the golden girl Tara if you're stuck on the outside?'

Patrick gave her a lazy smile. 'As a matter of fact, I've got a strategy on that front.'

'Sugar!' Shona laughed and moved her head closer to his. He had her full attention now, he could see. *Good.* 'You intrigue me! Do tell me what you've got planned. Does it have anything to do with Giles, and *Not Now*?'

She'd seen him come out of a meeting with the magazine's editor a couple of days before and had been probing ever since.

Patrick took great delight in tapping the side of his nose with his finger. 'My lips are sealed,' he said.

Shona giggled. 'Oh, is that so? We'll see about that later this evening, shall we? Your place?'

Patrick lifted his glass. 'My place.'

Perhaps their relationship had a bit more shelf life after all, but he wasn't going to tell her what he and Giles had got planned. Not before the time was right, anyway.

CHAPTER TWENTY-SIX

Blake watched Agneta Larsson remove her gloves and walk towards him, away from Luke Cope's body, which lay in the centre of her room at Addenbrooke's mortuary.

'Thanks for getting on to him so quickly.'

She smiled, her silvery blonde hair falling over one eye for a second. 'Hey, no problem, Blake. Frans is already home with Elise, so that's all sorted.'

Frans' work as a freelance web designer gave him the flexibility to pick up the slack when Agneta couldn't be around.

'As for the other subjects on my list,' the pathologist said, 'this takes priority given it's related to the Freya Cross case. And I know you,' she gave Blake a look, her blue eyes on his, 'you think there's more to this than murder–suicide, right?'

He and Agneta had been out together once, long ago, before he'd married Babette and she'd met Frans. They'd parted firm friends.

'Correct. Anything to hint my gut instinct is right?'

Agneta shrugged. 'That's for you to say, but there are several things here that make me wonder.'

'Go on.'

'Want me to start with the time of death?'

'Don't tell me. It's hard to be precise?'

She rolled her eyes. 'There's nothing to say he didn't die at around the same time as Freya Cross, so he could have killed her, driven to the mill and then put an end to it all.'

'But?'

She shrugged. 'Well, the open window and the lack of heating in the building mean he'll have been as cold as Freya Cross was until the thaw came, and still well chilled even then, thanks to the temperatures.'

Blake had known those elements would muddy the waters. And he'd doubted from the start that Luke Cope would have opened the window before settling down to take a lethal overdose. Why would he?

'There are other things of note that will interest you too,' Agneta went on, folding her arms across her chest and leaning back against the bit of worktop where her computer was stationed. 'Stomach contents for one. He'd eaten fish and chips a while before he died, but the last thing he had was salted nuts. Cashews, to be precise.'

'When say you the last thing – what? You think he ate the nuts at the mill?'

She shook her head. 'Cut me a little slack, Blake! I can't be that precise. But it will be interesting to see what's found at the scene. Any empty nut packets, for instance.'

Blake hadn't seen anything that obvious, but the CSIs might find trace evidence. Nuts were covered in loose salt and messy to eat.

'Either way, I can say he ate heartily at one point in the evening.'

That might still fit if he'd tucked in before heading out to meet Freya. But not so much if the food had been consumed just before he'd supposedly taken his own life.

'Analysis of his vitreous fluid, taken from the undamaged eye, shows high concentrations of alcohol and heroin. Looking at the distribution of the drug in his body, I'd say death came very quickly.'

'That would fit with the fact that the needle was still in his arm.'

Agneta shuddered. 'Yes. Which brings me to another point. The drug was expertly administered, yet I couldn't find any other injection sites on his body. If he'd used it before that would suggest that he'd smoked it, or it was rare, and long ago.' She stood up from where she'd been leaning and stretched. 'You can inject heroin several ways: into the vein, into muscle or into the fat just below the skin. This case was intravenous, which has the quickest effect.'

'What about the alcohol you found? How drunk would he have been?'

Agneta's blue eyes met his. 'Very, very drunk, Blake. I would honestly be surprised he was conscious to inject that drug himself, let alone steady enough.' She looked at him more intently. 'You're a bit pale. Do you want to get a coffee? I could use one before I head home anyway. Elise had me up at three this morning.'

That would be him soon, too…

Five minutes later, he sat with Agneta in the Costa on the Addenbrooke's concourse.

'So, how are things?' The pathologist's eyes were speculative. She'd be wondering how Blake was going to cope with the unexpected new addition to his family. Only she knew the full background to Babette's betrayal, years earlier, and about her subterfuge more recently, over the pregnancy she'd kept secret until she was over three months gone.

He pulled a face. 'I tried to get Babette to tell me more about Kitty's father.'

Agneta whistled. 'Any luck?'

Blake shook his head. 'Nothing of use. Her story was the same as ever – that he was a brief fling and he means nothing to her now. The only new information I got was his name: Matt Smith, apparently.' He raised an eyebrow.

'Seriously? Hard to track down then. I mean – not that you'd want to.' Her eyes were suddenly worried.

'No need to fret, Agneta.' Blake managed to laugh, albeit briefly. 'I'm not planning to seek him out and take my revenge. Besides, Babette claims he's still in Australia.'

'Claims?'

He shrugged. 'I don't think she'd tell me if he'd moved back to the UK. Assuming he's British in the first place.'

'What would you do, seriously, if you managed to find him?'

It was a good question. In truth, despite the obvious difficulties, he had googled the name, desperately trying to get past all the references to the *Dr Who* actor. Just before Babette had walked out on him, way back when Kitty was a toddler, she'd told Blake that their daughter was the result of a one-night stand with someone she'd met 'through work'. But having that extra clue hadn't helped. If he'd been a colleague, Blake hadn't found him. And had Babette even been straight with him about the guy's identity? He sighed. 'Nothing like what you're thinking. But I'd want to know how he and Babette met, and if it was truly just a one-night stand. Most importantly, I need to know what kind of a guy he is. Babette claims she decided to leave him and come back to me when she realised he wasn't paying Kitty the attention that he should.' He closed his eyes for a moment. 'Yet one day, Kitty has a right to know who her biological father is. I couldn't live with myself if I didn't tell her the truth. So I need to reassure myself that he wouldn't harm or hurt Kitty.'

Agneta put her head on one side. 'I can understand that. Nothing's more important than your child's well-being. When I think of how I feel about Elise…'

Blake was profoundly grateful that Agneta understood the bond he still felt with Kitty, despite not being her natural father. To her, she was his child, plain and simple, and that was just how he felt too. He'd thought she was his until she was eighteen months old, and his love for her was fierce. Nothing would change that.

'Is there something else?' Agneta said.

He shrugged. 'I still feel Babette's lying to me about what happened. She told me the guy – Matt Smith – convinced her to leave me because he was Kitty's natural father and he wanted to be there for her. She says she came back because he lost interest within days of them emigrating. But who makes the sort of dramatic, life-changing move Babette did, only to rush back home without trying to fix things?'

Agneta's anger was obvious in her eyes. They were a cool blue but they could convey hot fury as well as anyone's. 'I hate Babette for doing this to you. And for affecting you for so many years. As for her motivations, I could believe anything of her.'

CHAPTER TWENTY-SEVEN

Blake had missed Kitty's bedtime. At least he'd managed to call her before he'd left Addenbrooke's though. He'd talked to her before heading back to the station to do more paperwork and had found he could remember the whole of 'Red Riding Hood', from Roald Dahl's *Revolting Rhymes*, by heart. He wondered what information he was failing to retain in the bit of brain space that gem was occupying... but it was worth it to hear Kitty laughing.

Babette knew he'd be late, so he figured it didn't matter if he made it that bit later still. He wanted to quiz his mother. She wasn't one for small talk but she was happy to converse when there was a proper reason to. When he explained his mission she agreed to his visit without hesitation.

As with most streets in the city centre, there were very few garages on Alpha Road and parking was at a premium. He ended up round the corner and had to walk back to his mother's place. The rain had finally stopped but a thickening mist had descended. He wrapped his dark wool coat tightly around him as he strode down what – for Cambridge – counted as a hill. His mother's house was a bay-windowed end of terrace, close to the main road. From the front you'd think she was out, or away even; the place appeared to be in darkness, and she hadn't drawn the curtains. But that was par for the course. She'd have forgotten all about them, her mind focused on the research she'd got funding for currently, which was on the way in which art showed women's roles in society over the last hundred years. It included looking at how male artists viewed and used women. He always felt his mother's attitude towards him – as a man – was influenced by her work. If he turned up just after she'd been studying a particularly frustrating product of the patriarchy her ire extended to him. She seemed to forget it was she who had brought him up single-handedly and he'd learnt a lot of his guiding principles from her. That said, he still thought his way of spending his life was more useful than hers. It wasn't uncommon for him to be dealing with misogyny too – right there and in your face with no need to spend months analysing the subtext.

He rapped loudly on the door using the brass knocker, knowing he'd have to rouse her from whatever she'd been thinking about, even though she was expecting him, in theory.

His mother – Professor Antonia Blake – appeared. Her iron-grey hair was close cropped except on top, where she'd allowed the curls to grow longer. She was wearing a dark-blue sleeveless shift dress, with a scarlet top layered underneath, and knee-length boots. She always said fashion wasn't her thing, but Blake could see where his clothes-designer sister had got her sense of style.

'Come on in,' she said, ushering him down the hall towards the light at the end. It came from her kitchen, which she'd had extended to form a large room where she did most things, including her work. She lived alone, so she didn't have to hive herself off to get peace and quiet. The room's walls were painted dark red, and lamps dotted here and there gave the space a cosy feel. It reminded Blake of an old-style Paris bar.

'Whisky?'

He sighed. 'Can't, I'm afraid. Got to drive home. I'll grab myself a Coke, if you don't mind?' She tended to have a ready supply, preferring it to coffee when she needed a pick-me-up.

She nodded and he went to the fridge to fetch one, not bothering with a glass.

'What's all this about then?' She sat down at the weathered wooden table she used to eat at, a finger of amber liquid in a tumbler at her elbow.

He drew up a chair too. 'You saw the news of the woman found dead in the Paradise Nature Reserve?'

'I did. Freya Cross. I met her at the odd private view.'

'Do you know Zach Cross at all? Her husband? He's on the history faculty.'

She frowned. 'Name rings a bell, but nothing more than that. That's not what you wanted to ask though, surely?'

She'd be thinking he could have done that over the phone, rather than interrupting her evening. 'No. I want to talk you about the gallery Freya Cross worked at: Trent's, out on the Babraham Road. It's a curious place and the owner, Jonny Trent, makes my skin crawl. I can't justify it, but I have a feeling you'd agree if you met him.'

'I already have,' she said. 'And I can confirm that I concur with your gut reaction. I dropped in to the gallery once on my way past out of curiosity. Dark place. Full of atmosphere. I've got a friend who owns a gallery in Chelsea. She says it's amazing how readily some people will part with their money if you can simply create the right ambience. You have to make the place feel special, and your customers to feel that they're special too, by extension. It's all about psychology. Unbelievable what people spend their time and effort on. Still, it works for her. Never liked her all that much, honestly.'

His mother had always used the term 'friend' rather loosely.

Blake found the tactics she was talking about weird and fascinating in equal measure. But if people were vain enough to be duped into overspending like that, it was fair enough, he supposed. And everyone knew presentation made a difference. Otherwise, why were restaurants these days charging extra for food served up on roughly finished boards, rather than plates? Blake liked to eat off something with raised sides, so he could have a decent helping without losing any to the table.

'What influenced your opinion of Jonny Trent?'

'The way he behaved around Freya Cross, as a matter of fact.'

Her tone made him guess what she was driving at. 'You mean he was sexually harassing her?'

His mother nodded. 'That's what it amounted to, but he was just subtle enough about it to make it difficult for her to complain, I'd imagine. No hand on the bottom or anything like that, but he was invading her personal space and I could see him leering at her when her back was turned.'

'You think she was aware of it?'

His mother raised her eyebrows and gave him a disdainful look. 'If someone ogles you to the degree I witnessed you're bound to turn round and catch them at it sooner or later. And at one point, when she was busy tidying some brochures on a side table, she had to worm her way round him, he was standing so close to her.'

Could that be the trouble at work Freya had been facing? It would have put her in a horrible position if his mother was right, and there'd been no concrete accusation she could lay at Trent's door. Blake could see why she hadn't walked out. She'd clearly loved her work – why should she lose a job when she wasn't at fault? Jonny Trent was the one who should pay.

'As for the artworks,' his mother went on, 'I did see some that were of interest when I visited the gallery. I'd imagine Freya was so passionate about her work that she'd decided to put up with her horrible boss. I wonder if she ever confronted him about his behaviour.'

Blake wondered too.

'Was the other member of gallery staff there when you called in, do you know? Name's Monique Courville?'

Antonia Blake frowned. 'There was another woman – I remember wondering if she suffered from the same treatment. But it seemed to be Freya that Jonny Trent had in his sights.'

Blake found the gallery website on his phone and called up a mugshot of Monique. He showed it to his mother and she gave a quick nod.

'Yes. That was her.'

He remembered Tara talking about Monique's indulgent attitude towards her boss – though she'd speculated it might stem from a desire not to rock the boat. It had been clear Freya Cross's assistant needed the income from her role.

'Trent's gallery is on my mind for other reasons too.'

Antonia raised an eyebrow.

'One of the artists whose work they display, Luke Cope, seems to have had a disturbing relationship with Freya.' It felt odd, not sharing the fact that they'd found the man's body. His mother wouldn't talk – he knew that – but equally she wouldn't care that he'd not told her the whole story. It was best to wait until their discovery was public knowledge. So, instead of explaining further, he used his mobile again to call up the photo of the painting Luke had done of the dead woman.

She glanced from the screen up into his eyes and her expression was exhausted for a moment – almost defeated – but then she rallied. 'If this goes public I'll include the bastard in my research.'

'There's another example, I'm afraid,' Blake went on, scrolling so that she could see the portrait of Imogen Field. 'In this case the subject's not actually dead, thank God. But then there's one of a man too.' He didn't fill her in about the identity of the guy at the bottom of the stairs. He wanted to get her unbiased reaction.

She was quiet for some time. 'The paintings of the women confuse me,' she said at last. 'They're so exact in the way they are composed and executed… and yet the image itself speaks of white-hot anger.' She looked at him. 'You did a good job with the photos. I can see how controlled the brush strokes are. These weren't works slapped down in a hurry.'

'So what's your conclusion? They weren't painted in the heat of the moment?'

She shrugged. 'I think not. Perhaps Luke Cope doesn't experience emotion in the same way the rest of us do. And the one of the man is different again, because of the emotional distance between the onlooker and the body.'

Blake nodded. He'd have to digest that later. 'I was going to ask you a favour,' he said, taking a swig of his Coke as she took a slug of her whisky.

She raised an eyebrow. 'Out with it, then.'

'I wondered if you could drop in to Trent's again. Sniff around as an expert and just let me know if anything seems off to you.'

'And I suppose you want me to do this sooner rather than later?'

He gave her a look. 'Like, tomorrow, for instance?'

She pulled a face, but he could tell she was intrigued. 'All right,' she said at last, as though he'd just beaten her at a game of chess. 'I'm lecturing in the morning, but I can head over later in the day. I didn't let on about my background last time I visited; didn't talk much at all in fact, beyond a "Good morning", so I doubt they'll remember me.'

'Excellent. There are two front galleries but also one at the back that's Trent's pet project, apparently.'

'Am I looking for something in particular?'

He shook his head. 'Just anything that makes you wonder.'

She put her head on one side and watched him with her bird-like eyes. 'Got it. I'll make sure I take all the galleries in. If this Jonny Trent's up to something then I'd be glad to catch him out. The man's a toad.'

CHAPTER TWENTY-EIGHT

Tara had been in the doorway of the supermarket when Bea had called to invite her to supper. The food she was now enjoying at Bea's table was so good, she felt almost emotional. Game pie, parmentier potatoes, perfectly cooked green beans and a warming Pinot Noir. The one slight fly in the ointment was the presence of her mother. Tara couldn't help feeling she'd been lured to the scene because Lydia wanted something. She had that air of a person waiting for the perfect moment to spring their request. Each time Tara glanced up, her mother's eyes were on her. She looked swiftly in the opposite direction, though, when she realised she'd been caught out.

Bea's cheeks were rosy from the heat of the kitchen, where they were all sitting to eat. Lydia was wearing a beautifully cut suit, complete with a miniskirt – a style that she carried off far better than Tara ever would. Her warm, mid-brown hair glowed in the lights that shone from under Bea's wall-mounted units. Tara felt tatty in comparison. The woollen jumper she was wearing had bobbled. At least she had her good boots on.

Bea's look contrasted Lydia's. Her mother's cousin was still wearing a bright red and navy striped apron over a green linen shirt and jeans.

'Absolutely first-rate, Bea,' Lydia said, putting down her knife and fork and reaching for her glass of wine. 'And lovely that you could join us, Tara. Work all right?'

'Fine.' She didn't want to go into details; didn't want to think of the sight of Luke Cope, slumped dead at the mill with his eye pecked out.

Bea gave Tara a knowing look, but Lydia took her assurance at face value.

'Splendid. And are you coming to your father and Melissa's anniversary do? Nice of them to invite us all, don't you think? I spoke to him yesterday and he mentioned that he had.'

'Delightful.'

Lydia gave her a look. 'Don't be like that, darling. It's all a long time ago now.'

A long time since Robin had told Lydia she should have had a termination rather than bring Tara into the world. Funny how it still weighed on her mind… 'The invitation's a bit last minute. It wouldn't look odd if I made an excuse.'

'Last minute?' Lydia said. 'What do you mean?'

A creeping realisation came over Tara, coupled with fresh resentment. 'When did you get yours?'

Lydia met her gaze, then looked away hurriedly. 'Oh, um. I don't quite remember.'

Tara carried on staring until her mother glanced up again.

'Oh, for heaven's sake. About a month ago, I suppose.'

'Whereas mine's only just arrived.' As an afterthought, at best, but probably carefully planned that way, in the hope that she'd already be booked up.

'You know how it is,' her mother said, airily. 'So much to think about when you organise that sort of thing.'

'I can see how the odd daughter could easily slip one's mind.' She turned deliberately away from Lydia. 'Are you going to go, Bea?'

'I thought I might, in fact.'

'Please try to see it from someone else's point of view, Tara,' Lydia leapt in, before she'd had a chance to respond. Clearly, she'd picked up on the guilty look Bea had shot Tara. 'It might be quite nice for Bea to be waited on for a change, eating food cooked by someone else.'

Tara felt about two inches high. Lydia hadn't lost her touch. She decided not to address her mother's specific implied criticism of her own character. 'Kemp told me I should go too,' she said, 'for much the same reason. Eat drink and be merry at Robin and Melissa's expense.'

'Really, Tara!' Lydia said. 'I hadn't realised police force pay was *that* bad.' There was a pause as she sipped a little more of her wine. 'But enough about that. As a matter of fact, I wanted to ask you a favour.'

Here it comes. Tara had known there must be a reason for her mother to want Bea to invite her along to supper. She raised an eyebrow.

'It's Harry,' Lydia said, shooting a conspiratorial smile at Bea. 'He's had excellent news – his offer's come through to read natural sciences here at the university – Bosworth College – but,' she rolled her eyes, 'he's at that rebellious stage. UCL's offered him a place too, and he's talking about studying there instead.'

'UCL's excellent.' That was what Tara had heard, anyway, and a place at a London university would mean she wasn't in danger of running into her half-brother.

'Yes, but it's not *quite* the same, is it?'

Tara took a deep breath. She knew Lydia would be repeating her stepfather's deeply biased thoughts on the matter. But after being brought up in the sticks, Harry might want to head for the capital, instead of being press-ganged into accepting a place at his dad's old university.

'I was hoping you could convince him Cambridge is a lovely place to live.' Her mother's words seemed to confirm her theory. 'You know the city – and you might not have been a student here, but you must see them out and about in town all the time. You'll know the kind of things they get up to. I was thinking you could have Harry to stay for a few days. It would give him a chance to get to know Cambridge properly; fall in love with the place.'

Bloody hell! That was one of the most unappealing ideas she'd ever heard. If he was being rebellious Lydia would probably be glad of a few days' peace and quiet whilst Tara dealt with his teenage mood swings. *Great.* The silver lining was that there was no way he'd want to come. Chilling out with his thirty-one-year-old half-sister wouldn't be the stuff of his dreams. Just as well, as it certainly wasn't hers either.

So, her mother wanted Tara to jolly along the wanted child; to make him feel better about life in one of the most beautiful cities in the country. *Fine.*

Bea reached over and topped up Tara's wine, catching her eye as she did so with a pleading look. She'd never liked seeing Tara and Lydia argue.

'Mum, you know what my work's like,' Tara said. 'I'm not around enough to entertain him.'

'Darling, he's eighteen years old. He doesn't need you to hold his hand.' Lydia gave her a look. 'Try to remember what it was like to be that age.'

She'd rather not. She'd still been getting over the effects of being stalked for a year and a half. Going off to university had been a chance to escape, but because she hadn't known where the danger had come from she still hadn't felt safe. She didn't remember anyone except Bea paying her any special attention.

But the whole conversation was academic anyway. There was no way Harry would agree.

So she shrugged. 'If you think a short stay in a cold damp house in the middle of nowhere will convince him, then by all means,' she said. 'He'll need to bring a sleeping bag though. I haven't got a spare bed.'

Her mother rolled her eyes. '*Thank* you, darling. I'll let Harry know. He'll be so pleased.'

But Tara rather doubted that.

CHAPTER TWENTY-NINE

It felt weird for Max that evening, walking into the Flag and Diamond for his second recce, on this occasion with Megan in tow. It was the first time he'd been to a pub alone with another woman since his wife, Susie, had died. It was only for work, of course, but it was after hours, so it felt informal.

He glanced around the room they'd just entered, noticing it afresh now he'd got company. It was dingy, with grubby flock wallpaper – certainly not a venue he'd choose for a date. That made it less awkward; it wasn't the environment that would make either of them forget why they were there.

Megan had asked how she should dress to fit in, given that Max knew the pub. He'd advised jeans and a jumper, but thanks to the weather they'd both got more layers on top of that – the least self-advertising that they owned. He was in a black bomber jacket and she was wearing a brown faux-suede number with a fluffy hood. They'd waited until mid-evening, but Max guessed it wasn't the sort of boozer that ever really filled up.

Several of the clientele glanced round at them as Megan made for a table, but there was only one guy he recognised from the day before and he was in a corner, engrossed with something on his phone. Max didn't reckon they'd been spotted for what they were, but they sure as hell didn't fit in.

'They don't do food,' one guy with a grizzled-looking beard said. His eyes were small and beady.

'No problem, mate,' Max said. 'We're just after a beer on our way home.'

The bearded man took longer than Max would have liked to nod his acceptance. Megan was doing a great job of looking unconcerned, though, and managed to cast the sort of glance that made the guy who'd spoken defrost by a degree or two.

'You sit down,' she said, still smiling and sliding her eyes to meet Max's, her look rather intimate. 'I'll get them in. What do you fancy?'

Max caught the bearded guy's envious glance. The serious, methodical DS he worked alongside had great acting skills. It wasn't something he'd expected.

'Go on then, love,' Max said, still feeling odd himself. He hoped to God it didn't show. Was he blushing? 'I'll have a pint of Old Speckled Hen.'

Megan nodded, her dark curls falling over one eye, and went up to the bar. They'd arranged it that way in advance, in case the senior guy who'd served Max the night before was on duty. Max hoped if he lurked near the door and Megan bought the drinks, no one would notice that he – a stranger – had been in two nights running. He swallowed as he dropped into a seat. It was still a risk. He was half turned away from where Megan stood, queueing at the bar, but he could see there was a woman on tonight anyway. She wore a black hoodie and had more piercings than Max had ever seen before – and he'd seen a lot.

'Not often you get a woman telling you to sit down whilst they buy you a drink,' the man with the beard said, leaning across from his table.

Max grinned and tried to look natural. 'I know what you're saying.'

'Not used to it either, are you? New, is she?' He slurred slightly. Must have been in all evening, Max guessed. 'What made you choose this dump for a date?' He gave a low laugh.

'I don't know about dump,' Max said. 'Reminds me of one of the locals my dad used to go to, out in the Fens. I like traditional places.' They might have an edgy-looking bartender, but the venue itself was 100 per cent old-fashioned pub in its décor. 'But we were just passing anyway – found this place on the off chance.'

The guy gave him a look. 'You might want to take her somewhere else next time.'

There was nothing exactly aggressive in his tone; but there was a slight warning note to his voice. He was quietly pointing out that it wasn't really the place for him and Megan. Just making sure Max knew they weren't altogether welcome. What had he done wrong? He'd messed up in double-quick time.

'Okay,' he said, 'I'll keep that in mind.' And if he'd really just stumbled across the Flag and Diamond he wouldn't have needed a drunk guy built like a brick shithouse to tell him he'd picked the wrong venue.

As he glanced round he realised their exchange had caught the attention of a few of the other regulars too. Their eyes swivelled towards him and common politeness didn't stop them from staring when he looked back.

He felt a sinking feeling inside. He and Megan had decided to come together to avoid Max having to interact with the bar staff, but in fact they'd just made themselves more conspicuous. It wasn't a couples' pub. And now, no one would say anything telling whilst they were there. But he was loath to leave completely empty-handed.

'A mate of mine mentioned coming here a few times – guess he likes this place all right.' Max watched the bearded man intently.

He raised an eyebrow.

'Guy called Luke Cope.' It was the last time Max would be able to drop the artist's name casually into conversation and get away with it. The identity of the body at the mill hadn't been made public yet.

'Luke Cope?' The guy's unflinching gaze met his. 'Never met him.'

Megan had arrived back at the table with Max's pint and a Coke for herself.

'That all you're having?' the bearded guy asked.

She rolled her eyes. 'Got to drive, worst luck.'

The man jerked a thumb at Max. 'You could get him to do it.'

'Have him touch my car? You're kidding, right?'

At that, the large guy shook his head and turned away, but Max heard him say, under his breath, 'Your car? Assumed it went with the job…'

They'd been rumbled.

Megan caught his eye and gave him a sympathetic glance. He was hoping for promotion, just like her, and she knew it. For years, career progression had been the last thing on his mind, but suddenly he knew it was something he really wanted. This was hardly going to help.

Just for a second, Megan touched her glass to his and their fingers brushed.

They made small talk about a heist movie they both wanted to see, but even she sounded a bit stilted now. Max drank his pint in larger draughts than he might usually have done, though he was trying not to look uncomfortable.

At last he was able to make as dignified an exit as he could, with Megan at his side. He glanced over his shoulder as they reached the door to the outside world and saw the bearded guy was stirring in his seat. A knot formed in Max's stomach as he looked to see if he was going to follow them, but that didn't seem to be his plan.

In the fog-enveloped car park, Max paused for a moment. Standing well to one side of the window, he strained to see what was going on.

Megan was at his elbow and raised an eyebrow as he turned to her. The bearded guy had gone up to the bar, and was talking to the barmaid there. But instead of pointing to the beer he'd like to order, the guy had nodded in the direction of the table he and Megan had recently occupied. And instead of pouring him a drink, the barmaid had nodded, turned and walked out of the back of the bar.

They'd better get going…

As he got into the passenger seat of their car and Megan started the engine, he let out a sigh.

'It wasn't a total disaster,' she said.

Max sat back and closed his eyes for a moment. 'Which element would you say was successful?'

'Well,' she reached the end of the driveway and indicated left, 'we know it's a dodgy pub where they want to discourage genuine drinkers. And given Mr Beardy went straight up to the bar to dob us in, it seems likely they're hiding something specific, maybe from us in particular. Perhaps Luke Cope's sudden influx of cash has something to do with whatever trade they do at the pub, alongside watery beer.'

Max nodded. 'There is that. It's hardly evidence, though.'

'But it's something to consider.'

Max shrugged, unable to shake off the feeling of failure. But she did have a point.

'And beyond that,' Megan added, 'we also established we both want to see the remake of *The Getaway*. Do you fancy going along together?'

She'd taken him by surprise. Was this like a date? He glanced sideways at her but her eyes were on the road. She was smiling though.

A few of his friends had told him he should get himself back out there, but each time he thought of it, it felt like a betrayal of Susie. Hell – it was only a trip to the cinema. But part of him felt like crying just at the thought of it. It was something he and his wife had done together, as a treat. What if he couldn't control his emotions when the time came? Megan probably meant as friends. If he got all maudlin about it that would frighten her off in five seconds. And even though he didn't feel ready, he didn't actually want to put her at a distance…

He glanced sideways and realised she'd let her eyes drift left towards him. 'Don't worry,' she said. 'I understand. Seriously. But if you ever do fancy something similar, let me know, okay?'

CHAPTER THIRTY

Tara was in the Lord Butterfield Café on the Downing College site, her hands wrapped round a steaming mug of black coffee. It wasn't the only thing that was steaming: it was damp outside, the air thick with fog, and her coat, which she'd eased off, also had a humid fug coming off it, brought on by the warmth of the room they were in. At least the wet hadn't seeped through to reach her woollen dress underneath. It was cosy and fitted – designed to keep out the worst effects of a cold English spring. She glanced round at each of her colleagues in turn. Blake was next to her and Megan and Max opposite.

Her eyes roved over the café as she took a bite of her roll, which was stuffed full of halloumi. The place was thronging with students and academics, but they wouldn't be overheard – it was still the busy breakfast period and there was a relaxed level of hubbub and chat that meant they could talk. The halloumi was very, very good. Not healthy, but sustaining, and this was no time to quibble about diet. She could save her good intentions for when the weather was warmer and less insulation was required. At least she'd had Bea's home cooking yesterday.

It was Blake who'd suggested stopping off for breakfast – no doubt realising they'd all operate better on a full tank of fuel. She reckoned he wanted time for an informal chat too, after Fleming's headmistress-style briefing. (She'd had them writing suggestions on a whiteboard and putting their hands up in turn.)

They'd spent a moment eating in silence, but now Max and Megan were recounting their trip to the Flag and Diamond the evening before.

'And there's been nothing from the background checks you've done on the place so far?' Blake said, frowning.

Max shook his head. 'Nothing official on record.'

'Keep digging – take the search wider: gossip, rumours or more tangential links with past crimes.' He took a large bite of his bacon roll and appeared to swallow it whole.

Tara noticed Megan give Max a tiny, conspiratorial nod. They seemed to be getting on well together. She wondered if it was just professional rapport or something more. Max was owed some happy times, though Tara wondered whether Megan was the right person to supply them.

'So let's take stock before we head off,' Blake said, swallowing down more food and picking up his coffee. 'We think Luke Cope's death was staged to look like suicide. Agneta said he was so drunk she'd be surprised if he was conscious, let alone capable of accurately injecting heroin intravenously without messing up. Plus, there are no signs he was a regular user, so why would he choose that method? And where would he have got the drug? Or learnt how to inject it?'

'It just doesn't fit, does it?' Tara said, taking a swig of her drink. 'Unless he had the drug hanging about the mill then using it would suggest the suicide was pre-planned. That he knew he'd want to kill himself after he'd murdered Freya – and went to a lot of trouble to make sure he could do it via this particular method.'

'And then there's the evidence the CSIs found,' Megan put in.

They'd been filled in about that at the briefing. There had been traces of nuts and salt in the room at the mill and under Luke Cope's fingernails.

'I presume someone who was desperate to end it all would be unlikely to binge on cashews beforehand. Unless he ate and drank because he felt miserable.' The DS frowned.

Max shook his head. 'Except the CSIs couldn't find the cashew packet anywhere, don't forget. Someone must have got rid of it – presumably because they were worried about the conclusions we might draw. Maybe whoever killed Luke Cope was eating and drinking with him until they were sure he was far enough gone for them to administer his lethal dose.'

'I think you're right,' Blake said. His roll was finished. Tara noticed him reach absently to his plate and then glance down as he realised there was nothing left. 'And my guess is that same person locked up when they'd finished, using the missing spare key. They'd better hope they were careful. I want all of Luke Cope's contacts fingerprinted to cross-check against what the CSIs found at the mill. We can ask for DNA samples too, if people will volunteer them. And if they won't I'll want to know why.'

'Think the DCI will approve all that?' Megan asked.

Fleming was still hesitating over the theory of it all being staged. She probably wouldn't like Blake asking Professor Cross for a voluntary DNA sample – especially as there was no indication he'd know how to inject someone with heroin. But his son was diabetic. Tara had looked it up and found that insulin wasn't injected intravenously, but it would mean both Oscar and Zach Cross were familiar with hypodermic needles.

Blake sighed. 'More work to do there. Our job is to convince her as soon as humanly possible. It's true that everything we've got is circumstantial. But when you put it all together… I still can't think why Luke would open the mill's window on such a cold night if he was about to take his own life, but it would be a natural move for a killer. Especially one who murdered Cope, then took his phone and arranged to meet Freya Cross, in order to kill her too. The temperature at the mill means Agneta will never know which of them died first.'

'The perpetrator must have been holding their breath for the last twelve days,' Tara said. 'They had no way of knowing how long it would take us to find the bodies. Freya could have been discovered much sooner, and Luke might have told other people that he'd rented the mill. Maybe he had, in fact, but they haven't seen fit to let us know – or we haven't asked the right contacts.'

Blake nodded. 'Imogen Field's next on my list. As a GP, I presume she'll be familiar with administering all kinds of injections.'

And they knew she was Luke's ex, the subject of one of his grisly paintings, and rejected by him in favour of Freya Cross… She'd be a juicy interviewee for her and Blake to get their teeth into.

She watched as the DI raised his eyes to meet Megan's. 'You and Max take the son.' And then he turned to face Tara. 'And Tara, whilst I'm with Imogen Field I want you to head round to recheck alibis now we know we need to include the day before Freya Cross died, when Luke Cope's car was caught on the traffic camera. I reckon that's when he and the murderer drove out to the mill.'

Tara nodded mechanically. Of course. That was just the job for her, as the most junior member of the team. Why would he take her along to meet Imogen Field? Just because they'd paired up the day before, that didn't mean she was going be favoured with higher-level tasks in general.

But was this him putting some distance between them? Was she suffering because he felt awkward when she was near?

'All right?' Blake asked her.

'Boss.'

'Start with Jonny Trent and Monique Courville at the gallery. I've sent my mother there to pose as a casual visitor later on today, so it's best if you're out of sight before she arrives.'

Max raised an eyebrow.

'She's an art expert,' Blake supplied. 'I just want to get her take on the place in general. Luke Cope and Freya Cross were heard arguing there, and Freya clearly had some kind of issue she wanted to discuss with her boss. It makes me curious.'

So Blake's mother got to go undercover whilst she did alibi checking. 'Do the higher-ups know what you're up to?' Tara asked.

He raised an eyebrow and smiled. 'I can't believe you asked that. She's just an interested individual who happens to fancy a visit.'

Right.

'The tech gang are having a go at enhancing the traffic camera image,' Blake went on. At the briefing they'd heard that it looked as though Luke Cope had been carrying a passenger when he'd been recorded, but the picture was too grainy for them to make out whether they'd been male or female. 'I'm sending some officers back to Cope's neighbours too, to see if any of them clocked any visitors at his place on the night of Thursday twenty-second, before he headed off in his car. His passenger might have joined him at home first.'

And then there was the question of how the killer had got away from the scene, if they'd been travelling with Luke. Officers at the station were checking with the local taxi firms as a matter of course, but no one reckoned the perpetrator would have left that kind of trail. Tara guessed they'd most likely walked to somewhere where they could catch a bus. Cash was still accepted on the fenland routes, so their journey would be untraceable. The only hope was that someone had seen the killer walking away from the mill. But the road wasn't exactly a superhighway and the weather had already turned bad by then. Most people had probably stayed indoors.

'We'll reconvene at the station,' Blake said. 'By that time, I hope we'll have Luke Cope's bank records. I want to know just how much money he had coming in and going out, and where it came from.'

'I keep thinking of what Fleming said about his fingerprints on the syringe,' Max said, staring into the middle distance, a part-eaten sausage sandwich in one hand.

The CSIs had found his, and only his. And in just the right position too, apparently. It was true that only a real expert could have placed the man's dead fingers on the syringe so accurately. That was why Fleming still hesitated over the fake-suicide theory.

'It's Freya Cross's holdall that's on my mind,' Tara said.

Professor Cross had managed to dig out a holiday photograph of his wife carrying it, but no one had managed to find the item. Why had the killer taken it? Of course, it wasn't impossible that a down-and-out or a junkie had stolen it from next to her body, but surely in that case they'd have taken her phone and purse too?

'We definitely need more answers,' Blake said. 'But we'll get them. I'm not letting this rest. There's no way Luke Cope's death wraps this case up. We're looking for a third party that either wanted them both dead, or was ruthless enough to use one of them specifically to help themselves look innocent. And it has to be someone who knew Luke Cope had hired the mill, and who could access and administer heroin.'

'And who was possibly on good enough terms with him to go out there and spend the evening drinking and eating nuts,' Tara said. 'And who knew enough about Luke and Freya's relationship to be aware of their standard rendezvous.'

'And even to know they'd had some kind of quarrel,' said Megan, 'so they could write a convincing text from Luke's phone, suggesting the meet-up.'

The message had been sent from central Cambridge, so if their theories were right, the killer must have taken the phone into town and then replaced it at the mill, once they'd finished covering their tracks.

'Anyone want more coffee?' Blake asked. 'Apart from me, that is?'

Everyone went for it. Once they were settled again and Blake had downed half a cup in one swig, he said: 'Of course, our killer might not have a personal motive at all. What if Luke Cope was getting his mysterious extra cash from selling drugs? Maybe he'd crossed the wrong person? Freya could have known what was going on and that would have made her a target too. It would explain why Luke's killer knew how to inject heroin – and the fact that they had the drug to hand. And the set-up of the two deaths was pretty showy – it would be a good deterrent to point to, if anyone else caused them trouble.'

There was a moment's silence.

'Whatever the case, Luke Cope was certainly getting a reasonable income from somewhere.' He glanced at Tara for a moment. 'Despite the mill's dilapidated appearance, the agents were charging a fat rent for it.'

Tara pulled a face. 'And I presume we should treat inheriting Luke's house as a potential motive too?'

'Oh yes. The half-sister, Vicky Cope, has to be in the running. That's a two-point-five million pound motive right there if the estate agent's valuation is to be believed,' Blake said. 'She's no direct motive for killing Freya, as far as I can see, but we have to keep her in mind.'

'And I'd be resentful too, if my father swapped my mother for a new woman and forced me to move away from my childhood home.' Tara had nursed a grudge against her own father for years. She wouldn't commit violence over it, but she could imagine people who would.

'I agree,' said Max.

Tara thought once again of the legal provisions Luke, Matthew and Vicky's father had made for them all after his death. Vicky Cope had been left her father's business, and that was valuable too. Presumably her dad had thought she'd got the best skills and temperament to carry it on, whereas Matthew and Luke had been left their inheritance in trust until they'd reached an age that was well past maturity. But maybe the father had thought it would lead to arguments if he tried to make the business a shared venture. As it was, Vicky had something valuable, but which demanded hard work and a mature approach. Meanwhile the boys had bequests that wouldn't involve any effort on their part.

No doubt the arrangements had made sense to Mr Cope senior, but Tara could imagine each of the three children being angered by the provisions for different reasons. Vicky had been forced into a position of responsibility she might not want, carrying on a business built up by a man she had every reason to resent. And neither Luke nor Matthew had been trusted to behave sensibly.

'I wonder why the father picked Vicky to take over the business,' Blake said, as though reading her thoughts. 'I can understand he might write Luke off as unsuitable for the job – from what everyone says – but what about Matthew?'

Tara shrugged. 'His employer says he's a fantastic salesman – but it's clear he's one of a team. Not as senior as he had me believe, in fact. Maybe he's not a leader, and his father knew it.' But her mind was still on who stood to gain from the recent deaths. 'I know the house is the big prize, but I wonder if Luke Cope made any other bequests that might be significant?'

Blake swigged some more of his coffee and shook his head. 'I spoke to the Cope family solicitors after we got back from the mill yesterday. They can't release firm details until all the right paperwork's been signed off, but they did tell me Luke died intestate. Then again, beyond the house – and the furniture, which I understand goes with it – he didn't have much to leave.

'Matthew's his next of kin, and I'm sure he's looking forward to taking possession of his brother's eerie paintings, the contents of his wardrobe and his old paints… If there genuinely was any valuable jewellery, left by their mother, it sounds as though it will have been sold by now.'

'And if Matthew wanted to kill his brother to inherit something he could just have faked the suicide anyway,' Max said. 'He wouldn't have any need to bring Freya Cross into it, as far as we know. He and the half-sister, Vicky, are in the same boat there.'

'True.' Blake nodded.

And then, into Tara's head came the image of Jonny Trent once again. What had he got to do with all this? Why had Freya been so angry with Luke? And what was the problem she had at the gallery?

Her alibi-checking might just be routine, but she would make it count.

CHAPTER THIRTY-ONE

Oscar Cross looked at the two detectives sitting opposite him, one on a padded upright chair and one on the edge of his bed, for God's sake. Oscar was already seated in the office chair of his university room, so that left the guy, DC something, short on options, but it still sparked something like fury inside his chest.

It wasn't often that students studying at St Francis's College got visits from the police. If anyone ran into trouble, the institution's authorities stepped in first, meting out discipline and justice. For one second a flicker of pride rose up inside him. So much for the 'tame guy' down the corridor who nothing ever happened to. He knew that's what the others thought of him. Jack Paris, who'd almost been sent down last term for climbing the college chapel's bell tower – on the outside – sometimes patted him on the head. *Dear old Oscar, who's only really here, as we all know, because his father is a fellow of this very college. Family connections or no, he'll never be one of us...*

It was a lie! The rules for getting in were strict.

Oscar put his shoulders back. News of this visit would get around all right. There had been at least two people out in the corridor who'd heard Sam, the porter, announce the detectives by name when he'd opened up to let them in. Normally, Oscar had to fetch his visitors from the porters' lodge, but he guessed Sam hadn't wanted a couple of cops hanging round the official gateway to the college, even if they were in plain clothes. They might say something awkward and it wouldn't do to compromise St Francis's reputation.

Oscar could look forward to some curiosity from his contemporaries at the very least.

'So, let's just go through your alibis again,' the woman was saying. DS Mahoney or something like that. He hadn't registered. It had taken him a moment to calm down, if he was honest. He hadn't been expecting them to call. He'd have to ask about that. Shouldn't they give you some warning or something?

The woman glanced at the man who'd been writing down what he said.

DC thingummy referred to his notes. 'On the night of Thursday twenty-second February you were here in your room, working on an essay that had to be handed in the following day. You think you bumped into Patrick Jones, who's in room 4b, at some stage, but you're not sure when.'

The man glanced at him. Did he think Oscar was going to have changed his mind in the last two minutes? He nodded. Couldn't be bothered to speak to confirm that yes, that was the account he was sticking with. He was still irritated that they wanted to check his alibis at all. They had one murdered woman and one man, dead of an overdose. He'd assumed they'd put two and two together, but they had to 'cover all their bases' apparently. It was 'procedure'. How dull to be governed by a set of rules. They could have taken what they'd seen at face value, gone home and saved the taxpayers some money.

'On Friday twenty-third February you went to the dining hall at six p.m., where you had supper with Tom Cruickshank, after which you went for drinks at the college bar and then returned to your room by eight thirty, after which you saw no one.'

Oscar nodded again.

They went through Saturday and Sunday too, making him sound as unpopular as he felt. Each phrase: *you saw no one you knew, you missed your friends at breakfast, you stopped for two minutes to talk to Tom Cruickshank (him again)*, made him feel smaller and hate them – and himself – more.

'What kind of a relationship did you have with your stepmother?'

His stepmother? *Freya.* Freya was what he'd called her – and how he thought of her, too. There'd been nothing motherly about his father's second wife, closer to Oscar than she was to Zach Cross in age.

'By the time she came on the scene I was just about through my A levels,' he said, keeping his face expressionless. 'After that I moved out, so I've never had much contact with her.'

The woman raised an eyebrow. 'Wouldn't most students choose to live at home, if they're studying in the city where they live?'

She really didn't know anything. It was pathetic. 'You have to live in college accommodation. It's one of St Francis's rules. That's the case with a lot of the colleges. And besides, I would only ever have spent a couple of days a week at my father's house. Once he and my mother divorced I opted to spend most of my time with her.' Though he'd been glad enough to end that arrangement too.

'How did it make you feel, when your father told you he was leaving your mum for Freya?'

God, the woman had a fine line in questioning. How did she *think* it made him feel? But he was used to hiding his emotions.

'I was sad, but I understood. I knew he and my mother hadn't been getting on for a while and that not all marriages last forever.' He kept his unblinking eyes on the woman's.

'That was a very mature attitude for an eighteen-year-old,' she said. 'I can't imagine it was easy, what with the pressure of exams, your mum being replaced so quickly and the neighbours gossiping.'

She was pretending to sympathise, but he knew she was out to rile him – to keep poking until she got him to bite. He wasn't going to let her win.

'Lots of other people go through the same stuff. It's commonplace.' He couldn't believe he was having to sit there trying to convince some woman that he hadn't killed his stepmother. And all because his father hadn't the brains to see Freya was wrong for him. She was too young, too beautiful, too lively.

Oscar had been so angry at their wedding. He'd been shown up. People kept assuming he and Freya were contemporaries. Two people who only knew his father through work had asked if they were siblings. If Freya hadn't been in a wedding dress and hanging on the arm of Zach, they'd probably have assumed he and Freya would have made a more likely couple than Freya and his dad.

'And what about your father and Freya's relationship? Did you ever hear them argue?'

'As I said, I was seldom there.' He kept his gaze steady once again.

'Did you ever see anything that made you think your stepmother might have been unfaithful to your father?'

Their eyes were on him. They were staring at him like a couple of cats, watching a bird.

'Never.'

Why did they bother asking? They knew he'd lie if he needed to. In his head, pictures spooled. The memory of staying at his old family home in St Mark's Street during the Christmas holidays for his allotted time. Seeing Freya, dressed to kill in a low-backed black dress, ready to go to one her endless private views. His father had been going out too, to dine with some visiting professor, alone in the UK without his family over the 'festive' season. Why had Oscar even been there? He was just going to sit alone in the grand house with nothing to do. Freya had looked even more gorgeous than usual. Her cheeks were glowing. He knew the expression she wore; it was eager anticipation. She loved her work, but he couldn't believe that was the only thing behind her appearance.

In the end, he'd followed her. He'd kept a safe distance, but she'd made it easy – heading off through the nature reserve as a shortcut. It had been dry, and twigs kept cracking under his feet, but she'd been so wrapped up in her thoughts that she'd never noticed. He'd trailed after her, across Coe Fen and into town. On Magdalene Street, he'd seen her enter the gallery that was her destination, an eager smile lighting her face as someone opened the door for her. After that, he'd hung around in the shadows on the opposite side of the road, next to one of the gateways into Magdalene College.

He could see Freya through the steamed up, brightly lit window of the gallery. He'd watched her fine-featured face as she looked up at the artworks on the wall. And then he'd stared at that same face as it gazed upon another subject: a tall man with wild dark hair and angular features. A dangerous-looking man.

And he'd found himself crossing back over the road, and daring to stand in front of the shop next to the gallery so that he could get a better look. And that was when he'd seen the man and his 'stepmother', beautiful Freya, turn their backs to the window and face into the room. Everyone else did the same. One man was standing in front of them all, seemingly making a speech. And there, lit in the window, for only Oscar to see, Freya and the stranger's hands got closer and closer, until their fingers entwined.

He hadn't known the man was Luke Cope then. He only realised later, when he'd followed her again.

Suddenly he noticed that the two detectives were on their feet. He got up as well.

'Thank you for your time and your statement, Mr Cross,' the woman said.

Mr Cross... Some of his supervisors called him that. They meant it ironically, of course.

'You're welcome.'

CHAPTER THIRTY-TWO

Dr Imogen Field's house was on a quiet street running between Milton and Chesterton Roads. The news was out now, that Luke Cope's body had been found at the mill – and that he'd died of a heroin overdose. The medic had looked shaken when she'd answered the door and Blake had noticed her eyes glisten as he'd thanked her for agreeing to see him. She'd arranged for a colleague to cover her surgery so that they could talk. Once again, the latest developments in the case had leaked before the official press conference. Blake still couldn't work out who had fed the details to the media and 'a genuine, anonymous tip-off' was all he could get out of his contacts. *Yeah, right.*

Dr Field's house radiated calm and order, which interested Blake. How had this woman and Luke, who'd lived so chaotically, got together in the first place? It dictated the first question he addressed to her.

There was a gleam of amusement in her eye. 'You're not the first person to express surprise at our relationship,' she said, making him curse, inwardly. He hadn't meant to give away his thoughts. 'We met completely by chance. Our eyes locked over a cyclist who'd come off his bike down Mill Road. Luke caused the crash – he'd stepped out in front of the guy. He was carrying a large canvas and not looking where he was going. I stopped to see if the cyclist needed medical attention.'

'And did he?'

The woman shook her head. 'Even as I went over to him the stream of expletives led me to suppose his faculties were unaffected, and apart from a graze to his arm he was all right, thank God. Luke's canvas was similarly only slightly damaged. He wasn't too pleased about it though, and I tore him off a strip.'

The perfect meet-cute – but there'd been no happy ending for them. 'What was Luke's reaction?'

Field raised her eyes to heaven. 'He shouted back and I was furious. I stalked off up the road after I'd advised the cyclist on some first aid. I didn't look back, so I was pretty surprised when I felt a hand on my shoulder and realised he'd followed me.'

'He'd decided to apologise? Was he still carrying the canvas?' Mill Road's pavements were narrow and normally crowded. He couldn't imagine how the guy had managed to catch her up.

Imogen Field pulled a face. 'I'm afraid that was one of the things that charmed me. He'd just dumped it at the side of the road as it turned out, right by where the cyclist had come to grief, and run after me because he realised he'd been in the wrong. It seemed like a grand gesture. I didn't know at the time that the canvas was a work he hated. He painted over it later. You can bet your bottom dollar he wouldn't have left it there if it had been something he was proud of. His art always came first.'

'Was that the reason you broke up?'

The doctor had prepared them coffee and she took a sip of hers now. 'Partly. But I'd dealt with that state of affairs for three years. When he started to value both his work *and* Freya Cross above me, I finally decided to draw the line. I should have broken it off a long while before that.' Suddenly she put her hand over her face. 'I can't believe what he's done. He always had a temper, but I never imagined he'd kill someone. Or take his own life in a fit of regret, come to that. He used to shout and get things out of his system.'

Blake was glad she was being frank, but at the same time he thought he knew the type. Some people shocked you with their candour in order to blind you to the things they were really hiding.

'I genuinely didn't regret our break-up, even before I heard about this business. He wasn't an easy person to live with. And given what's happened, I guess I had a narrow escape.'

'What were his other relationships like? Did he have many friends?'

She shook her head. 'Friends would be the wrong word. He hung out with people who might be able to advance his career. Not that they ever did. That was another reason we broke up. I got impatient with him. He was stubborn about accepting help. Matthew, his brother, is in sales. Okay, I appreciate flogging medical devices isn't the same as convincing customers to buy art, but Matthew had ideas that Luke could have at least tried, but he wouldn't. Too proud, I guess. I had a friend too, a woman in the music industry who felt she'd got useful contacts. She had an idea she could make him trendy, get a buzz going around his work, but oh boy, he hated that thought. Said it would be selling out.'

Blake could see that one from both sides.

Imogen Field drank more of her coffee. 'I blame his parents in part,' she said. 'I don't know if you're aware of the way they made their wills? How they left Luke a house in trust?'

Blake nodded.

'They wanted the brothers to make their own way in life and they thought they'd manage that by making them wait for their inheritance, but it didn't work. For Luke, at least, it was as though he was treading water until he hit forty and he could release his assets. If he could just eke out an existence until then, he'd be home and dry.'

'But it was different for Matthew?'

'Well, his place is out of town. It's just as big as Luke's was – bigger in fact, I understand. Luke told me that. But it won't be worth as much. In fact, the combination of its size and location probably means it'll be hard to get rid of. But Luke still felt resentful of Matthew for having inherited it, for some reason.'

'He'd have preferred that property?'

Dr Field frowned. 'I'm not sure. But he wasn't happy with the arrangement. As I say, he was a tricky man. Fascinating – but in the event, that wasn't enough.'

Very sensible to cut your losses when a relationship wasn't working out. Blake sighed inwardly.

The leak to the press meant he couldn't try to trick Dr Field into admitting that she knew about Luke's bolthole. Everyone who listened to the news would be aware of the grisly scene out in the Fens. But at least their fake-suicide theory was still under wraps. Blake asked if Cope had ever taken Field to the mill – though their relationship would have been over by the time he'd got the keys to the place. Officially.

The woman shook her head. 'I had no idea he'd rented some-where.'

Blake nodded. 'And when did you last see him?'

'Oh, not for months. I bumped into Matthew recently, though. We had a quick chat and I gathered that Luke was his same old self.'

'Were you aware that he'd painted your picture?' Blake watched the woman's eyes. Her surprise looked genuine.

'What? I had no idea. I never sat for him.'

She wouldn't have lasted long if she'd posed for that particular portrait.

Suddenly her eyes sharpened, as though she was reading his expression. 'Was it an odd one? The painting, I mean?'

Blake hesitated. 'It was.'

She shook her head. 'Don't worry – you don't need to tell me. He painted a lot of peculiar pictures.'

Blake knew that for a fact.

'Just for the record, I need to ask where you were from the evening of twenty-second February, through to Saturday twenty-fourth.'

'I'll have to check my diary,' she said, flicking through the pages of a small Moleskine notebook. 'Though I don't know why I'm bothering. My life's nothing if not predictable. I have surgery on a Thursday afternoon. It's exhausting and I'm generally at work for over an hour after it ends. I would have been back here by seven thirty, say, and then – please don't tell my patients – sitting with my feet up on the sofa, watching TV and eating a takeaway curry. I get one every Thursday. On Fridays, I finish slightly earlier.' She gave him a look and raised an eyebrow. 'Consequently, I had the exciting chance to stop off at the supermarket on my way home and cook my own meal. But the TV bit's the same as for Thursday. On the Saturday – wahey! – I went to lunch with some friends in Newmarket. Then I had a scratch supper back here.'

'Thank you.'

'Do you want the address in Newmarket?'

But Blake shook his head. Nothing they could say would help, given Agneta couldn't be accurate about the timing. If Field had spent the entire week at a conference in Japan – now that would have made a difference. It was always going to be a long shot…

'One final thing,' he said. 'I could do with your advice on a technical matter.'

She raised an eyebrow. 'Let me guess, you're wondering how Luke had the expertise to inject himself with heroin. You haven't found any signs that he was a user?'

Blake nodded.

'I'm sure he wasn't,' she said, 'so I've been pondering the same thing.'

'Presumably it wouldn't be something a novice would pick up easily?' He watched her eyes. The papers hadn't got hold of just how the heroin had been injected.

It was a moment before Imogen Field replied. 'Some methods are simpler than others. Into muscle or subcutaneously would be easier than administering the drug intravenously, for instance. And users tend to be more nervous about injecting into a vein. They end up going for it anyway because they get a hit from the drug much faster that way.'

'And is there anything else we should be aware of? We're already looking into where Luke might have sourced the drug.' *Or where someone else might have.*

'Just the practical stuff. For instance, the kit he would have needed to do the job. There are different needle sizes and so on.'

'What size would Luke have needed?' Blake wasn't aware that the type of needle used had come up in any of the reports they'd had so far. It was probably information that was waiting for him in his crowded inbox.

Imogen Field went into some technical details, but what hit home was the type of needle she said was best for subcutaneous and intravenous injections, if the injection site was in the arm: a diabetic needle.

CHAPTER THIRTY-THREE

Jonny Trent's eyes popped slightly as he regarded Tara. When she'd first arrived, he'd looked frightened. He'd been anticipating something, she was sure, but when she started to talk the blow he'd been expecting hadn't fallen. Gradually, she'd seen his shoulders relax and that tautness of his face slacken. Why had he thought she was visiting? She must be very close to the truth. It was desperately frustrating. Her alibi checking didn't go down well.

'Forgive me,' he said, with a slight splutter, 'but why do you want to know? I saw the news that Luke was being sought in connection with Freya's murder, and now his body's been found. Given he died of an overdose, I'd assumed this was an open-and-shut case. Isn't that what you call it?'

Too much TV... Tara watched his features. Was that really what he thought, or could this be a bluff? He might hope righteous indignation was the best way to put her off the scent. It was hard to tell. Everything Jonny Trent did seemed larger than life – slightly phoney. 'When we investigate a case it's essential we cover everything,' she said. 'If we haven't looked at all the possibilities the coroner can't come to a proper conclusion. And Freya's family need to feel sure we've discovered the truth, too.'

Jonny Trent was twisting the gold ring on his right hand with his left. She looked at the movement pointedly and he stopped. Their eyes met.

Whatever you tell me, I won't believe a word you say.

The man let out an impatient sigh. 'I live here – above the gallery. More often than not I'm at home during the evenings. I spend a lot of hours on my feet, talking to clients, and by the time we close I've no desire to head out.'

'So you were here on Thursday twenty-second February, alone, all evening?'

He frowned and took a diary from his inside jacket pocket, leafing through the pages. 'Yes,' he said after a moment. 'After Monique and Freya went home at six.'

'And what about your movements on the Friday through to the Sunday? Was the gallery open each day?'

He nodded sharply. 'It was. Again, the girls were here with me on the Friday all day until it was time to shut up shop.'

The girls…

'And Monique was on duty on the Saturday, from ten until four. I caught up on paperwork and supported her.'

Tara rather doubted that final claim.

'Then I was here alone on the Sunday until two, when we close. We had a handful of visitors but none of them bought.' He sounded cross about that. 'So I can't give you their names.'

'And you were here alone each evening? You didn't go out on the Friday, Saturday or Sunday?'

He scanned his diary again. It seemed to Tara that he was making too much of a show of it. 'I didn't.'

It would take more than that to convince her, but there wasn't much she could do about it.

'Thank you. I'd like to speak to Monique now.'

He opened his mouth as though to protest before closing it again. He was probably worried he might actually have to do some work whilst Tara talked to the woman. He looked very at home behind his mahogany desk, his portly middle just nudging up against it.

'Very well,' he said, getting to his feet. 'I'd be grateful if you didn't keep her long.'

Tara decided to draw out their chat as much as possible.

Jonny Trent led her back to the front gallery. They found Monique in the room that overlooked the driveway. The space looked different somehow – lighter – in spite of the fog-darkened day outside.

Monique's eyes widened when she glanced up and saw Tara. She must have been out of earshot when she'd knocked on the gallery door earlier and been shown in by Jonny Trent.

'I thought we had an early customer,' she said, giving her an uncertain smile. 'I saw the news about Luke. It's unthinkable. I mean, I know he and Freya had argued, but I never thought…' She let the sentence tail off and bit her lip.

'I just need another quick word,' Tara said. She glanced at Jonny Trent. 'Somewhere private.' He raised an eyebrow. 'I wouldn't want to disturb your clients once they start showing up.'

Trent sighed. 'Very well. I will hold the fort.'

Tara went with Monique back to the office where they'd talked previously. Once the door was firmly closed and they were seated opposite each other, she explained her mission.

Monique's eyes widened. 'You don't believe Luke's death was suicide?'

She decided to sidestep that one. 'This exercise is purely routine. However obvious the evidence seems we can't skip dotting the "i"s and crossing the "t"s.'

Monique swallowed. 'I understand. I'm not sure how much help I'll be though.' She gave the same story as Trent about how tiring it was working at the gallery, which meant she liked a quiet night in.

'What about the neighbours? Would they have seen you come home? Been aware of your presence?'

She frowned. 'My landlady lives downstairs from me. I'm in a first-floor flat. We have a shared hallway. I think I did bump into her on my way in after work that Thursday.' She made a rueful face. 'Or it might have been the Friday.'

'And you were here with Mr Trent all day at work on the Friday and Saturday. Neither of you left the gallery?'

Monique confirmed the times and that they'd been together. 'And on the Sunday I went into town, shopping,' she said. 'I bought a dress, so I have the receipt if you'd like me to find it?'

Completely useless… 'There shouldn't be any need, thanks.' She was going to have to let Monique go straight back to the gallery and leave the place feeling sure there was something out of kilter, without knowing what. Maybe Blake's mother would solve the mystery later. The thought was the opposite of comforting.

As she imagined the art historian wandering around, casting her expert eye over Trent's contents, the image of the front gallery filled her mind again, lighter than before. And then suddenly she realised what had caused the difference. Luke Cope's painting had been taken down. Of course – it made sense. Presumably Jonny Trent wouldn't be allowed to sell any more of his work until probate had gone through. She mentioned the matter to Monique, who nodded.

'Yes, you're quite right, it's come down,' she said. 'It's amazing what a difference it makes, isn't it, having a sunny pastoral scene up there instead?'

'And Luke's painting will be taken back to Matthew Cope, I presume?'

But Monique shook her head. 'In the ordinary way it would have been, but I understand Matthew's agreed that Jonny can buy it.' She smiled. 'I think he might have let him have it for a reduced price, but Jonny would have bought it anyway. He runs this place as a business, but he really does love art, and when it comes to his personal collection it's his own taste that governs what he purchases, not the potential value.'

Blake had mentioned that Jonny Trent claimed to rate Luke Cope's work, so it fitted, but Tara still couldn't imagine the man doing anything for such a pure reason.

'I wonder if he's more sentimental than any of us realises, too,' Monique said. 'It's the last thing we had left of Luke.' She looked down at the table. 'I hardly knew him, but this business with Freya is so tragic. I can only imagine he killed her in a moment of madness and then couldn't live with himself. Such waste.'

They got up and Tara followed Monique back towards the front of the building. Trent was with a client when they reappeared.

'Ah,' he said, looking up, 'and here's our gallery manager, Monique Courville, who will assist you.'

He'd given the woman Freya's title then. He probably wanted to make quite sure she knew she was on the front line, with a duty to shield him from any mundane work he didn't fancy.

Monique switched straight back into professional mode, Tara noticed. She flashed the visitor – a tall, gaunt man with red hair and goatee to match – a charming, toothpaste-advertisement smile, and though she looked smart and conventional, and he a bit of hipster, he clearly warmed in response to her greeting and outstretched hand.

As Jonny Trent showed Tara out, she tried to imagine him having a sentimental side. It wasn't happening. Once again, she wondered at Monique's view of her boss, but then if working with someone was a big part of your life it made sense to make the best of it. Even if it meant lying to yourself.

CHAPTER THIRTY-FOUR

Before she went back to the station to share updates, Tara headed to Matthew Cope's home. She'd called ahead and found he'd been given compassionate leave from work. She strained to see the way ahead as she drove. Visibility was down to a few metres, the surroundings shrouded in fog.

'It was kind of you to sell Luke's painting to Jonny Trent,' she said, when he'd let her in. The gallery owner must have been bloody quick off the mark to request it, given the timing.

Matthew shook his head. 'He rang as soon as he heard the news to offer his condolences. I'm not even sure how he got my number. He mentioned that he'd take the painting down and keep it for me, unless I wanted to sell it. He said he'd always loved it and it would be something to remember Luke by.' He looked at Tara. 'I'm surprised he'd want to remember him, considering what he's done. But I told him to have the painting, by all means. I've got lots more. He insisted on paying something for it, so we reached an agreement.'

Tara explained her mission.

'You surely don't think someone else was involved?'

She trotted out the same explanation she'd given the others – passing the checks off as red tape – but Matthew's dark eyes told her he'd seen through her spiel.

On the night of Thursday twenty-second of February, he said, he'd stopped off on his way through town for a beer, sometime in the early evening. He'd stayed on for a bit, as he'd done his commute by bus that day. The landlord of the Clarendon Arms, near the bus station, might remember. And she already had his movements for the rest of the weekend.

By the time she reached Parkside police station she'd also spoken to Zach Cross again. He was still off work too, so she saw him at his home in Newnham. When she asked where he'd been on the Thursday night he told her he'd stayed in all evening with Freya, and then burst into tears. Nothing else he said was much help either, though he did mention he'd been out with a friend from his department on the Saturday night for a drink. Tara would be interested to know how he'd seemed, the night after his wife had been killed.

Back at the station, Tara reviewed the information she'd got to pass on to Blake, Megan and Max. She was sure it was going to be disappointing compared with what they'd managed to get hold of. She called the guy Zach Cross had met with on the Saturday evening, desperate for something more. She hoped her actions wouldn't come back to haunt her. Claiming her enquiry was alibi checking was stretching a point. There was nothing to suggest either Freya or Luke had been killed that night.

When she, Blake, Megan and Max were back together they exchanged their news.

Blake raised an eyebrow when she told him Monique Courville was still talking up her boss.

'My mother says that last time she dropped into the gallery she saw Jonny Trent harassing Freya – or at least, invading her physical space. Monique was there too, and my mother didn't see him treating her the same way, but I couldn't see him stopping at one. D'you think there's any chance Monique reciprocates his feelings, if I'm right and he's come on to her too?'

'Don't,' Tara said, 'you're making my flesh crawl. The alternative is that she's making the best of things. She clearly needs the cash from her job, so I'd guess she's stuck, one way or another.' She felt for her. She'd been in a similar position when she'd worked for *Not Now* magazine. You couldn't live off fresh air. Still, she'd got her own back eventually.

Blake frowned. 'What did the academic Zach Cross met say about their evening out that Saturday? I presume you managed to dig up more than just confirmation that they were together?' There was a slight smile in his eyes and Tara switched off her response to it. *Almost* as soon as it started. She noticed Megan's eyes were on her, her look unreadable.

'He was oddly forthcoming,' Tara had to admit. 'Not much digging required.' The guy had seemed glad she'd called, as though he felt he had something to say, but hadn't liked to pick up the phone.

'He told me Professor Cross got very drunk. Then he paused and said they both did. Struggling with loyalty, I think. Bottom line is, Cross had way more than he normally would, and the friend, another professor – Guy French – suspected something was up.'

They all looked at each other.

'But given by his own admission he thought his wife had gone off with another man, that seems like natural behaviour,' Tara added.

'And maybe he'd have been more likely to stay at home that night if he had killed Freya,' Megan said.

Tara nodded. 'Though I gather the professors' "lads' night out" had been in the diary a while, so he might have thought ducking out of it would look suspicious.'

Blake relayed his visit to Imogen Field. 'She was very matter-of-fact, very honest-seeming. She didn't gloss over her knowledge of how people inject heroin, for instance. She told me she hasn't seen Luke for months and that she didn't know the mill existed.'

Tara could see the hesitation in Blake's eyes. He couldn't pull the woman up on anything, she guessed, but he still wasn't sure he could trust her.

'That painting,' he said. 'The one Luke did of her struggling to free herself from a noose.'

With no hope of success.

'I had another look at the photographs the tech team took of the picture afterwards. The backdrop is at the mill.' His eyes met Tara's. 'She's hanging from a beam in the room where one of the millstones is still present. It doesn't prove she was ever there, of course, apart from in her ex's imagination.'

But it made you think, all the same. Someone had found out about Luke's secret getaway. What if Imogen Field had been to see Cope more recently than she was admitting? She had the motive and knowledge to kill both Freya and her ex. Tara could see why Blake was hesitating.

'Oscar Cross was interesting,' Megan said. 'The guy clearly thought he was giving off a really laid-back vibe but I'd swear he was hiding something. He was leaning back in his chair, smiling even, but his fists were clenched. When we walked off, down his corridor, I heard one of his "mates" laughing at his expense. I wonder if he has a hard time at college.'

Blake explained how the needle used on Luke had probably been diabetic-sized, according to Imogen Field. 'I cross-checked the notes the CSIs provided and they described the needle type differently, but it turns out they're one and the same. It might not mean anything.'

He sat back in his chair, his dark eyes on the middle distance, and took a swig of his coffee. 'The other item of interest that's just come into my hands is Luke Cope's bank records.'

Tara sat forward, waiting for him to share his spoils. She couldn't help it – when someone else had information she lacked, it was almost unbearable.

Blake flipped open his laptop. 'So, the surprise is, he really was selling jewellery, by the look of it. There are a few transfers into his account from a couple of jewellers in town.'

Tara raised an eyebrow. 'A few?' It didn't match the story Matthew had relayed, of Luke having inherited one stand-out item that he'd sold.

'Several. And there are also other deposits by cheque which we'll need to trace to their source. I'm wondering if they represent similar sales – to individuals maybe.'

'What sort of amounts of money are we talking?' She'd cut across Megan slightly. The woman closed her mouth again with a sidelong glance at Tara. She'd probably been about to ask the same question. Tara hadn't meant to drown her out, but Blake always encouraged them to chip in without hesitating. She had a feeling Megan's preferred approach would have been different.

'No single, large sum that would account for his move back into the family home as Matthew described it,' Blake said, 'but each individual transaction was for anything from five hundred to a couple of thousand. And they add up.' He raised an eyebrow.

'It would be interesting to know if Luke Cope's mother insured her jewellery. Or if there's any other way of getting an idea of exactly what she had,' Max said.

'When Matthew mentioned it, he said his mother had left him a few nice pieces too,' Tara put in. 'In which case, I guess her will must have itemised them.' Though when Matthew had told her that story she'd wondered if he'd made it up, to save face. Perhaps Luke had been his mother's favourite. From the way Blake had relayed Imogen Field's evidence, it sounded as though he'd been both brilliant and charming. His mum might not have seen his darker side.

'We'll need to find out,' Blake said. 'Has anyone got anything else before we carry on?'

'An update from the team who're continuing the interviews with Luke's neighbours,' Max said. 'They've found someone who thinks they saw him leave his street by car – alone – on Thursday twenty-second of February.'

The night his vehicle was caught on camera later, with a passenger…

'But they can't be absolutely sure it was the same day.' Max pulled a face.

'And the deep dig for information on the Flag and Diamond produced something,' Megan said. 'Though I'm afraid it's thin. And it might not even be relevant, if Luke really was getting his spare cash from selling jewellery rather than drugs.' Tara watched Blake, sitting forward on the edge of his seat, and knew he was restraining himself from telling her to spit it out. 'I've found one news feature on drug-related violence and crime which mentions the pub,' Megan continued, glancing down at her notes. 'The article refers to a mugging that led to the death of an eighty-five-year-old. The perpetrator was called Gavin Rawlings, and one of the newspaper's interviewees knew him from the Flag and Diamond. He told the reporter Gavin wouldn't have meant to hurt the woman. Described him as a gentle soul, at the mercy of his drug addiction and the need to get money for his next fix.'

Blake's eyes were on Megan. 'His next fix being?'

'Heroin, apparently.'

Interesting, I'll give you that. But Megan was right – despite Luke's apparent links to the pub and his death from the same drug, the connections were still tenuous.

'We should keep it in mind,' Blake said. 'For all we know, Luke's killer's not even on our radar yet. He could still be a connection through the pub.' He put his head in his hands. 'Just because we've got a paper trail that shows Cope was selling jewellery doesn't mean that's all there is to it.' He looked at them in turn. 'So many medium-value transactions looks like a front to me. So let's run through our suspects. We've got Zach Cross, who was pretty certain his wife was having an affair with Luke Cope, and Oscar Cross, who disapproved of his father's marriage to Freya. And then there's Imogen Field.' He paused and sipped his coffee, a double espresso, Tara guessed. She could never work out why he wasn't constantly bouncing off the walls.

'Then we have Vicky Cope, who stands to inherit Luke's house now that he's dead,' he went on. 'But I can't see why she'd kill Freya. Similarly, Matthew Cope inherits Luke's paintings and any other odds and bits we might not know about. But however much they're worth, he wouldn't need Freya dead in order to benefit either. And then, for me, the big question mark. Jonny Trent at the gallery. Monique Courville says Freya's argument was with Luke Cope. She heard them rowing. But given that it was at work, and Freya was shouting about how stupid Luke had been, my bet is the reason for the upset related to the gallery. Trent knew them both; he was definitely frightened when I first turned up, and I'm certain he's keeping something from us. Plus, the man makes my skin crawl. Anyone I've missed? Any comments?'

Megan didn't look as though she was about to leap in, so Tara did. 'So you're thinking this might still be drugs-related? Perhaps Luke supplied heroin and was paid in untraceable, legitimately bought jewellery? Whoever was supplying Luke would probably be ruthless enough to kill him and Freya, even if they only suspected she might know the truth.'

'But the drugs angle is seriously thin,' Megan said.

Tara had been thinking the same herself, moments earlier, but for a second she still felt affronted.

'That said,' Max put in, 'the guy I spoke to at the Flag and Diamond was warning me off, that's for sure. He had me down as a copper – maybe as a new boy: wanting to make something of myself but easily intimidated.'

Tara laughed. 'Or so he hoped. Poor judge of character, clearly.'

Max grinned at her, and she smiled back.

When Tara looked up, both Blake and Megan's eyes were on her. Something in Blake's expression reminded her she was still angry with him.

'I suppose we need to think who from our list of suspects might have gone with Luke to the mill,' Megan said.

Blake nodded. 'I can't honestly see him taking Oscar Cross over there for an evening of drinking and nut-eating. Why would he? There's no evidence they knew each other, and they're not even close in age. But Zach Cross? Even though they weren't on friendly terms he might have been able to swing it. Maybe if they'd met somewhere else first, had a drink, buried the hatchet. Zach could have pretended to be interested in Luke's artwork maybe. If his ego was big enough, it might have made him overlook the danger he was in. But why the mill? Why wouldn't they just go to his house in town?'

'So maybe Imogen Field's more likely?' Tara said. 'Perhaps she got dolled up, convinced him she wanted one final rerun of their affair and suggested the mill because it was romantic. We've only got her word that she didn't know about it.'

Blake nodded. 'It's possible.'

'And surely Jonny Trent from the gallery is just as likely?' Megan said. 'There's every possibility Freya knew about the mill, as Luke's current girlfriend, and she could easily have mentioned it at work. It was clearly inspiring his output, so it was a relevant topic. And all the clues we needed to figure out its location were right there in the gallery. We joined the dots, so he might have too.'

Blake nodded his agreement again. 'And I could also imagine him taking Vicky or his brother over there – but not why they'd need to commit this double crime, as I say. No... I like your thinking on Jonny Trent.'

Megan Maloney beamed. Tara was starting to find her smile irritating. She snapped her mind into neutral. She wasn't going to be thrown off course because of her feelings. It was true, she could imagine Jonny going off to carouse with Luke. And that the gallery owner might have some kind of motive. Hell, it could even be pure jealousy, given Blake's mum had seen Jonny pawing at Freya. He probably wished he could have what Luke was having. For a second, all-encompassing anger rushed through her, hot and powerful. Maybe he'd intended to kill Luke, then meet Freya in his place and give it a go. She'd put up a struggle, insulted him and he'd hit her with that stone before killing her. It might have played out like that…

'What about the way Freya was attacked?' Megan said. 'Do we need to look at that? The fact that her killer stunned her before strangling her?' It was as though the woman had read her mind. 'It might indicate the perpetrator was physically different to Luke Cope, in an obvious way, even in the dark. They'd need to act quickly to subdue her in that case, before she realised she'd been tricked.'

Jonny Trent was probably just as tall as Luke Cope had been, but pretty portly compared with the artist. But Tara wasn't sure Megan's hypothesis was right. 'If Freya got to the nature reserve first she'd have been on high alert,' she said. 'No one stands around in that sort of place late at night letting their mind wander. In the quiet, the slightest noise gets your attention. So the moment her murderer arrived all her focus would have been trained on him – or her.' A woman could have tucked long hair into a cap or under a scarf; the weather had been so cold. 'My bet is that even a killer the same build as Luke Cope would have to have acted fast. Freya would have known in a moment that the person walking towards her wasn't her lover.'

She imagined the woman's feelings: she'd have assumed for a moment that the person was simply another local, out for a breath of fresh air before bed. But then they'd have approached with hurried steps, making straight for her, and fear would have kicked in…

No one responded to her point, and a moment later, Blake let the team go. She wondered if everyone thought she was arguing for the sake of it. But she was sure she was right. The fact that anyone might think she was being childish brought her anger back.

CHAPTER THIRTY-FIVE

Patrick Wilkins was walking along St Andrew's Street in the centre of town, towards *Not Now* magazine's offices. It was nearly lunchtime and the pavement was crowded with office workers, scurrying into sandwich shops. When the hell was the weather going to get better? The damp of the fog played havoc with his hair.

It was as he crossed over Downing Street, towards John Lewis, that he saw a figure he recognised. Mostly, he didn't find pregnant women attractive, but DI Blake's wife, Babette, was an unusual specimen. She managed to look voluptuous. He wondered when she was due – she had to be quite far along. She was leaning down to talk to a small child – her and Blake's daughter, Patrick assumed. Strands of her golden hair had fallen forward. As she stood upright again she caught him watching her, and a smile of recognition crossed her face.

From the warmth of her expression, Wilkins guessed Blake hadn't mentioned his suspension. Unless Babette didn't remember who he was. They had met – at a staff drinks do only last year. For a moment, the thought that she might not be able to place him set anger bubbling up in his gut. But it had been a busy event. And it made sense to be friendly if that was how she was going to play it. It was too good an opportunity to ignore – chatting to the DI's beautiful wife, Babette the babe.

'Mrs Blake.' He walked forward, holding out his hand formally, whilst giving her a smile that also took in her daughter. Women liked it when you included their kids – treated them as though they mattered. 'Patrick Wilkins, from the Cambridgeshire Constabulary.'

He found he couldn't bring himself to put his subordinate position in relation to her husband into words.

'Of course – I remember you.'

Patrick wondered. *Did she? Or was she just well versed in managing people?* She probably didn't have a clue whether he was a DS or the Chief Constable.

'And please,' she added, her own smile widening, 'do call me Babette.'

'Well, it's lovely to bump into you again, Babette.' He bent down to look at the little girl, who had mid-brown hair with ringlets. *Sickly sweet*, Patrick thought. 'And who's this?'

The girl – she could have been anywhere from five to eight, Patrick had no idea how you could tell – clung to her mother's camel-coloured coat, half hiding behind her. *God, he hated it when kids did that. What did they think? That he was some sort of child molester? Did he look dangerous?*

But Babette laughed. 'She's shy. This is mine and Garstin's daughter, Kitty.'

Garstin. Patrick tended to forget his DI had such a ridiculous first name. He made most people call him Blake – if it wasn't 'boss', or 'sir'. He could see why. What mother would give a kid a handle like that?

He was tempted to back off, but he felt he had to keep going now, even if he couldn't convince the child he was all right, so he bent down again slightly, without fully committing himself, and smiled at her. 'Hello, Kitty. Pleased to meet you.'

The girl's grip on her mother's clothes loosened just a little, and slightly more of her face became visible. Patrick sought inspiration and at last had it, when his eyes lit on Babette's pregnant stomach again.

'You must be very excited that you'll have a baby brother or sister soon,' he said.

It seemed to have been a good move. A cautious smile spread across the little girl's face now, and she nodded. 'Mummy says it will be here in time for the summer,' she said.

He was ashamed at the relief he felt that Blake's daughter had accepted him. *How pathetic. Why had he even stopped to talk to them?*

'That's very exciting,' he finished, lamely.

The little girl nodded, setting her ringlets quivering. 'It is. Daddy was very excited when we told him. It was a big surprise.'

Babette laughed. 'It was a lovely surprise all round!' She ruffled the daughter's hair. 'Come along, sweetie. We need to go into John Lewis and get some baby gear.' She turned to Patrick. 'She's off school officially – just a cold – but I should march on with the shopping, so I can get her home again. Being out in this weather probably isn't the best idea.'

The child didn't look very ill. Patrick's mother had never let him go out when he was off school.

As they walked away, and he pressed on towards *Not Now*'s offices, he played the last bit of their conversation over in his mind. *'A lovely surprise'... very interesting.* People added to their families by accident all the time, of course. Patrick had vaguely gathered over the years that he himself had been the result of an unplanned pregnancy – he was the youngest of five. And Babette had clearly tried to pass their situation off as something similar.

But that didn't explain why it had been she and Kitty *together* who'd broken the news to Blake. *Daddy was very excited when we told him. It was a big surprise.* What woman told their child about a pregnancy before the father? Assuming Blake was the father. Babette must have been holding the news back for some reason. If he could get at the truth it might be worth his while...

He was thinking so hard that he almost walked past the entrance to the magazine's premises, between two of the shops on St Andrew's Street.

As he climbed the stairs to the first floor and pressed the buzzer he felt even more pleased with the way the day was progressing.

Five minutes later he was in Giles Troy's office with a skinny latte in front of him.

Giles raised an eyebrow. 'What have you decided?'

Patrick took a sip of the coffee and felt better than he had done in weeks. 'That a new career awaits. And that I'm happy to work with your proposal.'

A lazy grin crossed Giles's face. 'Excellent. I'm delighted that I'll be your first client.' He raised his coffee cup. 'Here's to making Tara Thorpe's life uncomfortable.'

'Amen to that.' He raised his drink, too.

Tara was standing by the coffee machine at the station, queueing for an after-lunch pick-me-up, when the text from Matt, her old colleague at *Not Now*, came in. He was the only person on the staff that she'd kept in touch with. As workmates, it had been their habit to let off steam about their boss, Giles Troy, over long evenings at the pub.

How goes it? That policeman guy who caused all the trouble's been in and out of here like it's his second home of late. I wanted to warn you in case something's up. He's just left the building with Giles. The boss said something about having cause for celebration.

What the hell was Wilkins up to? The news was more than ominous.

She was so distracted she hadn't noticed it was her turn at the coffee machine until Max – who was just behind her – nudged her elbow.

When he saw her face, he put a hand on her shoulder. 'Everything all right?'

She turned her phone so he could see Matt's message. Max frowned and shook his head.

'Wilkins is an arch stirrer,' Tara said, 'who hates people making him look small.' She pulled a face. 'And I've certainly done that – with Kemp's help. As for Giles, he'll hold his grudge against me until he's in his grave. Or I am. I feel as though I'm the common denominator, and whatever they're planning, I'll be at the centre of it. But I might not be the only one to suffer.'

When Shona Kennedy had written her poisonous article about Tara just before Christmas it had thrown a bad light on the whole team – and made Blake look like a two-timing lothario to boot.

Max gave her shoulder a squeeze and smiled before he took his hand away again. 'You can't stop people like them,' he said, 'but they're ten a penny. It happens all the time. The force has got broad shoulders and it looks after its own. If anything happens it'll be dealt with just as calmly as it was the last time. And six months down the line, it'll all be forgotten.'

She didn't quite believe him, but she appreciated his attempt to make her feel better. For all that life had thrown at him he was always calm and grounded. Tara took a deep breath.

'Thank you.' It didn't seem adequate, but when her eyes met his she somehow knew he'd got the message – and understood just how much she meant it.

She let the machine dispense her drink and then started the walk back to her desk. She was halfway along the corridor when she noticed Megan. Instead of going back to the room the team shared, the DS moved towards the station's main entrance and beckoned Tara to follow. She did so, taking a quick sip of her hot, black coffee, which was threatening to spill.

When they'd both come to a standstill, Megan opened her mouth, but then closed it again. She didn't look happy.

'Is there something wrong?' Tara asked. She didn't think she'd injected any antagonism into her tone.

Megan's dark eyes met Tara's. 'We just need to be careful of Max's feelings. That's all. He works for me and I've got his back.' She made it sound like a threat.

O-kay. So, Tara had been right about the connection she'd sensed between Megan and her fellow DC then – even if it was mainly felt by Megan, perhaps. And presumably she'd seen Tara and Max's interaction at the coffee machine and overreacted, big time.

'No problem,' Tara said. 'I agree with you. Max is the best friend I have here – I'd never be careless of his well-being.'

She turned and walked smartly back towards her desk. Thank goodness she'd already drunk her coffee down to a reasonable level. It would have been a shame to lose her dignity by slopping it everywhere.

CHAPTER THIRTY-SIX

Professor Antonia Blake wasn't worried about Jonny Trent recognising her: it had been months since she'd visited his gallery, and all the slimeball's attention had been on Freya Cross, in any case. But when it came to the crunch she decided to dump the turquoise and navy geometric tunic she'd been wearing over thick tights and boots and – going completely against the grain – change into the most boring, presentable skirt and jumper combination she owned. After a moment's hesitation, she added a set of pearls she'd inherited from her grandmother. Well-to-do but artistically ignorant was the image she wanted to convey.

An hour later, in the foyer of the gallery, she decided the effort had been wasted. Antonia doubted that Jonny Trent saw women in technicolour – separating out those that might be rich but clueless from potential experts in the field. She guessed the groupings he used were more basic: women he found sexually attractive and those he didn't. As he'd welcomed her in, he'd put a guiding arm around her shoulders, close to her but not touching, just to steer her in the right direction. But Antonia knew how to walk from the car park into the building. *Patronising* and *a predator*. It made her blood boil.

As they passed through the gallery hallway, a well-presented but unimaginatively dressed young woman joined them, accompanied by a balding man with grey hair, wearing jeans and a shirt. She recognised the female from her previous visit.

'Good morning,' the woman said to Antonia, with a bright smile, before turning to the gallery owner. 'Mr Fisk would like to see the back gallery now, Jonny.'

Trent beamed. 'Excellent, excellent.' He turned to Antonia. 'In that case, I'll leave you in my gallery manager Monique Courville's capable hands for the moment. Please, Mr Fisk,' he turned to the other visitor, 'follow me.' He began to manoeuvre away, whilst smiling at Antonia over his shoulder. Thinking of her son, and his mission, which might include putting one over on this horrible man, she managed to smile back. The sort of fixed grin she saved for buttering up the necessary people in her faculty. At which point Trent gave her a little wave. 'I do hope you'll follow us through, once you've finished out here,' he said. 'The back gallery's my pet project. I'd love to show it to you.'

'That would be wonderful,' she replied, skilfully supressing a shudder.

Monique Courville stepped forward now, her expression warm. It was a veneer put on for customers, clearly, but that was fair enough. They were running a business and there was no reason why either of them should be genuinely pleased to interact with her.

'Feel free to ask me any questions,' Monique said. 'We have information sheets here that detail the works that are on display, but I can tell you more about the artists and their backgrounds, which ones will take on personal commissions and so on.'

Antonia nodded, whilst trying to look vague. The work on show was all right – nothing she'd have been tempted to shell out for though, even if she'd had the money. Nonetheless, she peered closely at each piece in turn and asked a couple of questions. Monique accompanied her to the middle room where they followed the same pattern.

There was nothing that struck her as off – except perhaps that it was a large building to maintain and they had no stand-out works that were likely to bring in really big money.

'I think perhaps I will take up Mr Trent's suggestion now, and look at the back gallery,' Antonia told Monique.

The woman's smile faded ever so slightly, but she jacked it up again almost immediately. 'Of course.'

Antonia guessed Courville got commission on paintings sold from the main rooms, but no doubt not from Jonny Trent's 'pet project'.

The room at the back of the building was a revelation. It felt quite separate to the rest of the gallery – visitors had to go through two doors to get to it. These were both propped open with wooden wedges, but not to their fullest extent, so that you felt you were going somewhere slightly secret. The interior of the back gallery reminded her of a Paris flea market. The whole room was crowded with works of art – some mounted on the dark-red walls, lit by the glow of soft lamps, and many more stored in folding display racks that sat on the floor. Even she could feel its draw, old cynic that she was. It held that promise that you might find a bargain, an undiscovered treasure. For her, she'd be living in anticipation of stumbling across a new artist, as yet unrecognised by the establishment.

She gave Jonny Trent a smile as she entered the room. He smiled back, making her feel clammy all over. *The things you did for your children.*

As she'd expected, Trent was still dealing with his other visitor. The balding man was staring down at one of the paintings in the folding rack and biting his lip.

Torn, clearly. She could see the agony of indecision on his face and wondered what he'd spotted. At last he raised his eyes to meet the gallery owner's again. 'I'm going to think about it.'

Trent gave a wide smile, reminding Antonia of a frog.

'By all means,' he said. 'As I say, I wasn't intending to sell it today in any case. Ideally, I'd like to get an independent expert to look at it before I let it go. Believe it or not, I'm one of those people who buys on instinct. I'm not formally trained to value what we sell. My gallery manager knows her onions, of course – one of us has to. Personally, I operate on passion. This is my little find, my gamble. I don't suppose it's worth anything like what I hope, but buying it is my version of a flutter. For some, it's betting on the races, for me, it's art. You never know, maybe one day I'll make a packet! If you see in the papers that I've sold this one for millions then you'll know I finally got it right.'

The man in the jeans had been backing off, but now he looked at the painting again. More of the lip-chewing.

Antonia tried to glimpse the work they were talking about without moving closer. If she showed any interest she'd probably push the would-be buyer over the brink. Whatever Jonny Trent's game was, she didn't want to help him with it.

At last, the man turned and left the room. Antonia let Trent catch her interested look and then pottered over to where the other visitor had been standing. She found it hard to control her expression as she glanced down at the canvas. She ran her tongue over her lips and raised her eyes for a second to meet Trent's.

'I'm rather fond of it,' Trent said. His look drifted away from her for a moment. 'I don't suppose it could be the genuine article for a minute, but I should know by next week.'

'So you won't sell it now?'

The gallery owner shrugged his rounded shoulders. 'I've priced it quite highly. If someone's convinced they want to take a gamble, then I might let it go. After all, I could be wrong.' He let out a low laugh. 'Though I'll be kicking myself round the room this time next week if you take it off my hands and it turns out I finally backed a winner. I should probably hang onto it.'

'But a bird in the hand is worth two in the bush,' Antonia said, raising an eyebrow. 'You'll have done well if it turns out to be an imitation, or something done by an admirer.'

The man shrugged. 'Well, I suppose that's true… I wasn't even going to put it out today. One of the gallery hands was helping me shift stuff and it got mixed up with the other works.'

'It might be fate then,' Antonia said. It was a good fake. No signature. Based on one of Picasso's lesser-known paintings – one of the collection his electrician had had squirrelled away in his garage. The man had been accused of stealing them after the works were found in 2015. The treasure trove had been worth an estimated $98 million. Antonia moved the canvas gently so that she could see the back. Rusted nails – deliberately aged no doubt, and a nice touch. A stained label detailing an exhibition date in Paris, completed using an old-style manual typewriter. She caught her breath at the audacity of it. She met the gallery owner's gaze again. It was clear that Trent had taken her gasp as excitement rather than shock.

'I really shouldn't let it go,' he said, stepping forward. 'What if it's the genuine article after all?'

'What are you asking for it?'

'It's not really for sale.'

She was tempted to play with him – walk away like the other client had done. But she wanted to know what happened next.

'How much would you take to let it go now? I know nothing about art either.' *You'll wish I didn't.* 'But it does look interesting, and I like a gamble too. And it will be a gamble. There's no signature, after all.'

And even then, the art world was a murky one. Picasso had reportedly knowingly signed a painting that wasn't his to help out a gallery owner friend, whose wealthy client believed she'd coughed up for the real thing.

'True…' Trent spun the word out and frowned. Antonia saw his eyes flick for a second to her pearls – real, not cultured. 'But given what a gamble it would be for me, I don't think I could let it go for less than eighteen thousand.'

Antonia must look classier than she'd realised. If only Jonny Trent knew she was on a professor's salary. She managed to swallow back a laugh.

'That's a lot of money.'

Trent nodded. 'It is. I wouldn't blame you if you wanted to walk away. But I think I'd be a fool to let it go for less.'

At last, Antonia nodded. 'I have a feeling I'll regret this, but it's not something I've ever done before, and what's life if you never take a risk?'

Trent smiled with just the right amount of hesitancy. 'If you're sure.'

She nodded.

'Please do come through to my office then, and we can sort out the paperwork.'

And it was the paperwork that Antonia especially wanted to see. The ledger Trent got out and filled in described the painting as 'Artist unconfirmed. In the manner of Pablo Picasso.'

So neat. She noticed that the ledger was new. Was that the only one they had, or was there another, that contained the records of their legitimate sales? Was he keeping this little sideline a secret from his gallery manager? And had the previous post-holder found out the truth?

Antonia wasn't given to feeling afraid. She'd dealt with a lot of flak over the years. Her husband had turned abusive before their split, and her views got her endless hate from various male colleagues and critics, but this was something else. Trent was onto a valuable racket here; he had a lot to lose. And he'd told her no lies. He was relying on self-deception and clever psychology. If he got a reputation for this sort of thing, it might not land him in jail but it would certainly mean he'd go out of business. But probably the people he duped were too embarrassed to come back and admit how easily they'd been conned. And they had no way of proving Trent hadn't sold them the works in good faith.

'I'll give you a cheque, shall I?' she said. She could go straight to her bank and cancel it, but she didn't expect he'd accept that form of payment.

'I'm afraid I'll need a bank transfer,' he said, 'but you can arrange it now.'

She took a deep breath. 'You know what will happen, don't you? I'll get one of those wretched security calls they make, and I won't be able to remember any of my "memorable" details.' She let out a sharp sigh. 'If I write you a cheque for a deposit now and leave the painting with you, please will you promise not to sell it to anyone else whilst I go to my bank in the village and get them to sort it all out for me?'

'Of course,' Trent said, smiling as Antonia wrote a cheque for a thousand pounds.

Two could play at deception.

After she'd left, Antonia made two calls. The first was to her bank to stop the cheque. The second was to Garstin, telling him he might like to get straight over to Trent's gallery, with some backup and a warrant, in case the painting mysteriously went behind the scenes as soon as her back was turned.

CHAPTER THIRTY-SEVEN

Tara felt shut out. Blake and Megan were closeted in an interview room with Jonny Trent, whilst Max had been put in charge of liaising with the art experts and other technical staff who'd got permission to dig into Jonny Trent's dealings.

Meanwhile, she'd been asked to speak to Vicky Cope, Matthew and Luke's half-sister, who stood to inherit Luke's house. It felt as though she'd been flung a loose end to tie up, to keep her busy whilst the others worked on the important stuff. She'd no intention of being a prima donna about it – the job needed completing – but, deep down, it still rankled.

She called Vicky Cope's patent law firm and asked to be put through.

The woman sounded strained. *'I've actually just arranged to meet my half-brother, Matthew,'* she said. *'And I've got to be back here for a drinks do with some overseas clients after that.'*

Tara wouldn't be thwarted in completing the one task she'd been given. 'Where are you meeting him? I wonder if I could join you immediately afterwards. Perhaps accompany you on your journey back to the office to grab a quick word?' She knew she was being pushy, but it *was* a murder investigation, even if Jonny Trent seemed the most likely candidate for perpetrator.

There was a momentary pause and the woman let out a sharp sigh. *'Oh, all right. I was going to go and grab a coffee with Matthew at Café Foy, by the river.'*

'That's fantastic. I do appreciate it. Tell me when to turn up and I can meet you there.'

'Okay.' Another sigh. *'We haven't seen each other in ages, but I don't think we'll need long. Give me an hour.'*

Tara was glad she'd cycled to work: it meant she could whizz over to the river in minutes. She sat at the station completing reports on her visit to Jonny Trent – the contents of which, from his purchase of Luke Cope's painting to Monique Courville's promotion, now seemed like old news. After that she wrote up her latest encounter with Professor Cross, but there was nothing in that that she found interesting. *An hour...* She wondered how long it would really take Vicky Cope to talk to her brother, and what they would say to each other. Not much, from what Ms Cope had said. It wasn't surprising; talk about an awkward conversation. *Hey, I'm so sorry your brother's dead, and apparently a murderer at that, but let's talk about the family home I'm about to inherit...* Not that she'd probably bring that up at this stage. She'd want to break the ice and express her sympathy, ahead of Luke's funeral.

Suddenly, Tara knew she wasn't going to wait until the appointed hour. Even if she could only watch Matthew Cope and his half-sister for a moment before they spotted her, she was too curious to forgo the opportunity. She couldn't see why either of them would want Freya dead, but now that she'd had the thought, she couldn't abandon it. It would be like leaving the job half done.

She locked her computer, got her fitted woollen coat and did up all the buttons, ready to brave the fog. It tended to be worse by the river.

Five minutes later, she'd chained her bike to the railings on Quayside, under the noses of the tall office buildings, with food outlets below. Across the river, the imposing dark shape of Magdalene College loomed out of the mist. Anything more than a few feet away was indistinct. Dark shapes gradually morphed into people, walking up the boardwalk, their shoulders hunched.

She approached Café Foy cautiously, peering through the window at an angle.

It took her a moment to spot Matthew Cope. His upright bearing was now familiar, but even at a distance she could see how tense his shoulders were. He was looking across his table at the woman who must be Vicky. Tara could only see her from behind, but her posture was taut too – she sat leaning well forward. Matthew was talking – the conversation hadn't run out. He had a cup, clenched in his hand, but he wasn't remembering to drink. She waited a few minutes, watching Matthew's face, until they paid the bill.

After another moment, they appeared outside, and Cope's eyes lit on Tara. His eyebrows went up before he turned to Vicky. There was some discussion. Tara guessed his half-sister hadn't explained they were meeting. There was no reason why she should have; she wouldn't have intended them to interact. Tara was ten minutes early and had taken them both by surprise. It was her old journalist's tactics coming into play. It was often worth disturbing people's plans if you wanted to get under their skin.

'I'm sorry,' she said, striding up to them. 'I'm a little bit early.'

Vicky looked cross. To be fair, she'd probably been trying to steer the conversation away from the criminal investigation. She let out one of the sharp sighs that were now becoming familiar, and reached into her coat pocket, pulling out a packet of Marlboro Lights.

'I'm sorry,' she said, turning to Matthew. 'Do you mind? Would you like one?'

Her half-brother shook his head. 'No thanks, I don't smoke, but please go ahead. This is all a massive strain on everybody.' He gave Tara a look as he uttered the words. 'I should be going. I'll let you two get on with your *chat*.'

There was an edge to his voice, but he must know the police would be talking to everyone.

Vicky Cope put back the lighter she'd used to ignite her cigarette and turned to him. 'I meant what I said you know, about the paintings.'

He faced her and shook his head. 'You're welcome to have as many as you want. I certainly won't let you pay me for them. After what's happened I can't imagine I'll want them hanging up on my walls.'

She put her head on one side and gave him a look. 'That's crazy. Just because you don't want them doesn't make them valueless. I'll find out for myself.' She pulled a mobile from her coat pocket with her free hand and began to tap in her PIN.

Matthew put a hand on hers for a moment, stopping her mid-entry. 'All right, you win. The large ones go for around four hundred each. Once the police have finished with the house you can come and choose one.'

She put her phone away and nodded quickly. 'Thank you. I'll do that.'

'I'll see you soon then.' He gave Vicky a brief pat on the shoulder, nodded at Tara with his eyes narrowed, and walked off towards town, disappearing into the fog.

The woman took a deep drag on her cigarette, its smoke mingling with the water droplets in the air. 'Shit.'

'A difficult meeting?'

Vicky Cope raised her eyes to heaven. 'Clumsy, on my part. I feel so bloody guilty, now I've got the business *and* the townhouse. How must he feel, stuck out at that weird place on the fringes of the city? It's a pile, but it's falling down from what I remember. I've only been there once. And it's in a rough area.'

'Is that why you offered to buy one of Luke's paintings?'

'Great! If it was that obvious to you, I'm sure it will have been to him, too. And four hundred quid's not exactly going to help.'

'But the house on Trumpington Road *was* your family home first. And Matthew's place belonged to his mother's parents, if I remember correctly.'

'True… but I got the business, too.' She glanced at Tara, looking up at her from under a thick, dark fringe. 'And it's a valuable one. Patent law firms do a lot of trade in Cambridge. People seem to come up with three inventions before breakfast.' She rolled her eyes.

'Did your father ever explain his thinking, about the provisions he made in his will?'

Vicky Cope shook her head. 'I suppose he didn't get the chance, really. He died relatively young. You knew that? After falling down stairs?'

Tara nodded.

'He simply told my mother what he'd done. And of course it didn't seem so uneven when we each had something. Though I always felt that Matthew had drawn the short straw.'

'And you can't imagine yourself why your father divided things up in the way that he did, and left the houses to the boys in trust? I understand you get Luke's place outright now?'

Vicky Cope closed her eyes for a moment and took another drag of her cigarette before opening them again and facing the world. 'I suppose I got the impression I did a bit better than them academically. I wondered if that was why I got the business.' She gave a quick bark of a laugh. 'It was certainly the only bequest that involved serious hard work. And it was clear Luke had a talent for art, from when he was a teenager, so I guess our father wouldn't have wanted to doom him to life in an office.'

But that still didn't explain why Matthew hadn't got a look-in.

'Did you miss your family home?'

'I did, but it was the idea that I was hankering after, not the reality. I can see that now. My father made my mother miserable – I wasn't missing some idyllic past. Mum and I never set foot in the place after we left. I went to my father's funeral, of course, but we didn't go back for the wake. My mother didn't want to, and I didn't want to abandon her.'

Tara nodded. 'How old were you then?'

'Twenty-four. The boys – Matthew and Luke – were twenty and eighteen. But I was in and out of Cambridge all through my teens. My mother moved us to Suffolk after the split, but I came in to shop and see friends.' She sighed. 'I'd go and look at the house sometimes, from the outside. I think, because I'd never been back, it held a sort of fascination for me. Occasionally I'd glimpse some movement through the windows. Once I saw Luke coming outside, smoking, and I heard his mother, telling him off.'

'Do you still visit the house at all, just to look?' She wondered if Vicky could possibly know about Luke's hideaway at the mill. If she'd loitered round outside and followed him, it wasn't impossible.

'Oh good lord, no! I gave up that malarkey with acne and bad boyfriends.' She laughed now, but Tara wondered. There was something deliberate about the action – and if you'd been compulsively spying on a place throughout your childhood, wouldn't you be tempted to do it again, just once in a while? It wasn't as though she'd have to go out of her way. She worked in Cambridge, after all.

'Did you ever see your half-brothers as you were growing up? Socially I mean?'

'Once in a very blue moon. My mother and father thought it would be good for us to meet. But it was always very stilted.'

'What were your impressions of them?'

'Luke was rebellious. He didn't think the meet-ups were a good idea and he wasn't afraid to let it show. I agreed with him, so I wasn't offended. In fact, I felt he was a bit of a kindred spirit, only we were each so busy being stand-offish that we never formed a real bond.'

'What about Matthew?'

'He was more reserved, and that's true to this day.' She shook her head. 'I was cross when I saw you'd turned up. I didn't feel we'd said everything.' The woman fixed her with her gaze.

Tara waited, and at last Vicky sighed.

'I was hoping to round off our talk in private, but I don't suppose I'd feel any better about things if I had.' She shrugged. 'I guess I just want absolution – to know he doesn't hate me. But that's a bit childish really.'

Tara could relate to that. Half the feelings she had about her family would be quite at home in a five-year-old's head.

After Vicky Cope had faded into the fog, Tara checked her emails and messages. No one seemed to be telling her anything. If there was nothing for her to do, she decided she'd please herself. Whatever Jonny Trent's game was, Luke had been involved. If she returned to his house, she might find something fundamental that proved to be important. And deep down, she knew she was indulging her journalist's instinct too. The Cope family set-up was more than odd. If she'd still been a writer, she'd have dug into it for all she was worth.

Twenty minutes later, Luke's house loomed into view, tall and sombre in the saturated air. The police hadn't released it back to the artist's executors yet. Barry, the PC who'd been first on the scene when Freya's body had been found, was stationed on the door. Like Tara, his coat and hair were covered with tiny water droplets.

'Wotcha,' he said, clapping his gloved hands together and rubbing them. 'How's it going at the station?'

'I haven't heard the latest.' She didn't want to admit that she had no clue.

'You after going back inside? Max and some techs came to pick up a couple of paintings earlier, but there's no one in there at the moment.'

She nodded. 'I feel as though I've missed something. I'll be around for a bit if you want to go off and grab a coffee.'

His smile, already wide, broadened. 'That sounds good. I've got my thermals on, but this fog eats into your bones.'

'Go for it then. I can give you a call if you're not back by the time I need to go.'

'Perfect.'

He gave her the key and walked off up the road, his cheerful, tuneless whistle fading as the dark day swallowed his retreating figure.

Tara unlocked the house. Once she'd entered and closed the door behind her, it was almost dark. Little of what daylight there was filtered into the interior. She stood for a second, looking through the doorway to the front room, with its heavy William Morris curtains.

But it was only a moment before she turned to make her way back through the house to the eerie chaos of Luke Cope's studio. She spent some time there – switching on the stark lighting and searching all over again – but it didn't tell her anything new. She gave up and went from room to room, imagining what it must have been like growing up there. There was something oppressive about the stately grandeur that was still apparent in most of the house. She assumed Luke must have let it out furnished, after his mother had died. It would have been a hell of a job to put all that Chippendale-style polished wood into storage. He must have trusted his tenants to take care of it – or just not been bothered about its fate.

She stood at the bottom of the stairs, looking at the cold, hard tiles where Luke and Matthew's father had fallen to his death. At last, she started the climb to the first floor, her footsteps making no sound on the high-quality cushioned carpet. All around her, everything was quiet – as silent as the grave.

CHAPTER THIRTY-EIGHT

The moment his mother had called, Blake felt a massive piece of the puzzle had fallen into place. He was over at the gallery in less than fifteen minutes, screeching to a halt on the shingle driveway. The painting, as predicted, was nowhere to be seen, but they didn't need a warrant, given they were there to arrest Trent on suspicion of murder.

They found the artwork upstairs, in the man's private quarters. Most interestingly, it wasn't the only one. There were four more, each resembling the work of late nineteenth- or early twentieth-century artists. It would have been hard to prove that Trent knew the single Picasso lookalike was a fake, but four such paintings was way too much of a coincidence. With this little hoard, things weren't looking so sunny for him.

They'd left the gallery in the hands of the CSIs, Max and a couple of PCs. Monique Courville had left the premises on some kind of errand, apparently, just before they'd got there, but they were going to bring her in for questioning too, as soon as they reached her.

Now, Jonny Trent and his solicitor had joined Blake and Megan at the station for an interview. If he'd looked nervous the day Blake first met him, it was nothing to his demeanour now. He was twisting the gold ring on his right hand and chewing his lip. Blake could almost feel his held breath as though it were his own.

'We have an expert who says that all five paintings in your flat, which crudely imitate lesser known works by well-known artists, were in fact created by the same person.' Blake leant forward, his elbows on the table between them. 'And that person was Luke Cope.'

'You can't know that.' Trent was still attempting an airy bluster.

'That's an initial conclusion by an expert. We can bring in second opinions, and thirds. We can also look to trace the frames and the canvases that were used. And we can compare the paints between the fakes and Cope's works.' They'd need a warrant for that, given that it would involve scraping samples off the canvases, but Blake decided not to bother Trent with the details. 'And we've also got forensics looking at them.'

'Forensics?' Trent appeared surprised at the pitch of his own voice.

Blake smiled. 'Tacky paint's excellent at picking up fingerprints, fibres and all of that stuff. It'll be better for you if you're honest.' He stared into the gallery owner's piggy eyes. 'So, Luke painted the fakes for you. When did you make the deal? When he first came to visit you? You agreed to display his genuine works in pride of place in the main galleries, in exchange for the fakes in your back gallery. Was that it?'

Trent looked down at the table.

'Then Freya Cross found out – quite recently – what you'd managed to keep secret all this time. No wonder you were so precious about the back gallery being your pet project! The entries in your ledger looked innocent enough, individually. A single painting 'in the style of' a famous artist is one thing. But at some point, Freya must have noticed a pattern, and seen just how well you were doing out of the arrangement.'

A pattern. Suddenly he thought of Freya on the night she'd been killed, carrying the mysterious missing holdall. And then of the ledger they'd seized as evidence that morning: a brand new one, just as his mother had said.

'Freya somehow found out that it was Luke who'd been supplying you with fakes,' Blake said. 'Monique Courville heard them arguing about it. Freya asked Luke how he could have been so stupid.' Perhaps it had been after their row that Luke had painted the picture of his hands around Freya Cross's neck. Because she'd made him feel a fool? Because she hadn't 'understood' him? Blake felt a shiver of disgust run through his core. 'But because Freya was in love with Luke, instead of reporting you both, she stole the ledger, with its evidence of the past sales you'd made, and took it with her to meet him. I presume it was too bulky to get rid of at her house without raising questions, and she wouldn't have risked just throwing it away. She'd have wanted Luke to destroy it and promise to stop working for you. But it wasn't Luke who turned up to meet her.'

He paused for a moment, his throat dry. 'Our evidence is that Luke's suicide was faked, so we're looking for someone with a motive for killing both him and Freya.' It was all he could do to keep his seat when he thought back to the two dead bodies he'd seen; Freya's waxy skin, and Luke Cope's pecked eyeball. 'You fit the bill. You had no guarantee they'd keep your secret, and they had the ledger as proof. You'll face jail for what you've done, and your business and reputation will be in ruins.'

Trent's healthy colour had faded. His cheeks were slack and pallid with shock.

'When did you find out Freya knew your secret?'

'I—' He clearly felt the need to reply too urgently to think through what to say in advance. 'I didn't know. How would I know that she knew?'

'Oh come on!' The guy clearly took him for an idiot. 'I'm betting the first thing Luke did was to warn you you'd been found out. And we've searched your place, don't forget. My colleagues inform me that the meeting Freya Cross had marked on her kitchen calendar *was* in your desk diary too. So you did know she had something to discuss. Something so serious she booked an appointment rather than just knocking on your office door.'

'It could have been anything.' He was too slow. 'I…' Another long pause. 'I even wondered if she might want to ask about maternity leave. It's true!' A pathetic note of protest. He must have read Blake's expression correctly then.

'Besides,' Trent went on, 'wasn't Luke found dead in some place in the back of beyond – a bolthole no one knew existed?'

Blake raised an ironic eyebrow. 'Well, someone was clearly aware. You're telling me you had no idea about the place then?'

A splutter. 'How would I?'

Blake noticed the man's lawyer was trying to catch Trent's eye. He smiled again. 'That's a no, is it?'

'Of course it's a no,' Trent said. The lawyer's hand went down onto his arm just too late.

'That's fine then,' Blake said. 'Our tech guys will look at the journeys recorded on your satnav, but that won't cause you any problems, given what you've just told me.'

And now, Jonny Trent did look at his solicitor, and the solicitor looked back at him.

'I believe my client might like to revise his statement,' the lawyer said.

Nice.

CHAPTER THIRTY-NINE

At the top of the stairs in Luke Cope's house, Tara's gaze swept over the wide landing, with its tall ornate mirror and sombre paintings. She wondered if he'd viewed those artworks as a child, determined to paint something more dramatic. What would his parents have thought? Which of the children had they valued more?

She went back into Luke Cope's bedroom, with its clutter, the clothes strewn about the place, imprints of the man's character wherever she looked. He hadn't cared about anything except his art, that was what everyone said. Once again, she noted the books by his bedside. She wondered what he read for relaxation and went to examine a bookcase that ran along one side of his room, opposite the window. She'd got the main light on, but it was still shadowy over there. The colour of the walls, a moody grey, didn't help. She crouched down to scan the shelves.

A second later she'd forgotten the room around her. The first book she pulled out was *Snakes in Suits: When Psychopaths go to Work*. A second was called *Without Conscience: The Disturbing World of the Psychopaths Around Us*. And next to it were self-help books. *How to Escape Your Demons*, and *Your Genes Are Not Your Destiny*. She thought again of the Stanley knife she'd noticed, the first day she'd visited the house, jammed into a board as though it had been thrust there in anger. What had Luke Cope been dealing with?

Her legs felt wobbly as she stood up and dusted the bits of fluff off the hem of her coat. She hadn't bothered to take it off; it was bitterly cold without the heating on.

She exited Luke's room and crossed the landing now, to make her way up another set of stairs that were narrower and more confined. She hadn't got this far when she'd last visited, though the CSIs, Megan and Max must have covered the entire house. Once again she was conscious of her feet sinking into the high-quality carpet. The door at the top of the stairs was closed, leaving almost no light and making the space feel claustrophobic. She'd have to watch her step.

Once she'd opened the door, she found what must have been Luke Cope's dumping ground. There was no overhead light, and the room's floorboards were bare. She discovered a lamp on a low table and turned it on. Its feeble glow cast shadows beyond boxes and crates that were dotted around the space. The curtains were three-quarters closed and she went to pull them back, but the light was fading now and her efforts didn't make much difference. She looked down onto the street. There, below her in the foggy gloom, was a dark-blue Mercedes. For a microsecond she felt nothing more than a flicker of heightened awareness. But almost instantly the memory of the car that had nearly mowed her down sharpened in her mind. She took a deep breath. Vehicles like that were common in this part of the city. By straining her eyes she could just read the number plate. In a moment she'd called the station to ask them to run it. Might as well just check it wasn't flagged on the system, but it probably belonged to one of Luke Cope's well-to-do neighbours.

She went back to exploring the room, which contained trunks with paintings inside them. She moved them out of the containers one by one. They were unmistakably Luke's work. The first few were of similar subjects to the ones downstairs, fenland scenes, angry skies and seas, and bleak landscapes with isolated buildings. But then she came across a series of scenes that looked like stage sets. Characters were amassed amongst exaggerated furniture in garish colours. The subjects wore masks.

Suddenly, Tara's attention was caught by just one of them – a face she recognised, that appeared in each of the paintings.

Matthew Cope.

She examined one more closely. The mask he wore represented his own face. If anything, Luke had made it more handsome than his brother was in reality. But the face behind the mask brought the wobbly feeling back into Tara's legs, and sent the hairs on her scalp rising. It was recognisably Matthew too. Luke had given his brother a reddish pallor, sharp teeth and staring eyes. He'd painted him as the devil hiding behind the persona he presented in public.

In comparison with Luke's painting of Freya Cross it ought to have been nothing, but it wasn't. And she'd almost missed it: small figures, with faces that were smaller still, on canvases a child could handle. She could see why Max and Megan hadn't spotted them, especially as Max had had almost no contact with Matthew, and Megan none.

A message came through on Tara's phone, sending adrenaline coursing round her body. The Mercedes outside was registered to a man who'd been questioned in association with a drugs case. Heroin. There hadn't been enough evidence to charge him.

Was it the same one she'd seen near Matthew Cope's place? In her imagination she was back in the man's dreary kitchen, full of the tatty furniture he'd been landed with. *It had smelt of cigarette smoke, she suddenly remembered…*

And in that moment, she realised Matthew had lied to her. He'd told Vicky Cope that he didn't smoke when she'd offered him one of her Marlboro Lights.

He had had a visitor that day, just before she'd turned up. And it was likely that that person was the owner of the blue Mercedes. Someone who'd been suspected of dealing heroin…

She'd just started to dial Max's number when she heard movement behind her.

The sound of a footstep on the wooden floor.

CHAPTER FORTY

When Blake came out of the interview room he was frowning.

Trent had claimed he'd driven over to the mill to have it out with Luke, believing that he'd killed Freya Cross to keep her quiet. He'd said he'd been concerned, and after a while he'd claimed he'd wondered if Luke had harmed himself after killing his lover. And a little while after *that*, he'd confessed that he'd also hoped to get inside the mill to find the missing ledger that contained records of the multiple frauds before someone else did. That and to remove any fakes Luke might have stashed there, too.

That last bit had sounded entirely plausible. In his eyes, Jonny Trent was a heartless, selfish man, out for what he could get.

He'd told them he wasn't aware that Luke had told anyone else about the mill, but then he wouldn't be. And once all *that* had come out he'd started to confirm other details too, including the fact that he'd given Luke items of jewellery he'd bought, which, as they'd thought, Luke had then passed off as bequests from his mother. He'd sold them on to get his fee.

But what nagged at Blake's mind most of all was the messages Jonny Trent had left on Freya's phone. *Where the hell are you? Call me.*

Why would he send a text like that if he'd killed her? He doubted the double-bluff theory. The Jonny Trent he knew would have texted a 'concerned boss' message if he'd done it with an eye to the investigators who'd be assessing it later.

Fleming met him and Megan in the corridor, took one look at his face and sighed. 'Care to share your thoughts with me?'

'I don't think he's our killer.'

CHAPTER FORTY-ONE

Tara squared her shoulders and faced Matthew Cope head on. 'I was having a last look round. My boss has got a suspect in custody, and I imagine this place will be handed back to your brother's executors shortly. We're keen to find any last bits of evidence that might support the case we're making.' She smiled, but even as she said the words, she knew the bluff wasn't working.

Matthew's eyes drifted to the paintings his brother had done of him, which she'd left strewn across the top of one of the trunks in the room. His face twitched.

Multiple thoughts coalesced in Tara's mind. Matthew claimed he'd gone to the Flag and Diamond because it was where his brother drank, but the place had been associated with a heroin-related crime, just as the driver of the car outside his house had been. What if the pub had never been Luke's haunt? What if it was Matthew that drank there; Matthew that was linked to a drug outfit? Max had said Matthew raised his hand to the landlord before he left the Flag and Diamond. It was a familiar gesture. Why the hell hadn't she thought of that before? And Max said Matthew looked as though he was finding his ground with the people he was talking to. Negotiating? Matthew's boss's words came back to her now. He'd said he could sell oranges to the people of Valencia. And if he was there selling heroin…

Matthew's eyes were on her face. It was as though he was reading her every thought. And at that moment, he took out a gun from inside his jacket pocket.

There wasn't time to think. The information was all there in her head at once: a man who'd killed twice – she still didn't understand why. One person – more than one maybe – downstairs, outside in a car, with a lot at stake. Who knew how much money?

These people wouldn't muck about. And there, laid over the top of that immediate knowledge, was the need to act instantly, decisively. If Matthew Cope had any clue she was going to go onto the attack she wouldn't stand a chance.

In less than a second she had her left hand clamped around his wrist, vice-like, her nails digging into his flesh. In the exact same instant, she thrust her right hand up under the muzzle of the gun, shoving it towards the ceiling. It was no longer at an angle where he could hit her with a bullet, and she yanked the weapon out of his hand sharply, swinging her knee up violently to hit him where he'd hurt the most. Thank God her woollen dress was so stretchy. She laughed, the adrenaline making her crazy.

But Matthew Cope was down, not out. He'd howled and fallen back when her knee had connected, but now he struggled to his feet. He was limping towards her. She aimed the gun at him.

'Stop right where you are!'

His staring eyes bored into hers. He kept on coming.

'You think I wouldn't do it?'

Matthew Cope stood inches from her, ran his tongue over his dry lips and pulled a knife from under his jacket. 'The gun isn't loaded.'

CHAPTER FORTY-TWO

Blake was pissed off. And now he couldn't reach Tara either. He wanted to know what she'd found out from Vicky Cope. Not only had his DC gone AWOL, she was also ignoring her phone.

He could see – as he'd sent her off – that she hadn't liked being out of the main action, but she needed to learn you had to play your part, even if that wasn't an exciting one.

Deep down, he was pretty sure she was still angry with him too. Guilt made him more irritable. But whatever excuse she had for feeling resentful, she still needed to get over it and get on with the job.

'She put in a call for a vehicle check twenty minutes ago,' Max said, looking at a log on his screen.

Blake stood up straighter and frowned. 'Really? With what result?'

Max's brow was creased too. 'The owner of the vehicle in question has been interviewed in the past in relation to a drugs charge. Heroin.'

'Heroin?' *What was Tara onto?* 'What was the vehicle?'

'A dark-blue Mercedes.'

Blake felt cold. 'Wasn't it a navy Merc that almost hit her, when she went to visit Matthew Cope?'

Max nodded slowly. 'I think you're right. She might have headed back out that way, I suppose, after she'd finished with Vicky.'

'Without bothering to let us know? That's typical of her attitude.' Megan's voice was sharp.

Blake took a deep breath. Tara should have told them, but sitting around bad-mouthing her was hardly the right response, especially under the circumstances.

'Want me to head over there and check?' Max said.

Megan's eyes were on him, Blake noticed. Why was managing a team always so bloody complicated?

'Yes.'

'Though she might have gone to Luke Cope's house for all we know,' Megan said. 'If she was talking to the sister a moment ago they might have discussed the woman's inheritance.'

'True… we should check both locations. Get over there, will you, Megan? See if you can find her.'

Megan was too professional to tut at her boss, but he could tell the impulse was there. He wanted to accompany one or other of them. Tara's phone call and her unresponsiveness now told him there was a problem. His mind flitted from one option to another as he tried to predict Tara's moves. Where would she have gone?

She must have spotted the car again and, if it was linked with a drugs racket, he was guessing she might suspect Matthew Cope knew more than he was saying. Heroin – it was the common link. A heroin case associated with the pub where the older brother had been drinking, and with the car that had been seen driving back towards town from the direction of his house.

Blake made his decision. 'I'll come with you, Max. If she thinks she's onto new information about Matthew Cope, my bet is she'll have gone back to his territory.'

And now, Megan did tut.

CHAPTER FORTY-THREE

For a split second, Tara thought of using the same tactic on Matthew Cope a second time. Shooting wasn't the only thing you could do with a gun: smash it into someone's hand and you had a fair chance of knocking what they were holding clear. But the older Cope brother was one step ahead of her now. Even as she jerked forward he slashed at her with his knife, cutting across the fingers of her right hand. It was she who dropped her weapon.

For a second, she was so shocked she didn't even feel the pain. It was fury she was conscious of, rising up in her gut. She couldn't believe she'd bungled the move and couldn't bear the thought of him subduing her. She'd spent too much of her life at someone else's mercy, being made to cower. Fear and humiliation pulled at the edges of her mind too, as the blood dripped from her fingers onto her coat.

He'd stopped slashing when she'd dropped the gun. 'Get the cloth that's on the table and wrap it round your hand. Hold it tight.'

He didn't want her blood left on the floor. He was planning to take her away from the house, she guessed. Though how he thought he could get her out she couldn't imagine. Maybe he'd knock her unconscious, just as he had Freya. He could strangle her before removing her body.

Suddenly, Tara heard a tinny voice. It came from the direction of Matthew Cope's jacket pocket.

'What's going on up there?' He had a call open on his mobile. To the guys in the Merc downstairs, she guessed.

'An unexpected complication.' He took a step towards Tara. 'I'm going to need your help.'

There was a harsh laugh. *'You're kidding, right? We're not getting involved in your mess. Are we clear to come in and take what's ours?'*

Cope took a deep breath and moved a step closer still. He was between her and the door, and well within range if he decided to lash out again. Tara's eyes darted left and right, looking for something she might use as improvised weapon.

'You're clear,' Cope said. 'Get on with it. Don't take anything more than we agreed.'

The laugh was audible again. *'What's to stop us, Matty boy?'*

'I'll call the cops and take you down with me if you take anything extra. I'd rather do my twenty years than see you take me for a fool.'

'Whatever.'

Matthew's eyes were back on Tara's.

'My colleagues will know you've got me,' she said. 'You'll go down anyway, whether you give yourself up or not.'

The man raised an eyebrow and reached up with his free hand to cut the call on his mobile. 'I don't think so. I overheard you phone the station about the car outside. Your lot will assume they've taken you.'

It wasn't a good thought. Tara kept her expression steady. If he imagined he was winning it would give him a boost. Psychological advantage was a powerful thing.

'What are they taking?' she asked. She tried to swallow back her fear, but she could hear the slight tremor in her voice.

'Selected paintings of my brother's to sell. I owe them money. They're a charming bunch. I'd just been paid for selling a sizeable batch of product and I got mugged. Must have been someone in the know, who was well aware I couldn't go to the police. Probably one of them, in fact. The sum involved was substantial. I couldn't cover my debt.'

'But the paintings…'

'Were pretty much worthless before Luke died. But I'm a sales-man – marketing's my game, from the stuff I do in my day job to the heroin I sell to kids. I can tell you that artwork by a murderer escalates in value like you wouldn't believe. I told my brother I could make a success of his talent, but he was too proud to let me help. So now, I'm doing it without him.'

'You set him up in the role of a killer…'

'I knew I could make it work.' She could see the zeal in his eyes, but no emotion at all in relation to his sibling. 'Once an artist is sufficiently notorious their output develops a fascination for a certain sort of person. I've got a rock star interested, and a multimillionaire recluse. Both disgusting people, both very ready to part with their money. I need to make the deals before it gets out that Luke was a victim. The value won't be half as high then. Thank God the creeps downstairs don't know how precarious their pay-off is.'

'You killed Freya Cross, just to make your brother look like a murderer.' Tara was still trying to get her brain to accept the idea.

He shook his head. 'To make a fortune out of his paintings. We're talking a *lot* of money here, Tara.' He looked at her as though she was crazy; as if his motivation made his actions entirely explicable.

And suddenly Tara thought of the books downstairs, in Luke's bedroom – all about psychopaths. Had he bought them because he was worried he had one in the family, not because he'd been analys-ing his own make-up? What about the one on escaping your genes?

Outside, she could hear a car's wheels spinning.

Matthew Cope nodded. 'That's them off.'

'How did they know it was safe to come now? How did you?' They'd had people posted on the door almost constantly.

'I knew what would happen once you found Luke's body. You'd be bound to put someone on lookout here. But I had plenty of time to make arrangements. I put up mini spy cameras front and back, whilst I waited for your lot to take my worries about Luke seriously. When the time came, everything was in place. Even police officers leave their posts occasionally.' He frowned. 'But I wasn't watching when you entered the house this afternoon, clearly. By the time I checked I just saw that your colleague had left his post on the front door.' He was moving towards her once again. She shifted back, glancing sideways. She needed a heavy ornament. Or something. *Anything* within arm's reach. There was a tall pewter vase on a side table nearby, but she'd never get to it before he got to her. Yet if she let him take control, she'd be as good as dead.

She'd risk fighting where she stood, rather than let him make her disappear quietly. Her whole body shook at what might lie ahead. She tensed her legs. She mustn't lose control now.

Suddenly, she heard a noise beyond him, somewhere down the stairs.

'Tara! Is that you up there? What the hell are you playing it?' Megan's angry voice carried easily through the quiet house.

Matthew Cope put his finger to his lips and looked from Tara to the point of his knife.

Despite the warning, she almost called out. But even without the man's threat there were reasons not to. She guessed Megan would carry on searching for her when she got no reply, and whilst the DS was in the house, Matthew's attention would be divided. She remembered Kemp's advice: *Half the focus is half the threat.* Tara stood there, knowing her body was teetering on the brink, the tension pent-up, but liable to break out into full-blown shakes at any second. She listened hard. That was the way to beat it. *Focus and breathe.*

Footsteps. She guessed Megan was on the middle floor. There was no way she could let her come any closer. Dividing Matthew Cope's attention was one thing, letting him have a crack at one of the team was another. Her eyes went from the pewter vase to Matthew. The ornament was too far away, and his attention still too much on her.

But then she heard the sound of a police radio, crackling into life on the floor below.

There was a subtle shift in Cope's stance, a little more towards the door, a little less towards her. In that fraction of a second she crossed the room and swept the vase up in her hand, just as Cope moved towards the door, his knife still at the ready.

Tara couldn't hear if Megan had started on the stairs. The carpet deadened all sound. She might already be halfway up.

There was no time to think further. In an instant she judged the angle and method she'd need to use. She couldn't let Megan arrive in his line of sight unless she'd disarmed him first.

If she misjudged her move…

As she swung her arm she knew she couldn't risk staying silent. 'Run, Megan!'

In the same moment, Tara brought the heavy vase down with her full force across the metacarpal bones in Cope's right hand.

'What the—?' Megan exclaimed. She must only be feet away.

The vase landed. Tara heard bones crack.

Matthew gave howl of pain as his knife fell from his fingers and skittered across the wooden floor. Once again, Tara's knee went up, hard into his groin.

And this time, her aim was much better.

CHAPTER FORTY-FOUR

'It was an irresponsible way to behave.'

Blake looked at Megan. He felt exhausted. Tara's independence and her habit of keeping her plans to herself had almost cost her her life. But she was standing by her reasons for doing it, and even now he wasn't entirely sure she'd behave differently in future. How the hell could he make her see the potential consequences of her actions? What might have happened played through his mind like a technicolour horror movie. Matthew Cope's gun hadn't been loaded. Had that meant he'd fought less hard to hang onto it, knowing it hadn't the power to kill? How good were her skills really? Pretty impressive, he knew, but no one was invincible. How much of today's success was down to luck? And would she be emboldened to take even bigger risks next time? What if her good fortune ran out?

Megan was right. Tara's failure to follow protocol would have to be looked into.

'Ironic that she broke Matthew Cope's hand,' Megan said. 'It's as though she's moving up the scale of body parts.'

Blake thought back to the journalist with the broken finger. 'I don't think escalating violence is an ambition of hers; she was short on options.' But Blake knew Megan's sarcastic comment was born of frustration at Tara's overall attitude, not at her use of self-defence – which had been justified. He'd spoken to Tara shortly after that day's drama. He knew how scared she'd been, and how – in her eyes – she'd done what she needed to protect Megan by calling out a warning. At the same time, following her own rules would have been a no-brainer to her. He sighed. He was starting to understand why DCI Fleming sometimes treated them like a classful of recalcitrant children.

'Let's get back in there,' he said to Megan. They'd been taking a brief break from interviewing Matthew Cope. Their talk about tactics for their questioning had gone off-topic.

With the recorder back up and running, Blake weighed in. 'When did you first get the idea of setting up the murder–suicide scenario?' He still couldn't believe the man had coldly killed two people – including his own brother – to make money. And, Blake felt, to make a point too.

'When I saw that ridiculous painting he'd done of Freya Cross. The brainwave could have come to me sooner of course. I'd seen the picture he'd done of Imogen Field too, but it was only when I saw the second one that the notion took hold. And it was easier to set things up with Freya, because she and my brother were still seeing each other.' He smiled. 'The painting played right into my hands. It made Luke look guilty from the outset.'

It was strange. Luke had been the one to feel violent rage towards the woman, which had allowed Matthew – cold, calculating and reptilian – to make his move.

'He must have been very angry with her to paint that scene,' Blake said.

Matthew shrugged. 'I've no doubt he was. They had a massive row, I understand, when she found out he'd been defrauding gallery customers. But Luke was following some crackpot therapist's recommendations too.' He laughed and Blake quelled a shiver. He'd never come across someone like this before. Someone watching Cope's body language in isolation might have assumed he was chatting with old friends. 'She told him to paint the worst possible images going through his mind to exorcise them.' His calm eyes met Blake's. 'You see, Luke spent his whole life fearing that he had the same *taint* as me.'

Blake thought of the books Tara had told him she'd seen in Luke's bedroom.

'I'm a psychopath, apparently,' Matthew said conversationally. 'Interesting. Unusual. It's not something I can do anything about.'

The solicitor sitting next to Cope looked pained, but he'd clearly given up trying to get his client to stick to whatever party line they'd agreed before the interview started.

Blake's mind ran back to the other painting they'd found of Luke's. 'What made Luke paint that picture of your father? Was he angry with him?'

Matthew Cope laughed again. 'Oh no! I was the one who was angry with our father. He and my mother always prized Luke above me. So creative, so distinctive. Sensitive. I knew how the land lay.' Blake could hear disdain in his voice, rather than anger. It was as though he pitied his parents for what he saw as their poor judgement. 'The day my father told me he and my mother had arranged for Luke to have their town house in trust, and for me to have that mouldering monstrosity out on the edge of Cambridge, it was quite clear which of us they valued most. The day he passed on the news was the day my father died. As I told you before, *Luke* was out of the house when he *fell* downstairs. My mother was too…'

Blake felt a chill run down his back. Matthew Cope just smiled.

'Mr Cope, did you kill your father?' Blake managed to keep his voice steady despite his shock. To his left he could see Megan's eyes – wide and horrified.

The solicitor opened his mouth to speak, but he wasn't quick enough.

'I pushed him. He fell. He died.'

How many crimes went undetected, unsuspected, for so many years? But then this wasn't unsuspected, Blake guessed. 'Your brother knew what you'd done?'

'He had no proof, but he drew his own conclusions. That was why he was always so frightened of his own feelings of rage. And the reason he followed the quack psychologist's advice and tried to "paint them out of his system". I mean, seriously? I often used to tell him we were from the same mould, just to make him wonder.'

'So your relationship was poor?' Blake remembered Tara's notes from when she'd met with Matthew Cope's boss. He'd had Luke down as the difficult one. He said Matthew had tried to build bridges, but his efforts had been thrown back in his face. Blake could see why Luke had wanted to distance himself now.

'It wasn't good. I had to use all my acting powers once I had the idea of arranging his and Freya's deaths. Part of my plan relied on Luke letting me go with him to the mill, so we could get drunk together. I told him his suspicions about my involvement in our father's death were unfounded, and that I'd been so hurt that I'd played up to his fears. I said wasn't it time to bury the hatchet? We'd wasted too much of our lives, being at each other's throats.'

'And he believed you?'

Matthew nodded. 'Eventually, but not quickly enough. All the time I worked to break down his defences, the outfit I owed money to were putting the amount up. "Interest", they called it.'

'So you finally managed to persuade Luke to take you out into the Fens. Then you faked his suicide. You use heroin yourself?'

Matthew Cope sat up straighter and looked down his nose at Blake. Blake found it hard to hold back, never had a face begged for a punch harder than Cope's was now. 'I'm not that much of a fool,' the man said. 'But I know exactly how to inject. A lot of younger heroin users start off by smoking the stuff; they find it less frightening. But the dealers' aim is to move them on to using intravenously. It's an almost instant hit, and they get through more. And then more still. The profits are far better.' He gave that smile again; the condescending expert passing on his knowledge. 'As part of my salesman role, I played the friendly experienced user, able to show them just how to do it without harming themselves and acting as a go-between for my suppliers. It was a good sideline until it all went sour.'

For a second Blake's eyes met Megan's. He thought of the countless lives people like Cope sent spiralling downwards, out of control.

'Why the hell didn't you use your skills honestly?' Blake found himself practically shouting, the words reverberating around the room. It was Megan and the solicitor who jumped. Matthew Cope just sat there, as though Blake had criticised the design of his tie.

'I tried. But although I'm high-functioning, I'm a misfit. I overstepped the mark at work once. Syphoned off some funds from a deal. My boss is an old family friend. I swore to him that it had been an accounting error and he slapped me on the back and said he believed me, but I found myself reassigned after that. So you see, everything goes more smoothly if I make my income another way. The house I was left eats money, and no one would ever want to buy it. It's in a terrible area.'

Blake took a deep breath. This was why they'd taken their first break. He hadn't thought he could carry on without something internal bursting. The man seemed incapable of understanding what he'd done. In his mind, his needs trumped everyone else's.

He clenched his fists under the desk.

'So you had the skill to inject your brother with his overdose, making the positioning of the fingerprints you applied to the syringe accurate.'

'That's right.'

'It's very good of you to be so candid,' Blake said, his voice dripping with sarcasm.

Cope looked surprised. 'I'm not a fool. Your people are already searching my house. They'll find the key to the mill and the holdall Freya was carrying. I meant to get rid of it, but I've been busy.

And then you've already got the disposable phone I use to make contact with my dealers. All that, and Tara's evidence, make your case against me quite strong. If I hide what I did, it will just draw out this interview, and I get bored easily. I've been bored for over an hour now.'

Once again, Blake fought to control himself. He didn't believe Cope was finding the situation tedious; he was loving the attention – anyone could see that. He was proud of what he'd done.

After a moment, he managed to continue. 'And then you took his phone back into town – travelling by bus, I presume – and texted Freya Cross the following day to arrange the meet up, pretending to be your brother.'

'That's right. And when I turned up at the nature reserve I thought I could carry on pretending, for a minute or two at least. Luke was of a similar build to me, but my hair's different, so I wore a hat.' He shook his head. 'But Freya was onto me almost immediately. I suppose lovers get to know each other more intimately than I'd judged. But I'd gone prepared. I hit her with a stone I was carrying to stun her, then used her own scarf to kill her. I'd brought a tie along for the purpose but limiting the fibres you'd find seemed sensible. I wanted to imitate the scene my brother had painted as closely as possible but I'd read up on the subject. Using my bare hands seemed too uncontrolled.'

Blake thought of the man, sitting there in an armchair of an evening, carefully working out what would make life easiest for him… Freya Cross's dead face rose up in his mind's eye.

'And then you nagged us to try to find your brother.'

'It was all taking too long. I assumed Freya would be found almost immediately and suspicion would quickly fall on Luke, given that he'd disappeared. But it didn't happen. And until there was publicity to show my brother was a suspected murderer I couldn't make any money out of his paintings. I had my supplier breathing down my neck for payment, upping the bill. I needed to get things moving, so I made a fuss about no one taking Luke's disappearance seriously.'

And at that, another piece of the jigsaw slotted into place. 'The anonymous tip-offs to the press – telling them Luke was under suspicion; and then later that he'd been found dead? That was you?'

Matthew Cope raised a calm eyebrow. 'Of course. I needed the money. But there was some satisfaction in proving myself right, too. I always did have the know-how to market my brother's paintings. If he'd have gone into partnership with me in the first place, I wouldn't have needed the income from selling heroin, and he would still be alive. He didn't believe in me, any more than my parents did.' His smile was wide now. 'Foolish of him.'

Cope's pride was unbearable.

'You say you've still got Freya's holdall. But what happened to the ledger from the gallery that was inside it?'

'I burnt it. The last thing I wanted was evidence of other possible motives for the murders coming to light. It was essential for everyone to think it was a crime of passion. If people started to consider alternative possibilities, it could ruin my entire plan.'

'You knew what Luke had been up to at the gallery, then?'

Matthew nodded. 'I barged in one day when he was halfway through painting a lovely Matisse. Luke couldn't resist the deal Jonny Trent had offered him – and as he pointed out, Trent never lied to a single customer. It was their fault if they decided to believe in fairy tales. So Luke managed to excuse his own behaviour. And I think he was right to do so – I told him that.'

'I understand you let Trent buy the last genuine painting of Luke's that he had at the gallery.'

For the first time a flicker of anger twitched across Matthew Cope's face. 'He knew damn well how much it would be worth, with all the scandal surrounding Luke. Even now, when it comes out that I'm the killer and not him, there'll be a moderate hike in the value.' He put his head on one side. 'Trent suspected I was responsible for both deaths, once it became clear the police hadn't fully bought the murder–suicide theory. He didn't have proof, but it would have looked odd if I'd refused to sell the painting to him. It was the same when your colleague witnessed my half-sister offering to buy one of Luke's works. She thought she was doing me a favour, giving me a few hundred quid for one, and I couldn't contradict her. Or risk her looking up the latest value of his works online.'

He sat back and folded his arms. 'It's only through luck that you caught me out and I'm still glad I decided to carry out my plan. If my parents were alive to see me they'd understand just what I'm really capable of.'

CHAPTER FORTY-FIVE

Nine days later, Tara was standing on the lawn of her father Robin and stepmother Melissa's garden in leafy Glebe Road, close to the Perse pre-prep school, the fee-paying establishment their children had attended up until the age of seven.

The weather had swung from the bitter opening of spring to warm, balmy temperatures. The March day could have been mistaken for May, which was working well for the anniversary party. Though her father and stepmother had plenty of space inside their 1930s semi if needs be. Robin's architectural skills meant the interior had been remodelled to the highest standard. *All right for some.*

Tara was feeling clumsy. She'd got a too-small plate, full of slidey bits of food – vol-au-vents, cherry tomatoes, falafels and the like – as well as a glass of fizz. All of that, mixed with a bandaged right hand, which still hurt from where Matthew Cope had slashed her, made for a certain amount of awkwardness. She'd already dropped a chipolata sausage onto the shoe of Robin and Melissa's vicar. The look her stepmother had given her spoke volumes.

Nonetheless, it was Robin, not her stepmother, who'd been the most distant when she'd arrived. It had been half an hour before he'd finally allowed their paths to cross and when they had, his jaw had been tense. Then again, Melissa was moving round like an overwound clockwork toy. She'd probably been stewing about the event. It could have rubbed off on him.

On the upside, Tara had backup. Kemp had convinced her she should attend, to wind Robin and Melissa up if nothing else. And unexpectedly, he was there too, with Bea. He'd been due to stay anyway, and when Lydia had found out she'd taken matters into her own hands and called Robin to ask if he could come along. Of course, her father had had to say yes. So Tara had Bea and Kemp, her mother and stepfather Benedict (not that she counted either of them as 'support'), and her stepbrother Harry.

Harry was peering at her right now – uneasily. Tara already knew why. A moment later her mother sidled up to her, fizz and crostini in hand.

'Darling,' she said, 'thanks so much for agreeing to take Harry back with you after the party. He'll have to sort out his university offers soon, and Benedict will self-destruct if he doesn't accept his place at Cambridge.'

'I'm not going to influence him, you know,' Tara said. 'I won't do your dirty work.'

Lydia raised an eyebrow. 'You *do* surprise me.'

'And you might have given me more notice. What if I'd had plans?'

Her mother gave her a calm smile. 'You hadn't, had you?'

Majorly irritating. 'No, as it happens.'

'Well then.'

'I still can't believe he wants to come, anyway.' Certainly, the look on his face didn't give any hint of it.

Lydia stopped meeting her eyes.

'What?'

'We said he wasn't allowed to reject his Cambridge place until he'd been to stay with you to get to know the city.'

'So not only will he have to sleep on my floor, he's also coming under duress? Great!'

'Don't worry, darling.' She giggled. 'He's got a sleeping bag and when you're eighteen you don't mind roughing it. It's the perfect opportunity.'

Perfect for whom? She knew exactly why her mother hadn't shared her plans in advance. Any extra notice and Tara would have come up with a plausible lie to get out of it.

Moments later, as she went to talk to Bea, she caught sight of Harry's face. He was blushing and she had a feeling he knew her eyes were on him. He'd been sent to make polite chit-chat with Robin's kids, who were all much younger than he was.

'I hope you're eating a lot and talking to all your father's friends,' Kemp said. 'Nice move with the vicar and the sausage, by the way.' He picked up a chicken drumstick from his plate and tucked into it untidily for effect, looking to left and right and grinning as he did so. Bea slapped his arm and rolled her eyes, but she was grinning too, Tara noticed.

And they were standing quite close together.

'Speaking of nice moves,' Kemp went on, through the end of his mouthful, 'have to hand it to you over that turd, Matthew Cope.'

Bea's smile was gone in an instant. She balanced her wine glass on her plate for a second and manoeuvred to give Tara a hug, her face a bit pale. 'I keep reliving it,' she said, 'and I wasn't even there. Have you been having nightmares?'

Tara had had the odd one, but she couldn't talk about it. Especially not there.

'Sorry,' Bea said, picking up on her mood. 'No need to tell me. Though it's good to talk, sometimes.'

It wasn't something Tara found easy. She thought again of Luke Cope, painting his worst thoughts out of his system. Maybe she should pick up a paintbrush? Somehow, she couldn't see it happening.

'Tara knows what she's doing,' Kemp said, waving a crostini wrapped in Parma ham. 'It's all in the teaching.'

Tara rolled her eyes, but his jokey words brought relief. And he was right, anyway. He'd trained her so intensively when she'd been stalked that the old moves came back on instinct.

Suddenly Kemp's look changed. 'I'm proud of you, mate,' he said. *Don't do this to me. Not in public.* She blinked hard and swigged her champagne.

'And so am I.' Bea was blinking as furiously as she was.

Tara glanced from one of them to the other. They looked like a pair. Two parts of a whole. It was as though the parents she'd been meant to have had suddenly coalesced in front of her eyes. And *they* thought she was doing a decent job.

It was the strangest feeling. She and Kemp had a past. But they'd only ever been hugely fond of each other. It had extended to a physical relationship at one time, but it had long since subsided into something else: deep and lasting. And he was closer to Bea in age than he was to Tara. Neither of them had said anything, but she had a feeling things had shifted up a gear.

One tiny part of her felt a sadness. A sense of loss at no longer having quite the level of closeness she'd previously enjoyed with either of them.

But she loved them both. Wanting them to be happy outweighed everything else.

She put her plate and glass down on the uneven grass. Her flute fell over. For some reason Melissa saw it happen, even though she was right across the lawn, and deep in conversation with a man boasting a show-off moustache.

Tara turned her attention to Kemp and Bea and managed to embrace them both in the same hug. 'Thanks. I'm not sure where I'd be without you.'

There was a moment's pause, during which even Kemp's eyes glistened slightly. 'And the dirt you gathered on my *ex*-boss is continuing to pay dividends too.' Tara spoke to him quickly, whilst stepping back and managing a more normal smile.

Kemp raised an eyebrow. '*Ex*-boss? That's definite, is it? I mean, I never thought they'd let Wilkins come back to the same role.'

For a second her feeling of happiness was unadulterated. 'He's resigned. I only heard yesterday.'

Kemp whistled. 'Excellent news, mate.'

And it was. But Wilkins wasn't out of her life. The next thing was to find out what he and Giles Troy were cooking up together. And what impact it was likely to have on her…

Lydia seemed to have entered into the full party spirit. Tara watched as she moved from group to group, Benedict scampering after her like a faithful puppy. Her mother's laughter rang out and the people she spoke to seemed charmed – and in some cases a little star-struck – to meet her. Melissa's eyes were often on her, Tara noted, her expression one of irritation mixed with anxiety.

After a couple of hours Tara became desperate to leave. It had been a hell of a couple of weeks.

She went to find Harry. 'You don't have to come now,' she said. 'Just follow me on when you're ready.' *Or not at all, which would be fine.*

Harry had been talking to Melissa's mother.

'I'm ready now,' he said. She caught the fervent tone in his voice and the look in his eye. Maybe they had something in common after all.

The taxi ride back to Riverside was awkward. Harry sat there not saying much, clinging onto a backpack containing his overnight gear.

After Tara had paid the driver, as they were crossing the common to her cottage, Harry glanced sideways at her. His blush was back.

'Sorry,' he said. 'I know Mum forced you to have me.'

Tara raised an eyebrow as her glance met his. 'She forced you to come, too.'

Harry gave a shy smile. 'She's a bit like that, isn't she?'

Tara nodded. 'Always has been, always will be. So what's the deal with uni?'

He shrugged. 'I'm worried I won't fit in – but that's not just here, it's anywhere. Plus, the more Dad goes on about coming to Cambridge, the more I want to dig my heels in and do the opposite.' The second sentence came out in a rush.

'Do you and Benedict get on, generally?'

Another shrug. 'I guess he's not the kind of person you get close to, exactly – and he's away a lot. But he's all right. What about you and Robin?'

Tara explained about the abortion thing. 'Mum thinks I should have forgiven and forgotten by now.'

'Blimey.'

They reached Tara's front door. Harry had never visited her before. They'd only ever met at parties at Lydia and Benedict's house, out in the Fens.

'This place is crazy!' Harry said, but as though that was a good thing, which Tara thought it was.

He was looking not only at the house, but at its surroundings too: the river, the common, the branches of the greening willows stirring in the breeze.

Tara smiled to herself as she unlocked the door. The postman had been. She reached down to pick up the jiffy bag that had landed on her doormat, striding inside. Harry followed her through to the kitchen as she ripped open the seal on the packet. It took her longer than it might have, thanks to her bandaged hand.

She'd been chatting as she went, and Harry had gone to the kettle, ready to put it on for coffee at her suggestion.

Suddenly the room blurred, sounds faded and it was just her and her delivery. There, where she'd opened the envelope in one corner, she could see a single dead bee.

Instantly her mind was back in Bea's sitting room, where she'd been for her sixteenth birthday. It had been when she'd received her first 'present' from her mystery stalker. Bees for her birthday at Bea's.

She'd flung the open envelope away from her and the dead insects had showered the room, landing in her mug of hot chocolate and all over her other parcels.

Tara's hands shook. She was dimly aware of Harry asking if she was all right and then moving towards her, taking the open packet from her numb fingers and peering inside. And then the look of confusion and horror on his face as he dropped it, just as she had, when she'd been two years younger than him.

It took a minute for her to pick the packet up and look for a note. She reached gingerly for the single sheet of paper she could see, avoiding the rest of the packet's contents.

Remember me? I'm still here. If you don't want me back, call off the dogs.

CHAPTER FORTY-SIX

An hour later, Tara was in her sitting room overlooking Stourbridge Common. Blake was opposite her, the packet of bees and the note on a coffee table between them, though some of the insects were still on the kitchen floor.

'Thanks for coming out on a Saturday.' Tara still didn't know how the hell he'd found out what had happened. She'd just called the station. She knew she wasn't his favourite person right now, after she'd broken the rules and gone looking for clues at Luke's place. The fact that she'd managed to find and overpower their missing killer seemed to have gone by the wayside…

'I was in the office tying up a few loose ends on the Cope case,' he said. His voice was tight.

Not at home holding Babette's hand then… Was the paperwork really that urgent?

Blake looked at her closely for a moment, as though trying to guess what she was thinking. She worked to clear her face of all expression. Despite what she was going through, and all the old horrors it brought back, she had a feeling his mind was still on her wrongdoings in the case.

At last, he sighed. 'We'll start by contacting suppliers of dead bees.'

'Suppliers? Who the—'

'I understand they're quite widely available over the internet. People use them for alternative therapies. I'm hoping your sicko hasn't thought to cover their tracks too carefully.'

But Tara had a nasty feeling they would have. No one had managed to track them down back when they'd first tormented her.

'What about the note?' Blake said. 'Do you know what they mean by call off the dogs? You haven't been doing any investigating yourself?'

The idea had occasionally crossed Tara's mind, but things had been quiet for so long. Digging into the past had begun to seem self-destructive.

'I haven't. Nor done anything that would lead anyone to think that I might have.'

Blake frowned.

'It's a local postmark, just like it was before.'

'I noticed.'

At that moment Harry came in and put coffees down in front of them.

'Thanks.' Blake and Tara spoke over each other in the instant before Harry dashed out again.

'We can be guided by you on this,' Blake said. 'Which way you want to play it – how you want us to dig.' His tone was formal, almost distant. It contrasted with his physical closeness.

She nodded. Their differences and the stress of the past, opening up again where her future should be, made her feel uncharacteristically emotional. The champagne probably hadn't helped. She bit the inside of her lip until it hurt. The threat of tears receded but the emotion and frustration behind them didn't.

'I think you're still preoccupied with what I did before I overpowered Matthew Cope, despite *that*.' She indicated the packet of bees. Her words had come involuntarily, quick and full of anger.

'You're damned right I am, Tara.' His response was just as sudden and fiery.

'I felt cut out – and that you were keeping me at arm's length for personal reasons.'

'And you think that makes it okay to storm off in a huff? You still don't get it, do you?' His voice rose, his tone harsh. 'Going off to review evidence without telling the rest of us might seem like a small thing, but it had big consequences. It stopped us from backing you up and it put you and potentially Megan in danger. She's right to be cross. I need you to understand why this matters – whatever your feelings are towards me and any other members of the team.'

She felt everything well up inside her: a massive boiling mix of stress, hurt and anger. But the anger was 90 per cent because she knew his comments were justified. She'd been too proud to admit she'd been at fault up until now. It would have been a hell of a lot easier if she'd been more adult about it from the start. She looked him straight in the eye. 'I get it. Genuinely. I'm sorry.'

There was a long pause.

'That's good,' Blake said at last. 'It makes it less likely you'll end up on Agneta's post-mortem table – she's busy enough as it is.'

She rolled her eyes.

He put his coffee down on the table next to the bees. She saw his hand move towards her, and, for a second, she thought he was going to reach out. In spite of what she'd said that day in the mill, she wanted him too. It was a reflex reaction. But in the end, he held back.

'Megan asked the other day why I hadn't told the team that Babette and I were expecting a second child.'

Tara couldn't imagine Megan asking any such thing.

'The truth is, I didn't know the situation myself, until Babs was three months gone.' His dark eyes were on hers. 'We hadn't been trying for a baby – far from it. She told me the evening after you survived the fire. Kitty already knew.'

Tara sat absolutely still. What kind of relationship did Blake and his wife have? Why on earth would she tell his daughter before him? To make it harder for him to walk away? There was a hell of a lot about his family set-up she didn't understand. Stuff he couldn't share. She didn't know what he was going through, half the time. And then there was the reason he'd worked this into the conversation, so that she knew the truth…

For a moment, neither of them spoke. The questions in her mind seemed to hang in the air. She got the impression that he half wanted to tell her more.

At last he sighed. 'We'll talk again about that,' he indicated the envelope with the bees, 'on Monday. But call me any time you're worried in between, okay?' His dark eyes were on hers. 'It won't be like last time, Tara. I won't let it. We've all got your back.'

She nodded. The team thing went both ways. She should have treated them all with more respect. Tears threatened again as Blake got up to leave.

After she'd let him out, Tara went to join Harry in the kitchen.

'You can tell Mum that people who live in Cambridge get dead bees delivered to them, so you've decided against uni here,' she said.

Harry laughed but his expression was troubled. 'I can't believe you went through all that when you were my sort of age and I never even knew.'

'Not family-dinner discussion material, I suppose.'

'I guess not.' Harry went to the window, from where they could see Blake's retreating back as he cycled across the common, towards his home in Fen Ditton. 'Is that your boss?'

Tara nodded. 'For the time being.'

'Were you and he arguing?' There was a curious look in Harry's eye.

'He was telling me off.'

'What a git.'

Tara gave him a flicker of a smile. 'Thanks, but I deserved it.'

For a second her half-brother grinned. 'I hate it when that happens. So he's not a git then?'

Competing feelings struggled inside her – sadness mixed with warmth. Blake had wanted her to understand his predicament – at least enough to know he hadn't led her up the garden path.

'No,' she said at last. 'Definitely not a git.'

A LETTER FROM CLARE

Thank you so much for reading *Death Comes to Call*. I do hope you enjoyed it as much as I liked writing it! If you'd like to keep up to date with all of my latest releases, you can sign up at the following link. Your email address will never be shared, and you can unsubscribe at any time.

www.bookouture.com/clare-chase

This particular book evolved entirely from the idea I had for the motive. I don't want to give too much away, just in case anyone happens across this letter before they've finished the book, but it was inspired by a news story. Oddly, as I was editing the novel, another very relevant item hit the headlines. Perhaps you can guess which one I mean? The Cambridge backdrop was a bonus in this instance because the city is so compact. I feel almost everyone here is interconnected and that was useful for this story.

If you have time, I'd love it if you were able to write a review of *Death Comes to Call*. Feedback is really valuable, and it also makes a huge difference in helping new readers discover my books for the first time.

Alternatively, if you'd like to contact me personally, you can reach me via my website, Facebook page, Twitter or Instagram. It's always great to hear from readers.

Again, thank you so much for deciding to spend some time reading *Death Comes to Call*. I'm looking forward to sharing my next book with you very soon.

With all best wishes,
Clare x

 www.clarechase.com

ClareChaseAuthor

@ClareChase_

ACKNOWLEDGEMENTS

Very much love and thanks to Charlie, George and Ros – partly because I'd never miss the opportunity to say this when it presents itself, but also for the unstinting support, feedback and good humour in the face of mad panic. Much love and thanks also to my parents, and to Phil and Jenny, David and Pat, Warty, Andrea, the Westfield gang, Margaret, Shelly, Mark, Helen, Lorna and a whole band of family and friends.

Thanks also to the fabulous Bookouture authors and other writer mates both online and IRL for their support and insights. It makes so much difference. I'd also like to express massive appreciation to the book bloggers and reviewers who've taken the time to pass on their thoughts about my work.

And then, crucially, my heartfelt thanks to my wonderful editor Kathryn Taussig for all her inspiring feedback, as well as to Maisie Lawrence, Peta Nightingale, Alexandra Holmes, Fraser, Liz and everyone involved in the editing, book production and marketing process at Bookouture. And massive thanks as ever to Noelle Holten, who puts so much energy and enthusiasm into promoting my work, alongside the amazing Kim Nash. I feel hugely lucky to be published and promoted by such a wonderful team.

And finally, thanks to you, the reader, for buying or borrowing this book!